In the Shadow of the Spanish Sun

In the Shadow of the Spanish Sun

Tom Malone

Denver, Colorado · 2016

Library of Congress Control Number: 2016905175
ISBN-13: 978-1-945236-10-5
ISBN-10: 1-945236-10-8

Printed in the United States of America

Third edition, 2018

Published by Malone Media · Denver, Colorado

To my Adventurers:
For your desire to explore and understand the world.

"You can't get away from yourself by moving from one place to another."

– Ernest Hemingway

The Sun Also Rises, 1926

PROLOGUE

In 2010, United States citizens faced the greatest recession since the Great Depression. With unemployment rates rising to 10 percent, college students faced incredible odds as they prepared to enter the workforce.

While some United States students aimed to surmount these less-than-favorable odds, other students moved elsewhere. Some moved to South America to experience Latin flavor, while some moved to Europe to educate themselves in the ways of Eurocentric culture.

At the time, Europe seemed to be a popular destination for people from every continent. With civil wars erupting in African nations and the Arab Spring on the horizon, people fled their dangerous homelands in search of safety, but that safety came with a price.

Soon-to-be American expatriates aimed to select a European country with a low cost of living and a high standard of living. The United Kingdom's currency, the British Pound, was high compared to the U.S. Dollar. With the relatively recent strengthening of the European Union, travelers aimed for the EuroZone.

Spain possessed an appeal: it's language and cultural flare made it an attractive option. Even though the Euro's worth was incredibly high compared to the U.S. Dollar, Spain's cost of living was much lower than countries like Germany, Italy, and France. Plus, its quality of life was second-to-none. The cultural necessity to take two hours off in the afternoon to simply enjoy the day was an attractive option to those looking to flee the stressful rigmarole of the American lifestyle.

What U.S. students overlooked, however, was the fact that Spain was on the brink of revolt. Spain's unemployment rate reached 21 percent in 2010. Full-blown strikes occurred on a weekly basis from train operators, airline pilots, and construction workers.

Catalonia and the Basque Country, two autonomous regions within Spain's borders, were looking to break away and become their own countries. Catalonian football powerhouse, F.C. Barcelona, dominated world soccer; their rivals, Real Madrid, symbolized the rigid Spain political regime, which created a sporting atmosphere of civil war that begged for manifestation. Spain's national team just won the World Cup, which added fuel to the fire.

Young adults in Spain were fired up and their disapproval of the government's treatment of its citizens was on the verge of explosion. Spain's culture was hot, and the atmosphere was even hotter.

CHAPTER 1

An old Spanish woman sat next to me; she occupied the middle seat, while I shifted in my window seat. She looked sweet in her bonnet and scarf. I wondered if she could sense what was about to happen. I felt sorry that I didn't speak Spanish well enough to warn her.

Sweat dripped from my forehead onto my lap as I shifted anxiously in my chair. My sentiments of sympathy shifted drastically to sickness. The plane landed. I snatched the barf bag from the pocket in front of me and unleashed every ounce of last night's binge from Munich's Oktoberfest. One more beer sounded like a great idea last night, but, as always, I regretted it the next morning.

Without altering her genuine demeanor, the grey-haired woman handed a napkin to me and called for the stewardess to bring me some water. Her warm words comforted me somewhat, even though I couldn't understand the meaning. I thanked her and scurried off the plane.

The heat made me feel worse as I strolled through the

Madrid airport and I felt overwhelmed by the mass of people who hustled in every direction toward their terminals. The lack of English in the air dropped my confidence to an all-time low. My train to Oviedo left in three hours, so I had some time to kill. I mustered all my strength and dragged my massive red travel backpack to a food stand.

"*Uno jugo*," I said.

The Spanish clerk looked at me like I was speaking Japanese. I pointed to the orange juice in the glass refrigerator window.

"*Zumo*," said the clerk, though his attitude said, "This dumb American can't even order a juice!"

I paid and sipped my orange juice slowly while I stewed in embarrassment. After a few similar encounters at the Renfe train ticket window and a sandwich shop, I realized that many vocabulary words I learned in my minimal Mexican-based Spanish education didn't translate well in Spain. *Zumo*, not *jugo*.

In the train station's waiting area, I found an open seat next to a young Spanish family with two small boys. The mother scrambled around the seating area in countless attempts to control the boys' energy. The father sat quietly in the seat; his smartphone kept him occupied. Passengers boarded the train.

What the hell am I doing here? I sat alone in a window seat. The train inched forward. The September sun beat down on the semi-mountainous Spanish countryside and I watched with passive curiosity. The scenery provided more entertainment than the boring movie playing on the train's video screen. As I gazed through my translucent reflection in the window, thoughts of doubt, excitement, and pending adventure filled my mind. My confidence shrunk, partly due to my embarrassing entrance into the country, partly from my realization that the world was quickly becoming bigger and more complex than I originally thought.

I spent two weeks away from my home state while on a high school class trip to Mexico. Other than that, I stuck close to home. Now, I prepared for a four-month journey in a foreign country with nothing but my backpack and my wits to keep me afloat. *Am I ready for this?*

o   o   o

Five hours passed and the train pulled into the Oviedo station. I threw my backpack over my shoulder. It weighed me down since it carried everything I would need for the duration of my study abroad semester. After a few wrong turns, I pulled out the map. Finally, I made it to the front door of the study abroad office and rang the bell.

"*Sí,*" said the mysterious female voice coming through the wall speaker.

"Um, hi," I stammered. "I'm Jason. Is this the International Study Program office?"

The door buzzed open and I walked into a small courtyard surrounded by towering six-story apartments on all sides. I made my way to door number three, hoping this was the right door. A woman in her mid-thirties greeted me in rapid Spanish and led me to a small conference room. She motioned to the pastries on the table. I ate one out of hunger and another out of nervousness.

I sat alone in the room for a few minutes and wondered what to do. My eyes wandered around the room. Pictures hung from the walls that depicted students on previous study abroad trips with overly excited expressions in absurdly picturesque locations, none of which were in Spain. The yellow walls gave the room a warm atmosphere. Then I heard door number three open again.

An athletically-built black man walked into the room. His backpack looked similar to mine and he had my confused expression as the woman greeted him in familiar, rapid Spanish. He entered the conference room and sat across from me. Aside from the obvious skin color difference, we looked very similar. Dark hair, buzzed to match the five o'clock shadow. Thick eyebrows. Dark eyes. Six-foot frame. Relaxed demeanor with an upbeat attitude.

"What's up, man. I'm Devon Hendricks," he said.

"I'm Jason Cologne," I responded.

We shook hands and continued waiting in the well-lit room.

"Where are you from?" I asked.

"I'm from the San Francisco area. I live in a suburb about five miles outside the city. What about you?" he responded.

"I'm from Portland, Oregon. I'm a junior at the University of Oregon. I guess this is my first time being too far away from home," I admitted.

"Crazy. I'm a junior at U of O too. I thought you looked familiar. Are you a Spanish major like me?" he asked.

"No, I'm a journalism major," I said.

"Cool."

The program director burst through door with a wild attitude. She told Devon and I that we would be roommates for the duration of our stay in Oviedo. I felt relieved that my random roommate situation was working out well so far. She gave us the map to our apartment and we left the office with wide-eyed excitement.

We walked into the apartment building and laughed as we looked at the tiny elevator.

"You go first," I said. "I'll go up after you."

"I barely fit in this thing!" he exclaimed, as he and he backpack struggled to fit inside the lift.

The floor counter reached five, and then regressed to one. I stuffed myself into the elevator. It smelled like old wood. I heard the gears churning as the elevator rose and Devon greeted me as the elevator doors slid open.

"Well, here it is," he said.

He opened the door to our apartment and stepped over the threshold. It was a surprisingly spacious place. Aside from the small living room and kitchen, we each had our own small bedroom with a bathroom as a divider.

"We have a deck!" I shouted, opening the door through the kitchen to the small platform overlooking the city. On a nearby hill, a distant white statue glistened in the setting sunlight.

We threw our backpacks in our rooms and unpacked. After a few minutes, I decided that I was too anxious to stay in the apartment.

"Devon, what should we do?" I asked.

"Want to grab a beer?" he suggested.

My Oktoberfest hangover was finally fading, but drinking another beer sounded absolutely terrible.

"Sounds good to me," I said, for hospitality's sake.

We walked through the city's cobblestone streets with no particular destination in mind. We gravitated toward downtown, near the medieval cathedral. Oviedo buzzed with people. We passed a pharmacy and its clock flashed *18:00*. The after-work Friday crowd was out in full force.

"This place looks cool," Devon said.

"Let's do it," I replied.

We sat in the plaza seating area of some random bar without a visible sign and ordered two *cervezas*. Devon spoke Spanish well enough to order beers, which far surpassed my skill level. *I can't even order juice.* The sun set over the buildings a few minutes earlier, so my eyes stopped squinting.

"It's awesome that we can order beers here legally," I said. "Just don't ask me to order any *zumo*."

I read the label on my Estrella Damm beer bottle as Devon and I sat quietly. As a result of growing up in a house with four siblings, silence made me somewhat uncomfortable. I felt the need to say something.

"I can't believe that we're in Spain two months after they won the World Cup," I said. "I want to see a professional Spanish soccer game while I'm here."

"I'm down. Let's make it happen!" he encouraged. "These Spaniards go crazy about their soccer teams. Real Madrid and Barcelona are two of the best club teams in the world right now. Maybe we can catch one of their games."

Devon didn't strike me as a soccer player like me. Not that I was any good at soccer. I just played for fun. I looked at Devon's shoes. *Basketball shoes.*

Two more *cervezas*.

"Do you know anyone else in our program?" he asked.

"No, not at all. I figured nobody I knew would study abroad in Oviedo. It's such a small city and off the beaten path, you know? I wanted to get away and do something different," I said.

"That's cool. I respect that. That was my thought process exactly," Devon said.

We picked up our beers from the bartender and wandered further into the bar and sat next to four old, local men. Their walking sticks leaned against the wall in between our tables. One man wore an old school Oliver Twist cap and the other had a thick moustache.

The bar clock read *22:00* and the FC Barcelona soccer game was under way. Barcelona, wearing blue and red stripes, scurried across the fuzzy television screen. Barcelona's Lionel Messi dribbled around a defender at the top of the 18-yard box and shot and scored.

The old men shouted and hugged each other, a routine action that went back through decades of watching Barcelona teams succeed. The bartender told them to quiet down and they shouted back to him, making fun of his support of the opponent. One old man turned to me and I gave him a high five.

"*Te gusta Barcelona?*" The old man asked me.

If every soccer game was going to be like this, then yes, I loved Barcelona.

"*Sí!*" I shouted.

If people in Spain watched soccer with this much intensity, passion, and pride, then of course I would cheer for Barcelona. Anything that would bring me further into an authentic Spanish experience. Anything that would bring me closer to exploring this culture. Anything that would allow me to scream my head off with a few old guys in a dusty old Spanish bar in an ancient Spanish town. This was what I came here for.

The old men ordered another round of Estrella Damm.

The bartender placed four bottles on their table and two on our table.

"*Gracias,*" Devon said to the men.

One man looked at us and tipped his Oliver Twist hat.

"*Para Barcelona,*" the old man said. "*El equipo de España.*"

"For Spain's team," Devon replied.

PART 1

CHAPTER 2

The next day, Devon and I woke up early for a mandatory ISP program meeting.

"Ah, do you think they sell Gatorade in Oviedo?" Devon joked as he held his head.

"Man, I hope so. I need some hydration. Let's hit a café on the way or something," I said, groggily.

Naturally, our "welcome to Oviedo" beer turned into a few more than we needed. We got dressed quickly because we were already running late. We thought the program director told us that the meeting was in the library, but we couldn't find it.

"No way!" Devon exclaimed.

"What?" I said, halfway alarmed.

"We're actually going to have to say *Donde está la biblioteca?*" he laughed. "That's the first phrase you learn in any Spanish class. I always thought it was a useless line. When am I going to go to a library and check out a book while I'm on vacation?"

"Literally, that would never happen. Except today," I jested.

I saw a guy sitting on the steps of the library. He stood as we approached.

"Devon Hendricks," the guy said.

"Brad O'Reilly," Devon replied.

Brad and Devon shook hands.

"Brad, this is my roommate, Jason Cologne," Devon said.

"Jason, nice to meet you," Brad said enthusiastically.

"You too," I said. "How do you guys know each other?"

"We played football together in high school," Brad said. "Dev, what a coincidence that you're studying abroad here, man."

"I know," Devon said. "When I saw your Facebook post that you were studying abroad in Oviedo, I was amazed at how small the world is."

Brad's sandy-blonde hair flowed to his shoulders, even underneath his snapback backwards hat that was emblazoned with the San Francisco Giants logo. He stood a few inches shorter than both Devon and I, but he looked strong and solid, like a rugby player. His defined jaw line gave him the appearance of a dreamy Southern California surfer with an aura of humility.

Based on his chipper morning attitude, it was evident that Brad didn't drink last night. The three of us walked into the library and sat down in the back row of the auditorium. We didn't want our program director and future teachers to smell the Estrella Damm exuding from our pores.

I looked around the room at the one hundred students from across the world that joined us for the Oviedo study abroad program. It was impressive, yet intimidating. After a some "inspiring" speeches from faculty members, we dispersed throughout the auditorium. I lined up in front of a teacher for an impromptu Spanish skills test, which would determine my class level placement. Devon, Brad, and I were placed in the same introductory level.

The three of us walked out of the auditorium and passed some Swedish, Chinese, and Moroccan students who stood in the "advanced" section. I nodded in acknowledgement as we passed. The meeting was the only thing on our agenda for the day, so we decided to go on an adventure.

"I heard the hike to that Jesus statue at the top of that big hill is pretty cool," said Brad.

"I'm down," I replied. "Maybe I'll sweat out some Estrella Damm."

"Did you guys drink a lot last night?" Brad asked with a smirk.

"Boy, did we," Devon said. "Frat boy Cologne can really throw back some cervezas."

"So can super-athlete Hendricks," I said.

"Wait until you see Brad drink, man," Devon said. "He'll put both of us to shame. Just don't let him get into any brawls like he used to back in high school."

"Yeah, yeah," Brad said. "Are you guys ready to go on a little stroll up the hill or what?"

Already dressed in athletic shorts, running shoes, and cotton t-shirts, we aimed for the statue. El Cristo rose above Oviedo to the North with outstretched arms. It reminded me of the famous statue that overlooked Rio de Janiero, Brazil, but resting atop a shorter mountain. None of us knew how to get there or which path to take, so we found the sidewalk on the main road that pointed to the hill. It didn't look too far away.

The road wound up and up. City buildings quickly turned to broad grass fields, then to lush forest. The sun rose high into the air and beat down on our sweaty bodies with desert force. Miniature European cars whizzed by us as the sidewalk evaporated into nothing but mountain road. After a half hour, the statue didn't seem to be getting any closer.

"Woof," Brad said in between heavy breaths. "This is quite the hike."

"It sure is," panted Devon.

We reached a point where the road arched downward, toward the ocean. The statue stood to our left, but we still had a ways to climb. Looking left, we found a wide dirt path surrounded by thick forest and entangled vines.

"Let's see where this goes," I suggested.

"Sounds good. I've got nothing to do all day," laughed Devon.

Sweat dripped into my eyes, so I wrapped my shirt around my head like a pirate. My legs burned. My mouth felt as dry as the Sahara desert. The three of us didn't speak for a long time as we thought about reaching the top. The dirt path became skinnier as the forest grew thicker. It forced us to walk in a single-file line. With Brad in the lead, we pushed the pace.

"We're getting close. I can tell" breathed Devon.

The path opened up into a wide grassy field with picnic tables. We followed a man-made sawdust path to a nearly vertical incline. Each step seemed like it would be my last. Regret filled my mind. I wanted to take a taxi back to the apartment and nap for the next year to shake off the hangover and pure physical exhaustion.

Then, we reached the beautifully flat platform. El Cristo appeared alone before us. The marble-white statue rose high into the air, supported by a thick base emblazoned with a semi-Celtic/Spanish cross of some kind. It looked forward as us three sweaty American boys rested at the base of the statue. Brad broke the silence after we caught our breath for a few minutes.

"This is awesome!" he exclaimed.

"Look at this view!" I shouted.

This statue is massive," Devon said a few minutes later.

We stood in silence for a while and overlooked the entire city. I could see every corner of Oviedo from the top of this mountain. Oviedo sat in a bowl surround by snowy, mountainous peaks on all sides. It was the most beautifully fulfilling sight I had ever seen.

Our crew strolled to the other side of the mountain platform and passed a sign that said Monte Naranco, confirming that we had climbed a mountain, not a small hill, like we thought originally.

"Holy hell, it's the ocean!" shouted Devon.

The Atlantic Ocean touched the northern Spanish coast a few miles away and faded into the distance. The afternoon sun shimmered in its reflection.

CHAPTER 3

School started on Monday, so by the time Wednesday rolled around, we were already tired of structure and begged summer vacation to return. I enrolled in five Spanish classes: translation, vocabulary, grammar, phonetics, and Spanish history. Devon and Brad enrolled in the same courses.

On the way to our 8:00 grammar class, Devon and I stopped by a café near the Universidad de Oviedo campus. I ordered a *café con leche*, a simple drink, since I never drank coffee before crossing the Spanish border. I spotted a familiar face sitting on a corner couch. The guy wore a snapback Yankees hat, a plain black t-shirt, and skinny khaki pants. *I had translation class with him*, I thought. Devon and I walked over and sat by him.

"Hey, man. We have a few classes with you, don't we?" I asked.

"Yeah, I think so. History or something?" He replied.

"Something like that. I'm Jason," I said as I extended my

hand. "This is my roommate Devon."

"I'm Marcos Rodriguez. Nice to meet you guys," he said. "Where you guys from?"

"Portland and San Francisco. What about you," I inquired.

"Me? I'm a New York City kid. I go to Rutgers in New Jersey, though. Just started my sophomore year," he said.

"That's cool. How did you like growing up in NYC?" Devon asked.

"*Hombre*, it was fun. Always something to do, something going on. My parents moved there from Puerto Rico a year before I was born and we've lived there ever since," he said. He spoke rapidly with a thick Puerto Rican accent.

"Awesome. So you must be pretty good at Spanish then, eh?" I asked.

"Yeah, my parents spoke Spanish to my older sister and I at home, but we spoke English at school, so I had the best of both worlds, really," he said.

We continued to talk as we finished our coffees. I stood up to leave and Marcos made the same move. His head came up to my shoulder. Devon and I walked out of the café with Marcos after we paid 50 *centimos* for our drinks. He had class at the same time. The faculty placed him in the "advanced" classes, naturally. We parted ways with him at the front door of the main university building with a quick "Later, dude."

Three hours later, I was done with class for the day. Devon wanted to take a nap and Brad left for his apartment to do the same. Still full of energy from my life's third cup of coffee, I wanted to run around and explore the city.

I walked through the cathedral plaza and down a small street that I assumed was the old medieval portion of Oviedo. The three-story buildings looked like they hadn't seen a remodel since the beginning of time. They were beautiful structures and surprisingly well-kept, though. I walked through a familiar plaza and recognized the bar that Devon and I drank at the other night. I took a right and strolled down a more modern street that opened into a populated intersection. I noticed a large park across the street, so I decided to check it out. Passing a random bronze statue of Woody Allen, I crossed the street after the signal told me that I was permitted to do so.

The park was massive. Pathways intersected each other around every corner. Who knows where they started or ended? In the middle of the park, I saw kids skateboarding on a small halfpipe decorated in colorful graffiti. I sat on a bench by the main pedestrian thoroughfare and people-watched. Old men strolled slowly. Most walked alone with contemplative expressions. More than ten men walked by my bench within five minutes, all alone and in different directions. They strolled at a snail's pace, hands clasped behind their backs, promoting an upright posture. Heads held high. *People take their time here*, I thought. I could get used to this.

o   o   o

The next day, my history class took a field trip to the cathedral. Our professor led us out of the classroom and we strolled down the same path that I took on my exploration the day before. The walk took about 10 minutes yesterday, but our professor turned around to give us quick history tidbits every so often, so it took about 25 minutes today.

"Has anybody seen the cathedral yet?" our professor asked in Spanish.

Devon, Brad, and I raised our hands, along with two other classmates. Only five? That meant that more than 15 people in our class hadn't explored the center of the city yet.

"Who are these squares?" Brad whispered.

"Yeah. They've been here for a week and haven't seen downtown? What the hell?" Devon whispered back.

"I know, right? What have these squares done all week?" I joked, a little too loudly.

"Well, I've been studying for the grammar and translation tests coming up," said a snooty female voice in front of us, clearly responding to my comment.

Devon snorted quickly, holding back his laughter at my lack of social graces. Mistaking Devon's laugh for mine, the woman whipped her head around and caught my eye. I twitched my head back a bit to avoid her swinging dark-haired ponytail. Her piercing glare felt like a slap in the face. Her lips tensed as she prepared to fire.

"And who might you be?" she asked with a sharp tone.

"Jason Cologne. Glad to meet you. What's your name?" I asked with an overly-joyful tone in an attempt to cover my tracks.

"Audrey Reigert," she replied coldly.

I extended my hand, hoping the greeting would serve as a peace offering. She looked at it and turned around, continuing her conversation with the guy next to her. I received a sharp elbow to the ribs from Brad, who looked like a second grade kid trying to control the laughter swelling inside of him.

"Nice," Devon whispered to me after he suppressed his own childlike silent giggles.

In an effort to shake off my terrible first impression, I

tried to strike up a conversation with the guy talking with Audrey.

"What about you, man? What's your name?" I asked politely.

"Stan Johnson," he said awkwardly.

He stood at equal height to Audrey and wore a denim jacket with brown pants. His light brown hair was perfectly sculpted into a business-like combover, keeping in line with his freshly shaven face and thick-rimmed eyeglasses.

"Nice to meet you, Stan. How's your day going so far?" I replied.

"Oh, just fine. How about you-r's?" he said, more awkwardly than his first response.

"It's going great, thanks for asking," I said as I shot a quick glance toward Audrey, who was involved in our new conversation by default. "Where are you two from?" I asked.

"Well, I'm from Des Moines, Iowa. She's from," he paused.

"Paris," she interjected.

"Oh man," I said, halfway sounding interested. "We're some West Coast kids back here."

"Americans?" Audrey asked.

"Yeah buddy!" I said proudly.

"I should have known," she said before turning her head. Her ponytail flipped over her shoulder with significant torque.

We arrived at the front of the cathedral and gathered in a condensed group in the middle of the empty plaza. Our professor rambled on in rapid Spanish about the construction of the building and its improbable survival after the destruction that Oviedo endured during the Spanish Civil

War in the 1930s. She arranged a private tour for us, led by a Catholic nun from the adjacent convent.

My heart skipped a beat as we entered the main doors. The high-vaulted ceilings gave me a little bit of vertigo as I looked up. Brad and I walked down the main isle to the ornate altar area. I explored behind the altar and turned around to check out the church form the priest's view. For such a small town, the cathedral was humongous. As it turned out, Oviedo served as Spain's capital city during the Catholic reconquest of Muslim occupation during the late first millennium.

The nun led our group up a flight of stairs, bypassing the velvet rope that kept tourists out and faculty in. We entered a room held together by thick stone walls and a solid wooden door supported by steel security bolts. Directly through the door hung a version of the cross I saw at the base of *El Cristo*. The nun explained that we stood in Oviedo's sacred treasure room. Behind thick glass walls sat chests rumored to contain sacred Catholic relics and jewels gathered from centuries of military exploits. Then, she told the story of the cross.

By the late 700s, the Muslim Empire controlled most of the Iberian Peninsula. The area around Oviedo served as the last Catholic stronghold. An intense battle took place in a nearby town called Covadonga. A loss for the Catholic army meant the Muslim Empire would control the entire peninsula and Catholicism would be wiped from the area. King Pelayo, the Catholic hero, bravely fought and won the battle, prompting the gradual 700-year reconquest of Muslim Spain by the Catholic army. To inspire his troops to continue fighting future battles, he instructed a master metalworker to create a symbol made of luscious gems and gold. After working for weeks, the worker emerged with a giant cross, ornately woven with jewels of all colors. The original cross now serves as the symbol for Oviedo and its overarching province, Asturias. Pelayo's cross hung from the wall before my very eyes.

I stood in awe of the symbol. As a Catholic from Italian heritage, it was a powerful experience. I noticed Brad's gaze fixed on the cross as well.

"Pretty cool, huh?" I said.

"Yeah, man. I come from a big Irish-Catholic family, so I love stuff like this," he said. His eyes never left the cross.

"I'm not even that religious and this stuff is cool," whispered Devon. "Pelayo was a badass."

"Look at Stan and Audrey talking about the texture of the stone walls," I whispered, overcautiously this time.

"How can they look at something that boring when this thing jumps out at you?" said Devon, pointing at the cross.

"They were made for each other, I guess," joked Brad.

The tour concluded. With class done and our live history lesson for the day out of the way, the three of us decided to grab some food. We strolled down a wide cobblestone street with an unlit sign that read *Calle de Gascona*. The tables in the sidewalk area gave the appearance that the whole street was filled with restaurants, so we cruised down the middle of the road to check it out. We sat down at a table outside. This restaurant sat on the corner of two semi-populated streets, providing a prime people-watching opportunity.

Our waiter came to our table. He dressed in all black and looked a little older than us. Late twenties, early thirties perhaps. We chatted with him in basic Spanish, attempting to use the skills that we learned in class over the past few days. He asked us if we wanted to start off with some drinks, so we did. He returned a few minutes later with three small glasses and three bottles of something that resembled white wine.

"What is this?" Brad asked our waiter.

"*Sidra*," he responded. "Made from apples."

"*Bueno.*"

The waiter uncorked the bottle. He held the bottle high above his head, stretching his right arm to its highest capacity. With his left hand, he grabbed a glass and held it low by his waist. Then, he began to pour. The *sidra* flowed from the bottle to the rim of the glass far below, creating a frothy texture as it filled the glass. He quickly stopped the fountain-like pour, though there was only about a sip of *sidra* in the glass so far. He placed the glass in front of me.

"That's it?" I asked, looking at the nearly completely empty cup.

"Yes! Drink it! Quickly!" the waiter rambled in Spanish.

Panicked, I followed his directions and gulped the minimal contents of the cup. He poured the same amount for Brad and Devon, who drank the *sidra* in similar fashion. Then, he poured us three more glasses with impeccable accuracy.

"Why don't you fill it?" Devon asked.

"The pour gives the drink air. It needs to breathe," the waiter responded. "It's Asturian tradition. You can only find this style in Northern Spain. Oviedo is famous for its *sidra*!"

We ate a plate of *patatas fritas*. Our waiter returned to pour our second bottle.

"What's your name, sir?" I asked.

"Fernando," he said.

"Nice to meet you, Fernando. I'm Jason. This is Brad and Devon," I replied.

"Nice you meet you, *chicos*. Americans or English?" he

asked.

"Americans," Brad answered. "Spanish?"

"Venezuelan," Fernando replied with suave South American style.

"Cool."

Fernando spoke no English, so we talked with him in Spanish for a while longer in between *sidra* pours. He told us that he owned the restaurant. On Friday and Saturday nights, young Spanish girls around our age come to his restaurant to eat and drink before going to the *discotecas*. He encouraged us to come by around 22:00 and see for ourselves.

"Do you know those American girls at that table over there?" he asked as he opened our third bottle.

"No. Why?" I asked.

"They keep staring this way. Maybe they like you," he jested.

"No, we don't know them. I don't think we do, at least," Devon said.

"Well, I'll go talk to them for you," Fernando replied as he walked over to check on their meal.

We watched him as he conversed with the four white girls. They laughed and looked our direction.

"Oh man, what's he saying?" Devon asked.

"Who knows? He's either talking us up or embarrassing us, either way," I said.

"He seems like he's on our side. I bet he's talking us up," encouraged Brad.

A few minutes later, Fernando returned to our table.

"They think you *chicos* are very handsome. They want to meet you," he reported.

"Well that's good news!" Devon said, relieved.

"*Sí.* Two are American. Two blonde girls are German. But they speak English," Fernando continued. "Go talk to them. Maybe they want to date you," he said, halfway jokingly.

He poured the last of our third *sidra* bottle into our glasses, giving us enough liquid courage to approach their table.

"Hi, how are you girls doing this afternoon?" Devon asked.

"Fine. And you?" said one of the German girls.

"Fine, fine. Fernando told us you spoke English, so we figured we would say hello, since no one else in Oviedo seems to speak it," Devon replied.

"Where are you from?" Brad asked the two brunettes to our left.

"I'm from Seattle. I go to the University of Washington. She's from back East," said the prettier of the two.

"Oh, UW, huh? We can't talk to you then," I said, with a true hint of seriousness in my voice. I had bad experiences with Huskies in the past.

"Oh really? You must be a Duck, then?" she asserted.

"Of course I am!" I fired back.

The German girls looked confused, clearly unaware of the state rivalry between the college football powerhouses.

"We hear this place pops off early Friday nights. We're going to check it out. You ladies should join us," Devon said smoothly.

"We just might," said the pretty brunette.

She and Devon locked eyes for a moment.

"I'm Roxanne," she said, still gazing at Devon.

"I'm Devon," he responded, emphasizing his suaveness.

"Alright, well we have to pay Fernando, but we'll see you girls Friday?" Brad said.

"Yeah. Sounds like fun," said the German closest to me. "*Adios.*"

We entered the indoor section of the bar to pay. The walls shined with fresh bright green and contrasting black paint. Modern wooden tables covered the floor all the way to the back wall. The bar sat near the front on the left side, while booths encircled the remaining wall sections. The black floor concealed *sidra* drops and spilled drinks. Apple portraits hung from the walls. Though recently renovated, the bar gave off an authentic, old-world Spanish vibe.

Brad told Fernando about our conversation with the girls. We thanked him for helping us out and told him that we would be back on Friday night. He said he would have a table ready for us if we showed up.

"What's your bar called?" I shouted on the way out the door.

"*El Serpiente,*" Fernando replied.

CHAPTER 4

Friday rolled around. Thankfully, I only had to sit in class for two hours. I thought about the night ahead during my translation class. I hoped the girls that we met on Wednesday would show up to *El Serpiente*. One of the German girls was a babe. Her accent was unreal! Hopefully Fernando would save a table for us so we looked really cool.

"Jason!" demanded our professor.

"Uh, *si?*" I replied. *What the hell is she talking about?*

"*Numero 11, por favor*," she said.

"Um, well, um," I babbled, completely unaware of the page number or section our entire class was in the process of discussing.

Devon tapped on his open book slyly; his pointer finger indicated page 17. I flipped my book quickly to the correct page and rattled off a decent response.

"Thanks, dude," I whispered.

"Audrey, *numero 12, por favor*," our professor said.

She read her response, which she said with a ridiculously

forced Spanish accent that made me wince.

"*Perfecto*," our teacher hailed.

Audrey looked around the room as if she expected applause and a parade for her flawless sentence translation.

"Of course," I whispered to Devon.

Class ended at 11:00. Devon, Brad, and I sat in front of the main building and kicked a soccer ball around in the courtyard. We brainstormed a list of activities for the rest of our day.

"We have to kill time until late tonight. Fernando said people show up at the bar at ten and the *discotecas* open around two in the morning," I reminded them.

"Yeah, that's crazy. What a different schedule than we're used to, uh?" said Brad.

Marcos walked out of the building.

"Hey, dude. You done for the week?" I asked.

"Yeah, man. I just finished. First week of class is over. I'm ready to see what an Oviedo weekend is all about," he replied.

"Yeah, me too. We're going to this bar called *El Serpiente* around ten. I guess that's where all the girls our age go before the dance clubs open. You can cruise with us if you want," I told him.

"Sweet! Sounds good to me," he said as he dropped his backpack and jumped into the passing circle.

We kicked the ball around for a little while, and then decided to explore the city.

"I cruised through this huge park a few days ago. They had some cement soccer fields and a small basketball court. You guys want to check it out?" I proposed.

"Let's do it," Marcos affirmed.

Our conversation focused mainly on Marcos, since we

didn't know him that well. He told us some Spanish words he picked up in his advanced classes that would make us sound less like tourists. The four of us walked through the park for about ten minutes until we found the cement soccer pitch. When we approached the fence surrounding the pitch, it was packed with people already playing. We leaned against the fence and watched.

"Woah, these guys are good," Brad said.

"Yeah, dude. Look at the guy in the yellow Brazil jersey. He's schoolin' the other team all by himself!" Devon exclaimed.

"No way, the other team has huge guys on the team. I bet they play some mean defense," I refuted.

"What language are they speaking?" Marcos asked. "It's definitely not Spanish."

"Who knows, man," I responded.

The game increased in intensity with every pass. Each team consisted of four players and a goalie. The cement pitch was the size of a basketball court with metal goal posts that were about my height and double that in width. One team had five black players. The other team had three South Americans and two Spaniards, I assumed, but it was hard to tell. The crowd of 30 surrounding the fence matched the ethnicities of both teams. We stuck out immediately.

The guy in the yellow Brazil jersey looked Brazilian himself. He danced around an opposing defender and ripped a shot to the top-right corner of the goal from mid-court. Every fan along the fence went crazy, no matter which team they supported. Some with excitement and some with angry disappointment.

"What's the score?" I asked a guy next to me in Spanish.

"2-2," he said in Spanish with a thick African accent of some kind.

"What do they play to?" I persisted.

"First team to three," he said.

"Cool, thanks."

A few minutes later, a chiseled African forward chipped the ball above two defenders and his teammate headed it passed the goalie's left side. The Spaniards and South Americans hung their heads, but shook hands with the opposition as the onlookers shook the fence with wild excitement.

"Where are you from," I asked the guy next to me.

"Senegal," he responded. "The whole team out there is from Senegal and Cameroon. Where are you guys from?"

"We're from the U.S.," I responded.

"What about those guys?" Marcos asked, pointing at the losing team.

"Brazil and Colombia, mostly," he told us.

"Not Spain?" I asked.

"No, not in this park," he affirmed.

The African team grabbed water, then headed back onto the pitch. A new team of presumably South Americans walked on to oppose them.

"You guys want the next game?" the Senegalese man asked us.

"Oh no, not today," Devon responded quickly.

We watched the next game intently. An African forward took the kickoff and shot immediately. The ball whizzed past the goalie before he had time to move. The fence shook as his 15 fellow Africans banged on it. A South American ripped a shot from the halfway line a few minutes later. It nailed the crossbar and found a South American teammate ready to head it through for the tying goal. Kickoff.

A South American dribbled up the sideline and received a swift elbow to the chest from a defender, sending him to the ground hard. The fans went crazy, but no one called for a foul. The African possessed the ball in dribbled fancifully into the goalie box, where he received a hard shoulder to the chest before he had time to fire a shot. They played rough out there! The fresh South Americans scored two quick goals on the tired African team, who barely had time to recover from their first victory.

We left after watching another game, not wanting to play ourselves. Those guys were significantly better than us, we concluded.

After a nap and some dinner, Devon and I got ready for the night. The clock read *19:00*, so we still had two hours until we needed to cruise to *El Serpiente*.

"What should we do, man?" Devon asked me.

"I don't know? We got ready way too early," I laughed.

"We could grab a beer, I guess," he suggested.

"Cool, cool," I affirmed.

We took the elevator to the first floor and strolled out of the apartment building. The market next to our building was open, so we walked in and browsed through the beer isle.

"Check it out! They sell 40s in here!" I said, looking at a liter of beer.

"No way! Old English?" he joked.

"No, San Miguel, whatever that is. It's pretty cheap. Way cheaper than a six pack," I said.

"Cool, let's each get one and see where that takes us," he suggested.

We each bought a 40 (technically a liter, but we called them 40s out of college-bred habit). We heard a rumor that Spanish law allowed open alcohol containers on the street, so we took our 40s to the park with the soccer pitch. We sat on a bench near the middle of the park in a heavily shaded area. I cracked my bottle and took a sip.

"Well, it's no Estrella Damm, but it'll do the job," I said.

For Spain, the night was just getting under way. Couples strolled through the park and walked typically small Spanish dogs that were bred for apartments. Kids ran through the fields and trees and played games. Old men sat on benches and watched life happen.

"This is the life," Devon said after a few minutes of silence.

"Yeah, man. People move at a slower pace around here, and I like it," I replied.

"Yeah, I could get used to this."

We finished our San Miguels and walked toward *El Serpiente*. On the way, we rang Brad's doorbell. He hustled downstairs and we continued on our mission. We found out where Marcos lived earlier that day, so we took a slight detour to pick him up as well. The four of us walked into *El Serpiente* with a bit of uncertainty. *Would Fernando remember us?* He saw us immediately and called us over.

"*Chicos!*" he said, as he motioned to a table across from the bar.

"*Hola, Fernando,*" we said, almost in unison.

"What would you like? More *sidra?*" he asked.

"*Bueno,*" I responded, receiving affirming head nods from the group.

He returned with a bottle and four glasses, which he

poured with awe-inspiring accuracy from above his head.

"You'll have to teach me how to do that," Brad asked, half serious.

"It's easy. Fill a bottle with water and practice in the shower," Fernando responded. "Where are your ladies tonight? I thought they were coming with you."

"Yeah, maybe they'll show up at some point," Devon said.

"Hey, Fernando. This is Marcos. He's from New York and he's in our program," I said.

They spoke in rapid Spanish. I couldn't understand them well. Judging by the look on Brad's face, he was having trouble understanding the conversation as well. We finished our first bottle quickly with the help of Marcos as a new teammate.

Fernando brought us a second bottle as the four girls walked through the front door. They spotted us, but we were engaged in a conversation with Fernando and didn't notice them. They approached our table shyly. Fernando moved four chairs to our table and strategically placed the seats so that each of us could sit close to a girl. It was kind of hilarious actually. Roxanne sat next to Devon and they hit it off immediately. The pretty blonde German girl sat by me.

"Hello. How are you?" she asked me with her thick German accent.

"I'm great. How are you?" I responded.

"Good."

"How's you night going so far?" I asked.

"Good."

A real chatterbox, I thought.

"So, what part of Germany are you from?" I asked.

"Munich," she said after pausing to digest the translation.

"Her Spanish is much better than her English," Roxanne whispered, noticing the growing discomfort I was having with the conversation.

"Cool, thanks," I replied.

"*Hablas español, si?*" I asked the pretty German girl.

The conversation picked up quickly after that. I found that once I got in the groove of speaking Spanish, I spoke well enough. The *sidra* helped. It took away my inhibitions regarding perfect conjugation and all of that nonsense. The German girl's name was Heidi. Coincidently, she went with her family to Oktoberfest the same day I did, though we never ran into each other in the crowd of thousands. It is the biggest festival in the world, after all. Brad grew less and less interested in his American companion by the minute, though it wasn't too obvious. Marcos didn't seem interested in the German girl sitting next to him, either.

Fernando brought more *sidra*. Eventually, the clock struck one, so we left *El Serpiente* to find the *discotecas*. We paid for the *sidra*, which wasn't expensive at all, thankfully. Fernando told us that we needed to walk a few blocks south to reach *Calle Mon*, which had 30 or so *discotecas* lining the street and surrounding area.

We stopped at another bar near the beginning of *Calle Mon*. A man outside told us that we could get free shots of liquor if we went in, so we obliged. After accepting our free *chupitos*, which tasted liked mysteriously flavored green juice, we wanted to leave and find a dance hall. Heidi and Roxanne followed us four guys, but the other two girls wanted to stay, so we said our goodbyes. Roxanne and Devon led the pack on our mission to dance. Heidi and I talked throughout the entire walk, with Marcos and Brad trailing as the caboose.

Heidi was somewhat of an interesting girl. I grew a little infatuated by her exotic appeal. Her fit body and pretty face helped, also.

Finally, we found a *discoteca* that was packed, so we figured it must be fun. Roxanne and Devon disappeared into the crowd and Heidi and I followed. We walked to the second floor and into a large dance room. Thumping techno beats blasted through the hall. Blacklights and neon lasers danced on the walls. The occasional smoke from the smoke machine filled the room, making the shoulder-to-shoulder crowd nearly invisible. Sweat poured from my face.

Heidi grabbed my hand and led me to the middle of the crowd. She could dance. I kept up. I saw Marcos at the bar, where he and Brad bought beers. They wandered through the crowds, presumably searching for girls to dance with. To my left, I saw Roxanne and Devon making out. *Yeah, go roommate!* I thought. Heidi saw them, too.

She looked back at me and tried to make seductive eye contact, but my mind had shifted. For some reason, I didn't want to dance with her anymore. Sure, she was attractive, but there was something missing in our conversations, something intangible. I needed more time to figure her out.

Heidi leaned in further toward me as the song shifted beats. I looked back at the bar and feigned a wave to Marcos and Brad. As Heidi continued to move closer, I stepped away and disappeared into the crowd.

○   ○   ○

I woke up late Saturday afternoon. The oven clock in the kitchen read *15:00*. I got back to the apartment at six in the morning after a crazy night of dancing, drinking, and dancing. And drinking. Devon emerged from his room about 15 minutes later. He looked like death.

"Ouch. I have to stop drinking, man. These Spanish hangovers are killing me," he mumbled as he reached aimlessly into the refrigerator.

"I feel you, Dev," I replied. "How'd your night turn out?"

"Dude, great," he said. "I walked Roxanne home super late. Or super early. However you want to look at it. I got a little lost walking back to our apartment, though, but it worked out. How was your night? How'd things work out with you and Heidi," he said.

"Heidi's a babe and everything, but she's a little dull, man. I lost her in the crowd shuffle a little before sunrise, but I found Brad and Marcos. We walked home around six, I think," I replied.

"Cool. Maybe you'll see her again. I know I want to meet up with Roxy again, that's for sure," he said affirmatively. "Are you into Heidi or what?"

"I don't know. She seemed fun some of the time. It could have been the *sidra* thinking for me, though. Who knows?" I responded.

"It happens. I got Roxy's phone number last night before we said goodbye. I'm amped!"

"Cool. Well, hey. You want to grab a coffee?" I suggested.

"Let's do it."

I put on a backwards baseball hat to cover my bed head and opted for flip flops instead of shoes. Devon threw on his classic green "Oregon" sweatshirt and we took the elevator to the first floor. A middle-aged woman struggled to open the front door to the building as she balanced two grocery bags in her left arm. Devon mustered some hustle to help her before she dropped her food. I grabbed the door.

"*Gracias*," she said as she made her way to the elevator.

I expended little energy throughout the day. Devon and I sat outside of the café near the university for about an hour. The sun hung in the sky, but the awning kept us cool. The other two outdoor tables were empty, but plenty of people walked down the street to satisfy our people-watching fix for the day. Our waitress tended to our table every ten minutes.

"More coffee?" she asked, noticing our small cups looked nearly empty.

"Please," I responded.

She returned a few minutes later with two more *café con leches*. After a quick stint behind the counter, she brought a newspaper to our table. Devon thanked her and set it on an empty chair at our table.

"What's your name?" I asked the waitress.

"Anna," she answered. "And yours?"

"Jason," I said. "We're students at the Universidad de Oviedo."

"Oh, and what do you study?" she inquired.

"Spanish," I said, perhaps a little too confidently.

Her Spanish increased its speed.

"I see. I graduated from the university last year. Where are you from?"

"The United States. We're here for four months to learn…and stuff," I replied awkwardly, intimidated by her quickened pace. "Are you from Oviedo?"

"Yes. I live three blocks away from here. My parents own the café, so I work here now. I'll probably take it over one day. I studied political science, but it's impossible to find a job here, you know," she admitted.

Sensing she released too much personal information too quickly, she returned to a universal surface topic.

"Are you going to watch the soccer game tonight?" she asked.

"What game?" I replied.

"*El Clasico!*" she erupted. "Barcelona against Real Madrid. The two best teams in the world!"

"Oh, I didn't know they were playing tonight," I said sheepishly.

"You didn't read the newspaper I gave you?" she asked.

Glancing at the front page headline of the newspaper on the empty seat, I saw the faces of Barcelona's Lionel Messi and Real Madrid's Cristiano Ronaldo posed against each other in a style reminiscent of pre-fight hype in the boxing world.

"Yeah, we'll watch it. What about you?" I asked in an attempt to cover my tracks.

"Of course! Go Barca!"

"Where's a fun place to watch it?"

"*El Serpiente*, usually. I'll probably go there with my friends before the game starts to grab a table," she said.

"We drank there last night. It's a fun place," Devon interjected.

Another customer passed our table and entered the café, so Anna hurried to greet her. On our way out, we paid for our coffees.

"Maybe we'll see you at *El Serpiente* tonight," I said wishfully.

"Yes, you should go. Only if you cheer for Barca, though," she said. She shot me a quick smile, and then returned to her customer interaction.

As Devon and I strolled back to our apartment, thoughts of Anna replaced any memory of Heidi. Anna's confidence attracted me. Her tan, exotic complexion paired with her long, black hair emblazoned my mind. Her smile. And those dimples!

"Did you see that? Our waitress had some big... *café con leches*," Devon said as we turned the corner.

"Yeah, she was a babe!" I said.

"Is it just me, or do all Spanish girls look like models?" Devon asked.

"I know, dude. We picked the right place to study abroad, uh?" I said.

"Yeah, man. They should change the name from Oviedo to Ciudad de Babes," Devon joked.

"Good one," I jested.

"Let's go to *El Serpiente* and try to watch the game with the waitress and her friends tonight," Devon said.

"I'm down."

Babe City.

We hopped on the elevator and exited on the fifth floor. Devon dropped his keys and a laughed at him. He picked them up and unlocked the door. I sat in the kitchen and attempted to read the newspaper that Anna gave us. I didn't want to be embarrassed again, after all. The headline underneath the Barcelona vs. Real Madrid story indicated something about a strike next week. I read part of the story, but the details escaped me. It sounded like the buses would be closed, but that didn't affect my daily routine. I paid close attention to the statistics on the sports page. I needed to know everything about Barcelona's season so I could match my soccer wits against this unknown crowd of Anna's friends.

Devon and I left the house a few hours later. I wanted to arrive early so we could secure a table and grab a drink before the game started. Hopefully a little *sidra* would give my Spanish some fluidity. We entered *El Serpiente* as the dinner crowd exited. Fernando saw us and motioned toward a table in front of the largest of the bar's two television screens. About 20 minutes before the game started, large crowds walked through the door. Most people were close to our age, though some middle-aged groups filtered through the crowd. I watched each passing group avidly, hoping to catch Anna.

"Dude! Look who's here," Devon said excitedly.

My heart jumped as I whipped my head around to look at the door. I expected to see the Spanish beauty leading her group of equally pretty friends through the door. Instead, I saw Roxanne, followed by a few friends, including Heidi.

I had forgotten all about the blonde German girl from last night. My new fixation with Anna shadowed the already cloudy memory of the *discoteca*. And we bonded without *sidra* involved, which I liked. That didn't matter now. Heidi inched closer to our table as she shuffled through the crowd. Roxy caught Devon's eye and waved. We waved back.

"Here they come. What are you going to do if Anna shows up?" Devon whisper quickly.

"Who knows? Make it up as I go along, I guess," I replied.

Devon and I sat calmly at our table in the back corner of the room. Roxanne, Heidi, and three unfamiliar female faces sat in a few empty chairs awkwardly placed around the table. Heidi sat directly across from me. When the game started, she would turn to watch, taking the pressure off of me.

"What did you two do all afternoon?" Roxanne asked me

casually from across the table.

"Nothing. Coffee," I replied in an attempt not to sound panicked. "What about you?"

"Oh, nothing much. I bought some food at the market around the corner from my apartment building. I emailed my parents. I figured I would let them know that I'm still breathing," she joked in her seemingly usual chipper tone.

I attempted to control my breathing as I saw Anna walk through the door. Two female friends and a male accomplice followed her. Devon shot me a look that said, *Here we go!* I tried to avoid eye contact with her, as Heidi sheepishly conversed with me in English. I knew Heidi didn't interest me. She was a sweet girl, but my feelings of infatuation with her left as quickly as they arrived. I couldn't help but take fleeting glances in Anna's direction during my increasingly dull conversation with Heidi. *I shouldn't have kissed her last night,* I thought, kicking myself. This situation wouldn't be so difficult if I used a little more self-control at the *discoteca.*

As I conversed passively, I watched Anna approach the bar. She ordered a drink. Estrella Damm. A beer-drinker. I respect that. She looked even more stunning than she did in her café uniform. High heels, miniskirt, and a loose sweater. Her friends ordered something, but the growing crowd inhibited my detective-like stakeout.

One of Roxanne's friends stood up and made her way to the bathroom, forcing me to stand and let her pass. I saw Anna look my direction as I stood, so I looked toward her. We locked eyes and she waved. I returned the gesture. Our whole table looked that direction to see who I was waving at. *Damn,* I thought. I walked over to her table to say hello. Their table seemed too small for their group, so I invited them our direction. They accepted the invitation. *What was I getting myself into?*

I introduced my friends at the table and Anna and her Spanish counterparts did the same. We squished together to fit everyone in the same table vicinity, forcing Heidi further away from my stationary booth position. The Spanish male in Anna's group sat by Heidi. Anna sat across from me, forcing Roxanne to shift directly across from Devon. The bar volume increased by the second. I could talk to the people in my immediate radius, making conversation with Heidi impossible. I made small talk with Anna for a few minutes, and then the bar erupted in a deafening roar.

El Clasico kicked off. Barcelona's midfielder dribbled down the sideline and set an accurate cross to the top of the 18-yard box. Barcelona's Lionel Messi leapt, but the ball exceeded his reach by mere feet.

The bar erupted at the early display of near-perfect accuracy from the midfielder's cross. Real Madrid's Cristiano Ronaldo sprinted ahead of his defender a few minutes later. He faked right toward the sideline and the defender bit hard, sending Ronoldo to the corner of the box. He fired a shot that sailed over the crossbar. A passing defender impeded his direct aim. Ronoldo hit the ground and grabbed his face as the defender barely nicked his left arm. The crowd booed incessantly at the Madrid star's flop. I gathered that the majority of the crowd wanted Barcelona to win.

Ten minutes into the game and the atmosphere was already this intense? I noticed Heidi glancing in my direction, clearly not interested much in the game. The Spanish man said a few words to her, but *El Clasico* captured his attention, as did mine for the time being. After a scoreless first half, the table members turned inward to chat during halftime. Now the Spanish man refocused his attention on Heidi. Gradually, she gave him the same passion-induced glances that she gave me the night before.

I saw my opening. I focused on conversing with Anna and one of her female friends, using Devon as my midfielder on the sideline for support and comic relief. The flow of conversation intensified. I noticed Anna smiling at me as I made her laugh. I liked it. Heidi seemed content with the Spaniard.

The second half kicked off. Fernando placed an Estrella Damm in front of me and one in front of Devon. Ronaldo scored a quick goal with a selfish run down the right side of the field. He faked a pass to an open forward and ripped a shot from the top corner of the box to put Real Madrid up 1-0. Ten minutes later, Messi retaliated with a give-and-go, placing the ball inches above the goalies reach.

Time ticked faster. Five minutes of regular time remained. Barcelona's David Villa danced with the ball on the left sideline, closely guarded. I caught Anna's eye and she smiled, looking back at the television. Villa booted the ball through two defenders, finding Messi's right foot near the penalty kick dot.

Anna wetted her lips with her tongue. Messi feigned left. Anna's femininity protruded through her loose grey sweater as she leaned forward in anticipation. The goalie dove low as Messi chipped the ball into the top left corner. The bar erupted with wild excitement. Fernando placed a beer in front of Anna and told her that I bought it for her. He shot me a wink as she turned to thank me. Her large brown eyes captured me. Lust filled my body. *Heidi who?*

Our entire group left the bar about ten minutes after the game ended. I walked with Anna toward the front of the group for a bit.

"Did you enjoy the game?" she asked.

"Yeah, it was crazy!" I replied. "Did you?"

"Yes! Barca won. I love Barca. Did you like my friends?" she questioned.

"Yeah, they seemed nice. Who was the guy?" I said.

"He's my friend from elementary school. I think he likes that German girl. He made her laugh a lot," she deduced. "Is she your friend?"

"Kind of. I met her last night. She knows Roxanne," I deflected. "Hey, we should get together sometime. I want to practice speaking Spanish."

"Yes. That sounds fun! I can teach you," she said excitedly. "Let me see your hand."

Anna pulled a pen from her purse and wrote her phone number on my wrist.

"Cool."

Anna and her friends took a left near *Calle Uria* and headed for home. *Calle Uria* was lined with expensive designer clothing stores, but they were closed at this time of night. Heidi and the Spanish man hung back a ways, stalling. I saw them exchange phone numbers. I caught Roxanne's eye and she looked a bit sorry for me.

"Heidi, I'm going home, I'll see you later," Roxanne yelled.

"Fine. I'll walk with the other girls. I'll be fine," she said awkwardly in an attempt to conceal her plans with the Spaniard.

Devon, Roxanne, and I walked under a small tunnel

through some apartment complexes into our Pumarin neighborhood. Roxanne lived five blocks from our place.

"Rough, dude. Heidi stepped out on you, huh?" Roxanne said in an effort to console me.

"Yeah, it's cool though," I said calmly.

"Don't worry, man," she added with genuine spunk. "I just met her the other day and she agitates me already."

"He's into Anna now, anyways," Devon assured.

"Oh, big Jason, the ladykiller!" she jabbed.

"Whatever, Roxy! You go to UW. I can't take you seriously," I jabbed back.

She pushed my right shoulder enough to throw me off balance. I pushed back lightly in the same fashion. We laughed a little. Roxanne had a spark to her that I liked. She was small, but athletically built from years on the water polo team and summer surf outings in California. Her light brown hair accentuated her lightly freckled face. Her green eyes sparkled a bit. In a way, she reminded me of my younger sister. Bold with a firecracker personality, yet she possessed a mature sweetness.

"That game! I can't believe Barcelona won like that. Messi is the man!" Roxanne said.

"I know! I want to go to a Barcelona game so bad," I added.

"I wish I went to one while I was there a few weeks ago," Devon regretted.

"Would you go back?" I asked.

"Hell yeah! Barcelona rocked," he retaliated.

"Let's do it," Roxanne said semi-seriously.

"Yeah, why not?" I added.

"Seriously? Let's do it," she replied.

"I'm down," Devon said.

"Alright then."

We half-heartedly brainstormed potential plans for a few blocks until we arrived at Roxanne's door. I hugged her goodbye. She followed it up with a swift punch to the left shoulder. She hugged Devon and kissed him. Devon and I walked home and discussed the night's events.

Devon went to bed. I stayed up and sat on our small deck for a while. The dark night obscured our view of *Monte Naranco*, but I saw *El Cristo* hover in illumination. I thought about Anna. For a minute, I felt jealous that Heidi flirted with the Spaniard, but those feelings passed as I thought about Anna more. Then, I pondered the crazy idea of visiting Barcelona with Devon and Roxanne. *I don't know this girl.* The uncertainty worried me, but something about the positive vibe surrounding the situation pulled me closer.

CHAPTER 5

Another week of school ended. Our ISP group scheduled a weekend class trip for the 30 American students to a neighboring coastal town called Llanes. In a Thursday group meeting, our program director told us that the bus left at 8:00. She heavily emphasized *on time*. Pity and waiting for late arrivals didn't exist. She canceled our Friday classes because the bus left Friday morning, allowing time to fit a day trip to the small mountain village of Covadonga into our excursion. She emphasized punctuality multiple times throughout the meeting to ensure that no student arrived late. She had a schedule and she intended to stick to it.

With the extended weekend, Devon, Brad, Marcos, and I decided to go out for a drink on Thursday evening. We told ourselves that we would return home early to ensure a full night of rest before our big weekend adventure. My 21st birthday began Saturday at midnight and my new friends wanted to take me out for a real American celebration, so I planned to rest up.

We walked into *El Serpiente* and Fernando greeted us. He placed an Estrella Damm in front of me and he asked about our evening after *El Clásico*. We raised our Estrella Damm bottles. *Salud*!

○　　○　　○

I jolted upright in my bed. My clock read *7:52*. I busted through Devon's door and yelled for him to wake up. He remained immobile and dormant. I grabbed a magazine from his desk and threw it at him. He rumbled.

"What time is it?" he murmured from beneath his covers.

"7:52 in the morning!" I shouted.

He shot out of bed and looked at the clock in the kitchen.

"Ahh! We're done for!" he yelled.

"Hurry up and pack. The bus leaves at 8:00 on the dot!" I shouted as I ran into my room.

My head throbbed as I put my basketball shorts on over my boxers. Still shirtless, I ransacked my drawers and threw necessary items of clothing into my backpack. Devon ran out of his room in shorts and a sweatshirt with his backpack hung from one shoulder. I grabbed our toothbrushes from the bathroom and Devon snagged a day-old baguette from the kitchen table. We sprinted out of the apartment, remembering to lock the door behind us.

7:55.

I forgot to put a shirt on before we left the house. I reached into my backpack and threw one over my head. Devon and I darted between crowds of suited men strolling to work. We avoided a screeching taxi by feet without breaking our stride.

7:57.

We ran up the stairs and through the small tunnel that signified the exit from the impoverished Pumarin neighborhood. My head throbbed harder. I contemplated stopping to throw up, but we pushed forward.

7:59.

We rounded the corner and our jelly legs carried us down the hill toward the departure point. We burst through a few tall bushes and planted our feet with the bus stop in front of us.

The bus engine rattled with energy as it anxiously awaited departure.

"Yes! We made it!" Devon shouted.

"You certainly did, *chicos*. We almost closed the doors and took off," our program director scolded.

I placed my hands on top of my head and breathed deeply through my nose. The thought of vomiting crossed my mind again.

"Hurry up!" the director urged.

I slowly walked onto the bus with Devon behind me. Nearly all the seats were filled except the ones toward the rear. Every pair of eyes glared at us as we walked down the aisle. Brad and Marcos laughed as we walked passed them.

"Congratulations! You boys made it. Three hours of sleep and we're still excited," Marcos said with inflected volume.

Brad added a light clap to assist our victorious entrance. Devon and I sat in the back row and rolled down the window to catch some air. Brad and Marcos sat together one row in front of us, but on the opposite side of the aisle. Devon cracked the baguette in half and gave a piece to me.

"Thanks, man," I panted, handing him my water bottle.

"That was too close," he wheezed.

We smiled and bumped knuckles in silence.

"Did you two go out drinking last night?" inquired a familiar, rude voice from the seat in front of us.

Audrey raised her head above the seat and turned around to stare at us with judgmental intent.

"Yes. Yes we did," I replied stoically, in no mood to deal with her square attitude.

"Wow. You guys would," she said, rolling her eyes.

"And what did you do last night, Audrey?" asked Brad.

"I went to bed and got a good night's rest, of course. We have a long weekend ahead with a two-hour bus ride," she said.

"Team Fun strikes again," Devon said under his breath.

Another silent knuckle bump. I fell asleep quickly and opened my eyes two hours later as our bus exited the highway into Llanes. Our bus stopped after he weaved through the small streets. The cobblestone roads narrowed so much that the bus couldn't fit, so we exited the buses in an orderly fashion and walked a few blocks to our hostel, where we would stay for two nights.

"Check this place out!" Brad exclaimed to me as we prepared to walk through the front door.

The hostel rose five stories. Its façade looked like it hadn't changed since the middle ages. Four people stayed in each room, so Brad, Marcos, Devon, and I each grabbed a key to room number 407. We took the stairs to stretch our legs from the bus ride. Four short beds spanned the right wall with no space in between them. The left wall provided a broad beach view through sprawling windows. A desk sat in the back-left corner, so we threw our bags on top of it.

"Let's check out the beach," I suggested.

"I'm down. Let me change first," Devon said, still wearing his bus ride hangover outfit.

As we left our room, Audrey entered the door to 408, which sat across the hallway from ours.

"Oh, great," she said, followed by her usual eye roll.

"Get ready for a fun weekend!" Marcos said sarcastically.

"Party in your room tonight?" Devon asked.

She cocked her head and looked at him for a few seconds, then continued into her room to unpack. We scurried toward the stairwell, where we unleashed ironic laughter at the brewing room placement situation. The four of us hustled across the street to the main beach. Huge crowds of people splashed in the tide.

"Man, there has to be a few more beaches, right?" Devon asked.

"Yeah, let's find one without so many people. I want to swim," I said.

We cruised through the city without a destination. We crossed a bridge over a river that ran through the middle of the city. A shopkeeper nodded to us as we passed his bar. *We'll see you in a few hours*, I thought. We wandered toward the ocean after backtracking into the city center. Extending our stroll to a vast lookout point, we noticed a small cove a hundred yards to our right.

"Let's explore that place," Brad said.

"Yeah, it looks like there's a beach down there," Marcos noticed.

We followed the cliffed coast line for a while until we stood above the cove's beach. We climbed down and found ourselves standing on soft, brown sand. I took my shoes off.

I looked around and saw towering cliffs above us in a "U" formation, opening into blue ocean. The beach itself was half the size of a football field. The only exit was the rickety staircase which we descended minutes earlier. The four of us were the only life forms in the secluded cove.

I found a small cave on the right side of the cliff wall and explored for 30 seconds until I came to an abrupt wall. I turned and exited.

"Let's go swimming!" Brad shouted. Echoes reverberated.

Swimsuit-clad, we sprinted into the ocean and dove. The cliffs extended into the ocean. A few girls from our group appeared atop the viewpoint from which we discovered our hidden cove. We waved to them and they ran to join us. Midday hit and the sun beat down on the beach. The ocean was clear and the sky was deep blue. We found paradise.

"I'm hungry," I said after a few hours.

"Me to, want to find some *comida?*" Marcos asked.

"Yeah, let's do it," Devon affirmed.

We sundried and then headed toward the city center to find a cheap restaurant. The girls continued toward the hostel to nap. I looked at the menu and recognized the word *pizza*, along with a few ingredients. I ordered a pizza and a *cerveza*.

"Do you know what you just ordered?" Marcos asked me.

"Some kind of pizza," I commented nonchalantly.

"Some kind of pizza is right! You just ordered octopus pizza, *hombre!*" he laughed.

Our server brought my pizza to the table. Black crust dyed in octopus ink topped with cheese, tomatoes, and tentacles. Out of pure curiosity, all four of us tried some. It was delicious, thankfully.

We paid and returned to our room to nap and get ready

for the night. We had free reign until our ISP group dinner. We attended that and returned to our room. We bought a few beers at the market and drank them. A few more group members entered the room with beers in an effort to spend time with "Team Fun".

Audrey never showed. I fell asleep early, still recovering from the long night in Oviedo. I wanted to be in prime form for my birthday the following evening.

I woke up early. I strolled to the main beach from a swim, followed by push-ups and sit-ups. I felt good. Alive with energy.

I returned to our room and showered before my roommates awoke. Our group met in the hostel's main lobby at 10:00 and boarded the bus. We departed for a day in Covadonga, which was only miles away. The bus snaked through the mountain roads, leaving the flat coast behind it.

The bus stopped after 30 minutes and we exited. I was awe-stricken immediately.

Covadonga's pink cathedral sat on top of a large hill in front of me. Imposing and strong, yet artistic and delicate. Our group pushed up the hill.

Devon and I branched left once our group stopped in the village. We walked toward the mouth of an imposing cave that bore into the mountainside. Its iron gates were open, so we strolled through them. Candles lit the tunnel. We walked deeper into the mountain, unsure of our end point. The candles provided the only source of light as the cave grew darker. Then, we saw natural sunlight illuminate the walls. We came to an opening, and what an opening it was.

In a cavernous room, we entered a chapel. Pews rested on the cave's floor and continued for five rows, followed by an altar at the room's ending wall. My eyes drew left almost instantly. An entire wall was missing. The cave opened and dropped directly into a pool surrounded by mossy rock. The opening served as a window with a view of the cathedral. A waist-high climb would give me a perfect opportunity for a 50-foot jump into green water, but I elected to keep my feet on the ground.

A waterfall poured from the side of the mountain. It seemed as if there was a river flowing through the mountain rock and running underneath the cave chapel. I absorbed my natural and holy surroundings. I had never encountered any environment like this before. After a silent minute, I looked at the cave's right wall. A coffin rested in a carved hole in the rock about three feet above the floor. I read the inscription. *Pelayo.*

In front of me laid the remains of King Pelayo, the Spanish Catholic war hero who defeated the Muslim occupants of the Iberian Peninsula. His legendary battle took place here, in Covadonga, 1,300 years ago. And here he was in eternal slumber.

I sat in a pew. Silence allowed me to think. I thought about my upcoming birthday. *What have I accomplished up to this point in my life? School? Nothing, really. Nothing compared to the legendary King Pelayo who is immortalized by my side in this epic mountain cavern cathedral.*

Devon and I left through the only safe exit: the cave entrance. We made our way down to the pool to get a view of the cave chapel from another perspective. The waterfall flowed from solid rock.

I found a small, mossy path that led me around the pool. It ended at the base of the waterfall. The mist sprayed my face. An old stone fountain stood near the end of the path. Its water source flowed from the mountain as well. I drank from one of the six spouts of the round stone and returned to the road by the pool. An old Spanish woman told me that if I had sipped from all six spouts, I would be married within the year. *Thankfully I wasn't too thirsty*, I thought.

After hours of exploration, we loaded the bus and drove to Llanes. Around seven, my roommates and I left our room and found a restaurant. We sat and a round of *cervezas* appeared.

"I know you don't turn 21 until midnight, but it's time to start celebrating," Devon said. I ate full pasta dinner in an attempt to fill my stomach with some substance. After that, we walked to a bar. The same old shopkeeper from yesterday served us. We sat at the bar and another round of Estrella Damm appeared. Already feeling the *cervezas*, we strolled back to our hostel room as the sun set.

Seated at the edge of my bed, I poured a *calimocho*, a sweet mixture of red wine and cola. Team Fun sipped on those as a few girls from our program knocked on the door.

"Happy birthday!" they squealed, followed by a round of hugs.

"Thanks," I replied.

They drank *calimochos* with us for a while. We talked about superficial topics and joked about the lack of fun that Audrey was having across the hallway. Then I had an idea. I stood up without saying a word. I opened our door, took two steps across the hallway, and knocked.

"Hey! Come have some *calimochos* with us for my birthday," I offered sincerely.

"Seriously? You guys are drinking in the hostel?" she

asked, astonished.

"Yeah! It's a celebration," I replied.

"No. Stan and I are going out to dinner. Have fun," she said, followed by that infamous eye roll.

"That went well," I said as I walked back into our room and shut the door.

"She snubbed you, eh?" Brad asked.

"Of course! She's going out to dinner with Stan," I said.

"I bet that's going to be full of exciting conversation," Devon joked.

"Man, if Roxy came on this trip, you two could have double-dated with them," I fired.

"They wouldn't let us. We don't talk about the intricate art of wall-making," he retaliated. "You and Heidi could have joined them, though!"

"Oh, good one!" Marcos chimed.

"Hmm. Alright you got me there, Dev," I admitted. "And your cup's empty. You should fix that."

"Yes, sir. Got me!"

"And the birthday boy strikes hard," Marcos jested.

Around 11:30, the four roommates and the five female tagalongs left the hostel. Brad led the way with a plan in mind. We cruised into the town and crossed the bridge over the river. The empty streets looked less familiar in the dark.

"Where are we going?" I asked.

"To da beach, mon!" Devon said in a Jamaican accent.

We descended. All nine of us struggled on the steep staircase carved into the side of the cliff. The moon illuminated the beach, but cast a shadow on each step. The *calimochos* coursing through our bodies didn't help.

I kicked my shoes onto the sand and rolled my jeans to

my shins. I spread my arms and soaked up the moonlight and sea breeze.

No one could see us down here, but we could see the ocean perfectly. The moon glistened with every ripple in the water. After a few seconds of silence, Brad burst into a less than harmonious rendition of "Happy Birthday." The others joined in the song. *Pop.*

"Here you go, *hombre*," Marcos said as he handed me a bottle of *sidra* and a clear plastic cup.

"Thanks, dude!" I said.

Pop. Pop. Pop. Pop. Four more open bottles appeared.

"And here are glasses for everybody," Brad said.

We sat in the sand. The tide touched our toes every fifth wave, but we never got wet. Despite my drunken state of mind, I felt at peace. I sat with new friends, yet we felt so comfortable, like we had known each other for years. Our adventurous spirits aligned. The *sidra* continued to flow.

After an hour, Devon suggested that we find a bar. We left and climbed the stairs. A few minutes later, we entered the same bar we stopped at earlier in the night.

"Back again, *chicos*?" the bartender asked.

"Yeah. More drinks for us!" Brad said.

"You brought some ladies with you this time," he whispered to the guys.

"Yeah, just for you," Devon joked.

"*Que quieres*?" he asked.

"Four whiskey and cokes, *por favor*," Devon replied quickly.

"Whiskey?" Marcos asked?

"Yeah, man. It's my favorite liquor, for sure," I replied.

"Gross. I'm a tequila guy, myself," he said.

"Of course you are!" Devon joked.

"I know, I know. Puerto Rican, I get it," he said, mocking himself.

The bartender poured our drinks quickly during our short conversation and pushed them toward us. Each six-ounce glass was filled nearly to the brim with whiskey and without ice.

"Coke?" Devon asked.

He dashed each glass with cola.

Devon shot the three of us a look that said *Oh no!*

"*Salud!*" Brad toasted, raising his glass. We knocked glasses and sipped. We all had the "strong drink" aftertaste expression, but we continued to power through the stiffness.

After we finished those, one girl in our group asked if I wanted a drink. I agreed and she brought a beer to our table for me.

"Thanks," I replied.

The girl had brown, curly hair with an athletic body. *Soccer player*, I thought. She had a pointy face with high cheekbones and a broad forehead. Pretty, but not the sharpest intellect, I gathered. This was the first time we had spent time with these five girls. They seemed adventurous like us. All fairly pretty. Some appeared more intelligent than others, while others appeared more social than some. They meshed with Team Fun well enough, at least for tonight.

After everyone had a few drink at the bar, the bartender turned on the television. *Monday Night Football* popped onto the screen. Real, American, professional football. It was a replay from last week's game, but we didn't care.

"No way!" Brad shouted as a 49er's jersey moved across the screen.

"Go Niners!" Devon echoed.

"What a birthday present. American football," I awed.

The girls barely took notice and returned to their conversation about some reality TV show. The clock struck 3:00 and we made moves to leave. Stepping onto the street, we all realized we drank more than we should have, but we were in control and still having fun.

"Alright, I'm ready for bed," Marcos declared.

"Let's go back to the beach," the curly-haired girl suggested.

"I'm down," Brad said.

"Me too," said another girl.

"Let's do it," I chimed.

"Naw, I'm going back to the hostel. I'm tired," Devon said.

"I'll go back with you guys," said another girl.

Marcos and Devon walked two girls across the bridge as Brad and I followed three girls back down the stone staircase.

"Let's go swimming," the curly-haired girl said.

"The hostel's too far away. I don't want to run back and get my swimsuit. Let's just hang out," I said.

"Who said we needed swimsuits?" said the blonde girl.

"Yeah. Let's go swimming now," the curly-haired girl affirmed.

"You first," said Brad.

"Alright," she said with a challenging demeanor.

The three girls walked into the small cave in the cliff. A few seconds later, they ran out half-naked, darting across the sand. They dove almost simultaneously over a small wave and into the ocean. They popped up with quiet yells.

"Well, here we go," I said to Brad. "Let's throw our

clothes in the cave so no one sees them in case they look down here from the stairs or something."

"Oh, quit being paranoid! No one can see this place unless they look backwards from that viewpoint up there," Brad said. "But seriously, we should do that."

We tossed our clothes into the cave next to the girls' clothes and raced to the water. I dove and glided underwater for a few seconds. The sensation of the saltwater felt liberating. I sprang upwards and only my chest and head were above the water. The girls swam around us, exposing only their heads.

"You boys looked good running into the ocean," the blonde girl said.

"It's dark," Brad replied. "You couldn't even see us."

The five of us swam around and then decided to head back to the hostel. My feet touched the sand and my shoulders lifted above the ocean. The girls stood in much shallower water in front of me. The moon shimmered off their footsteps in the sand. Beauty in its rawest form.

I walked with the soccer player and her friend in an effort to give Brad some time to talk with the blonde girl; I knew he was becoming even more interested in her after this spontaneous, daring night adventure. Brad and the blonde girl sat on the stairs, already fully clothed and engaged in a conversation of pure surface depth. I walked into the cave to retrieve my clothes. I envisioned myself as a pirate treasure hunter searching for gold, like so many Spaniards must have done centuries ago in the Caribbean.

The tight cave drew narrower, but the moonlight lit the cave just enough for me to find my shirt and shoes. The girls waited impatiently outside, so I grabbed their clothes as well.

When I emerged from the cave, we all laughed at our own spontaneity as we left the secret beach and walked toward the stairs.

o   o   o

Marcos opened the blinds and sunlight filled the hostel room. Devon groaned. I rolled over to shield my eyes. Four girls were sprawled across our beds; while I slept on the hard ground in the corner of the room.

"Where's Brad?" Marcos asked.

"Oh, I think I know," the soccer player replied, adding a girlish giggle.

"Yeah, why do you think the four of us slept in here?" another girl said.

I brushed my teeth and packed my backpack. The girls left to do the same. Brad strolled into our room a few minutes later. We made fun of him while we packed.

"Some night, huh?" I said. "What a birthday party."

"Yeah, man. Wild Spanish nights," Brad said.

I told Devon and Marcos about our swimming adventure while we walked to the main floor. I hadn't showered and I smelled like ocean and alcohol. I passed our program director as I hopped on the bus.

"Wild night?" she asked me.

"Uh, a little," I stammered.

"Looks like the four of you aren't feeling too great this morning," she said with too much energy.

"Oh no, we're good," Brad fired back unconvincingly.

We passed the five girls, who sat near the front of the bus. I made eye contact with two girls from the cave and the smiled at me. I smiled back. They all laughed as Brad walked by.

Halfway through the bus ride (and a great nap), our director called the bus riders to attention.

"Remember, tomorrow is the strike, so we're cancelling your classes. I repeat, don't go to school tomorrow. We just want to make sure you're all safe," she bellowed.

"What strike?" Devon asked me.

"I don't know? I saw something about it in the paper a while ago, but I don't know what's going on," I said.

"The whole country is going on strike starting at midnight, man," Marcos told us from his seat to our right.

"How does that work?" I asked.

"Well, since the Spanish economy is so atrocious, the whole country is taking tomorrow off to protest or something. I'm talking no trains, buses, flights, stores, nothing," he told us.

"So, no one is working tomorrow at all?" Devon asked.

"No, man. I guess they think it might be dangerous or something. That's why we can't go to school. Teachers aren't teaching tomorrow. If we cross the picket line or whatever, who knows what will happen to us," he warned. "They say it's supposed to be peaceful though, so we'll be fine."

"Crazy, man. I guess Spain's unemployment rate is at 20 percent or some insane number like that," I said, quoting the article as accurately as I could.

Devon and I walked toward our apartment as we exited the bus. We made plans to see Marcos and Brad tomorrow since we didn't have school. I showered and ate dinner. Around 11:00, Devon asked if I wanted to go to the store with him, since it wouldn't be open the next day. We walked into the store near our building. The clerk let us in, even though the store closed a few minutes ago. I grabbed an orange juice, a *zumo de naranja*, as the airport clerk so kindly informed me upon my arrival to the country. Devon bought some bread and water.

"Want to cruise to the park?" he asked.

"Yeah. Let's do it."

We strolled for a bit until we found a well-lit bench on a main walking path. I sipped my orange juice. We discussed the events of the weekend, and then our thoughts moved to the strike.

"I wonder what's going to happen?" I said.

"Who knows? Oviedo's pretty small. I bet it won't be a big deal. Maybe in Barcelona or Madrid, but not here," he guessed.

"Yeah. That's terrible that the whole country has to strike just for the government to take notice. I bet families are in terrible situations right now with the unemployment rate," I said.

"I bet. I feel bad. Here we are spending all this money on booze at some beach bar and the rest of the country gets ready to strike because they can't find work. It's a crazy world, man," Devon stated.

"I feel you, dude," I said. "Let's head back soon. I'm tired."

"I'm down. It is almost midnight."

Boom! Thump, thump. Boom!

"Oh, wait! What was that?" Devon shouted.

"It sounded like a bomb!" I replied.

"Yeah, it did! I think it came from the other side of the park," he said.

"Hey, dude. Let's get out of here," I said nervously.

"Yeah, quickly," he affirmed.

We walked briskly down the well-lit path. We reached the street. *Boom! Thump, thump.* We ran across the street without waiting for the signal. Sprinting toward the Pumarin neighborhood, we heard another faint explosion. I skipped two steps at a time as I vaulted up the stairs to the fifth floor of our apartment building. Devon jammed his key into the lock and we hustled inside, bolting the door behind us. *La Huelga* had started with a bang.

PART 2

CHAPTER 6

I sat on a wooden bench and tied my left shoe. Devon used a street sign for balance as he stretched his hamstrings. Brad put his hands on his head and caught his breath.

"Alright, we're already halfway up the mountain, hombres," Brad said. "El Cristo is up there waiting for us."

"Yeah. That statue's huge, man. It looks so small from down here, though," Devon said.

"I'm feeling better than our last hike up here, that's for sure," I added. "No Estrella Damm excreting from my pores."

"Yeah, you drunk-ass," Devon joked.

"Whatever, man. You were in the same boat," I replied.

We walked higher and the road narrowed. The sidewalks ended. I poured with sweat. The smattering of rural houses began to thin and trees became more abundant in the landscape. Brad stopped suddenly and looked left into the forest, but Devon and I kept walking.

"Hey guys, was this the trail we took last time?" Brad

asked.

"You mean that wide, dirt path that led us straight to the statue?" I asked.

"Yeah," Brad said.

"No, that's not it. Our path is another 20 minutes or so up the mountain," Devon said.

"Where does this one go?" Brad asked.

"I don't know," I said, walking closer to investigate. "Let's take it and find out."

"You sure?" Devon said.

"Of course. Why not?" Brad said.

We turned left. A soon as the asphalt road became the dirt trail, bushes ballooned onto the path and forced us to walk in a single file line. I led, Devon took the middle, and Brad played caboose. The dirt was damp, but not muddy. The sun hung low in the sky and a chilled breeze flowed through the trees. I sweated from exertion, not heat. We talked early, but our conversation dulled after 15 minutes on the path.

"Where the hell is this path taking us?" Devon asked.

"I don't know, Dev," I said. "We're going up, though, so I'm assuming we will find the statue."

"Man, it looks like we're the first people to walk on this path in 100 years," Devon said.

"Yeah, they should bring a landscaper in here to groom these vines," Brad said.

I looked upwards for El Cristo, but I didn't see it. The trees blocked my view. We came to a small clearing ten minutes later, but the statue still eluded my sight. The tree line tapered inward toward us. I felt like we stood inside a giant cereal bowl made of trees.

"Check that out," Devon said. "Over there in the forest."

"What is that?" Brad asked. "Is that a house?"

"Way out here? No way," I said.

"Dude, I think it might be," Devon said. "It looks big, but it's covered in nature, so I can't see much."

Without exchanging words, we left the trail and stomped through the bushes. The vegetation rose to my knees. We walked into shadows as the trees became sequentially taller. As we stomped closer, we saw a few more buildings through the vines. Red clay. Window frames with no glass. Decrepit roofs.

"No way, dude. Three houses?" I said. "They're in total ruin. No one has lived in these for 200 years, at least."

"Yeah. Look at that tree growing through the middle of that two-story building," Brad said.

"It shot through the roof," Devon said.

"Check out this wall. It looks like someone threw a grenade in here," I said as I jumped through a window frame.

"Spanish Civil War?" Devon suggested.

"I see you," Brad said to me, looking through another wall hole blown between two connected buildings.

"Check out all the vines on the walls, man," Devon said. "I bet this is what the Ivy League schools look like."

"What are these places?" Brad asked.

"Who knows?" I said. "People used to live here though. There's a wooden bed frame in the corner of this room. It looks like it's growing back into the ground."

"This is crazy. Did we just make a discovery, or what?" Devon asked.

"Looks like it. I feel like Indiana Jones," I said.

"Let me take some pictures and let's get out of here," Devon said.

"Yeah. It's kind of scary in here," Brad said.

We climbed out of the ruins and stomped back to the trail. The sun began to set. We followed the thinning path as it weaved through the forest. I felt nervous. What were those ruins? And where is this path taking us? Judging by my friends' silence, they felt the same way. Another 15 minutes passed. No conversation occurred. The low sun cast long shadows through the landscape. We climbed higher and my fears smoldered. The ledge to the left heightened my vertigo. I glared at every step to ensure my footing was secure. Then I heard Devon shout.

"We made it!" he yelled.

El Cristo emerged from the trees. It beamed as the sunset hit it. Our path led us directly to its feet. We walked from the forest's edge to the cement platform surrounding the statue and turned to look at the familiar view of Oviedo.

"We made it, boys," I said.

"I thought we were goners," Brad said.

"Me too," Devon said. "I thought something was going to get us. Crazy forest people. Bigfoot. Audrey Reigert. The list goes on."

"Nice, Dev," I said. "Man, that path was awesome. I'm glad we decided to take a little adventure."

"It is fun when you don't know what's ahead of you, isn't it?" Devon said.

"Yeah. I guess sometimes you just have to ask, *What's the worst that could happen?*"

CHAPTER 7

Devon and I heard the intensity as soon as we walked into the park. I hadn't dared to walk through here since the bombs exploded before the national strike. Now, we prepared ourselves for another kind of explosion.

The noise from the cement soccer pitch reverberated through the park. Africans lined the fence on one side and South Americans on the other. I saw the ball fly through the air. An African knocked the intended South American recipient to the ground with a hard shoulder as we approached. The South American fence shook with disapproval. Devon and I weaseled our way to the fence through a crowd of 30 African fans.

"What's the score?" I asked the man next to me.

"2-2," he replied without taking his eyes off the game.

"I guess next goal wins, eh?" I said to Devon.

A short African dribbled the ball from fence to fence across the pitch, or *La Concha* as they called it. He passed to a fat man a few yards in front of him. He feigned right, then pushed the ball left. He took one step and fired a left-footed shot that bounced off of the goalie's chest. The goalie gasped for air. A familiar Brazilian swept in front of his goalie and recovered the loose ball. He dribbled to the midline without contention.

The Brazilian cocked his leg back for the shot. A defender darted toward him to deflect the ball and turned his head to avoid a direct shot to the face. Noticing his lapse in attention, the Brazilian rolled to his right, chipped the ball over another defender, and a fellow South American headed the ball past the goalie's outstretched leg.

The South American fence shook with wild excitement. The African fans shouted what I assumed to be profanities in their native Senegalese and Cameroonian languages. Another African team strutted onto the pitch to face the day's South American victors. The challengers stretched and dribbled while the South Americans took a break at the drinking fountain.

"I thought I saw you guys over here," Marcos said as he rounded the fence.

"What's up, dude?" Devon said.

"I just watched that game with Brad. It was crazy," he said. "I'm still nervous to play with the guys, but I like watching."

"Yeah, they're physical. That Brazilian guys can dribble," Devon said. "Get Brad over here."

"Hey, guys," Brad said as he jogged to our side of the fence.

"Who's playing the winners after this game?" the Senegalese man next to me shouted.

No one stepped forward.

"What about you Americans?" he asked me.

"Um, *sí*," I responded.

"Are you crazy?" Brad said.

"Yes. I am," I replied.

"We can't play with these guys," Marcos said. "They'll destroy us. And besides, I'm wearing jeans."

"Are you sure you're down to play?" Devon asked me.

"What's the worst that could happen?" I said.

"Alright, then. I'm in," he replied.

"Me too," Brad said.

"Well, I can't let you guys go out there alone. I'm in," Marcos said.

"We need a goalie, though," I told the African.

"If you can't find one by the time this game is over, I'll play goalie with you *chicos*," he said.

"Cool. Thanks, *hombre*."

The current game ended quickly. The Africans routed the tired South Americans by scoring three goals in five minutes. They allowed one South American goal after a botched trick pass off the fence.

"Game time," Devon said.

We strutted onto the field. Inherently, I puffed my chest to project dominance, but I felt insecure. I was out of my element. All four of us were. I wore green Oregon athletic shorts and a white cotton shirt with running shoes. Devon rocked a Ducks long sleeve shirt and black basketball shorts with basketball shoes. Brad wore khaki pants and a collared shirt, while Marcos looked equally as prepared for a day at the office.

Our Senegalese goalie walked behind us and stepped into the goalie box (roughly the size of a middle school gym's three-point line). He appeared calm. *La Concha* brought him comfort and familiarity. His muscles rippled in his thin tank top. His bald head produced beads of sweat in anticipation for kick-off.

"*Hombre*, you're playing for the wrong team," an opposing African player shouted.

"Yeah. Why are you playing with *los americanos?*" yelled another.

"The black one isn't even African," the opposing goalie shouted.

"*Pssh,*" Devon said, deflecting the comment.

Our Senegalese goalie ignored each comment with calm fire. To him, the opposition's taunts seemed to signify the other team's fear. He used the trash talk to fuel his adrenaline. His eyes focused with each verbal lashing.

"We won, so we start," the opposing African goalie declared.

"Let's go, boys!" shouted a familiar voice from the fence.

"Roxy's watching," I said to Devon.

"Oh man. I hope we don't get out asses kicked in front of her," he said.

Brad and Marcos positioned themselves as forwards, while Devon and I took defensive stances. A Senegalese defender dribbled along the fence as the game started.

He tested Brad's skill with a few quick left-to-right jukes. Brad stuck his foot out and stopped the ball. He aired the ball to Marcos across the field. Marcos swung his right leg in an attempted one-touch shot and missed the ball by an inch.

The sturdy defender possessed the ball and dribbled up the sideline. He took far strides and long-yet-controlled dribbles. I rushed to meet him at the top of the goalie box. He cocked his leg back and fired a shot at my face. I turned my head and the ball whizzed by my ear and into the top corner of the goal.

Africans lead 1-0.

"Damn!" I shouted.

"It's cool, man. It was a good shot. You'll get him next time," Devon said.

"*Lo siento*," I said, apologizing to our goalie.

"*No pasa nada*," he said. "No worries."

Our goalie rolled the ball to my feet. I took two dribbles toward my defender. I felt a dormant aggression building. I passed to Marcos along the fence. He possessed the ball at the midline and a defender met him quickly. Marcos feigned left, then spun to the right with the ball. The defender lurched forward with a bewildered expression and Marcos sprinted toward the goal.

He passed to Brad quickly and the remaining defender had no choice but to attend to the ball. Brad gave the ball back to Marcos in the middle of the box. One touch. Through the goalie's legs.

1-1.

I guarded the incoming Cameroonian. Thoughts of his previous goal haunted me.

He dribbled left toward the fence. I pursued. I nicked the ball as he attempted to pass me. We entangled against the fence in a fight for possession. He threw a swift elbow and caught my chest. I gasped for air. He took advantage of my immobility and evaded our scramble.

Devon met him and stole the ball, sending it up the field to Brad. He lost it and the opposing goalie sent it flying toward the Cameroonian near me. He faked left, then, right, then left. I rushed toward him and threw a familiar lacrosse check into his chest. He hit the ground.

The Africans along the fence erupted with disapproval. I dribbled across the midline. Marcos yelled for the ball. I faked a pass in his direction and my new defender took the bait. I wound up from the box line and ripped a shot past the goalie's hip.

Americans lead 2-1.

The Cameroonian possessed the ball at midfield. He was on Devon's side, but he caught my eye. He dribbled toward me with bull-like force. He shot from inside the goalie box. The Senegalese goalie punched the ball into the air, saving a goal. The Cameroonian followed his shot with a two-step run through me. I flew to the ground.

Our goalie helped me up and shouted something at the Cameroonian in my defense.

Fair enough, I thought.

The Africans looked tired and agitated. Devon took advantage. He chipped the ball over two walking defenders. Brad trapped it. His defender took notice and dashed toward him. Brad flicked the ball in front of the defender and over the goalie's left shoulder. The both sides of the fence went crazy.

Americans win 3-1.

"We won!" Marcos shouted.

"Hell yeah, dude!" Devon said.

We bumped knuckles. Our team shook hands with the African team and thanked them for the hard-fought match. I made a point to look the Cameroonian in the eye during our handshake.

"You played tough, *Americano*," he said.

"So did you," I replied.

I sensed a mutual respect.

"Thanks for playing with us," Devon told our Senegalese goalie.

"No problem," he said. "You guys played better than I thought you would."

"Thanks."

We played against a team comprised of two Brazilians, one Mexican, and two Colombians next. We lost 3-1. Their fresh legs and artistic footwork stalled us. I guarded the Brazilian in the familiar yellow jersey and he made me look like a statue. We shook hands after the game.

"Next time, *hombre*," he told me. "Next time."

Brad and Marcos stayed by the fence to watch the next game. Devon and Roxanne left to eat dinner. I walked home to eat by myself.

I saw our Senegalese goalie walk away from *La Concha* as I began to leave. We converged at the main path toward Pumarin.

"Thanks again for playing on our team," I told him.

"No problem," he said. "What's your name?"

"Jason." What's yours?"

"Az."

We shook hands. He spoke in broken Spanish in a thick Senegalese accent, but I understood him. I'm sure my Spanish sounded equally as rough, but we communicated effectively nonetheless.

"You're from Senegal, right?" I asked.

"Yeah," he said. "Where are you from in the U.S.? New York?"

"No. I'm from the West Coast," I replied.

"*Bueno*. Why are you here?" he asked.

"I'm studying Spanish for four months at *la universidad*," I said.

"All of you Americans?" he asked.

"Yeah. All the guys on our team study in my program," I said. "What about you? What brought you to Oviedo?"

"Work," he said. "I sell watches."

"You came all the way to Oviedo from Senegal to sell watches?" I asked.

"*Sí.* Things are bad in Senegal. It's hard to find a job," he said. "My mother, my father, and my sister were murdered, so my brother and I left. We had to leave if we didn't want to die, too."

"That's terrible. I'm sorry, man," I said.

"It's fine. It happens to a lot of people in Senegal. Thieves and rebels," he said nonchalantly, though I sensed repressed sadness.

"How did you pick Oviedo?" I asked.

"My boss sent me here. My brother and I talked to our friend and he connected us with a man who told us that he had a job for us if we could get to Morocco. This man paid for us to sneak onto a ship in Morocco. We got off the ship in Italy."

"Why didn't you stay in Italy?" I asked.

"Well, we don't have passports. The Italian police are hard on immigrants with no passports, so we snuck into France," he said.

"Then you and your brother came to Spain?" I asked.

"My brother and I separated. The French police almost caught us, so we fled to different towns. My boss said Oviedo's police are relaxed about immigrants, as long as we don't cause trouble. And Oviedo has a lot of African immigrants, so I'm comfortable here."

"Is your brother joining you here?" I pried.

"I don't know. I haven't heard from him in five months. I think he's still in France, but I don't know. I might never know," Az said.

We walked through the University campus. He lived a few blocks away from my apartment. We passed through the tunnel and walked down the stairs into Pumarin. His story hooked me.

"I met my wife in Oviedo. She lives in the building next to mine," Az said. "She's beautiful. We have one son."

"Cool, man," I said. "I'm happy for you."

"You should meet her. She's wonderful," he added.

"So, who's your boss?" I asked. "The one who got you to Oviedo."

"He's an African," Az said. "He gives us housing and food. We sell his watches. We take the watches into restaurants, street corners, cafes, and places like that."

"Wait, how many people work for him?" I asked.

"About 20."

"All Africans?"

"Yes," Az said. "We all live in the same apartment. I think he owns the building. Other people from Cameroon and Senegal live there, too. They sell videos, jewelry, sunglasses, and things like that."

"They're friends of yours now, I'm guessing?" I asked

"Yeah. They're good people who needed a change like me," he said. "We have to pay our boss almost all of our money that we make from selling his things, but we live in better conditions than we would in Senegal."

"Well, that's good. As long as you're happy," I said.

"Yeah. Here's my apartment. I'll see you on *La Concha*," Az said.

"*Adios*, Az."

o   o   o

I met Anna at a quiet bar that night. We met twice a week for an hour of language practice. I spoke Spanish with her, then we switched and she practiced English. She mixed up her words often and frustrated herself. I thought it was adorable. I used Spanish enough in class, but this gave me an excuse to spend time with Anna. I grew more and more enamored with her every time we met. Her voice, her intelligence, her innocence, and her beauty captured me with every passing moment.

She waited for me in a booth near the center of the bar. I was ten minutes late. Her Coke glass was half full.

"*Hola*, Jason," Anna said. "You're late."

"I know. I'm always late, aren't I?" I said. "*Como estas?*"

"*Bien, y tú?*" she asked.

"*Bien*," I said.

The waiter approached our table. I ordered an Estrella Damm. He brought me a glass and set it in front of me. He didn't pour it well. The glass had too much foam and not enough beer. I didn't complain. If Devon was with me instead of Anna, I might have complained. Sitting at a table with someone this exotic made the thought of a complaint seem ridiculous.

"How was your day, Jason?" she asked in Spanish. The tip of her tongue rested in between her teeth as she formed the "S" in my name. It gave her voice an airy sound. Her eye brows danced as she asked the question.

"My day was great," I replied. "I played soccer with my friends. You met some of them at *El Serpeinte* during *El Clasico*. You remember Devon, right?"

"Yes. He dates the girl with brown hair," she said.

"Yeah. That's him," I said.

"The black one?" she asked.

"Um, yeah," I said.

"Is he black or *mexicano*?" she asked.

"He's black."

"Well, he looks Mexican."

"Nope. His dad is black and his mom is white," I said.

"*Interesante*. So, he doesn't belong to a group," she said.

The comment froze me for a moment.

"What do you mean?" I asked.

"He's not all black, so he doesn't fit in with that group. He's not all white, so he doesn't fit in with that group. He looks Mexican, but he's not, so he doesn't fit in with that group."

"Why does it matter?" I asked.

"It matters to society," she said. "Everybody belongs to a group."

"I guess," I said.

"But he doesn't," she added.

"He belongs to both," I said.

"He can't," she said. "I read that your American census makes each person chose a group according to race."

Her backward thinking frustrated me. Did Martin Luther King, Jr.'s message impact Spain?

"Who cares what he marks on his census," I said.

"Society," she said. "You're white. Africans are black.

What is he?"

"Ask him. He can identify himself."

She sensed the rumble in my voice. My face smoldered. I gulped my *cerveza* and pondered my next sentence. I wanted to change her mindset with one phrase, one carefully planned verbal assault. She wasn't being overtly racist, but she wasn't thinking as progressively as I would have liked. I took another drink and finished my beer. The waiter saw my empty glass and hustled to our table. I ordered a coffee with milk.

"Do Americans discuss race?" she asked. The question interrupted my thought process.

"I guess we do," I said. "We talk about the Civil Rights Movement and the history of slavery in school."

The waiter brought my coffee to the table. He set a small pitcher of milk beside it.

"No. I mean do you talk about different races today," she said. "Do you talk to your white friends about what it's like to live with a black roommate? Do you talk about how white people and black people fit into society?"

I poured some milk into my coffee. I stirred it with a spoon. The black coffee and white milk swirled. I watch the contrast blend into one cohesive drink.

"No. The fact that Devon's black doesn't matter. He's my friend and that's all," I said.

"I had a friend who had a black roommate in college," she said. "My friend said her roommate used funny shampoo."

My *café con leche* steamed.

"Anna, do you know any black people?" I asked.

"Of course," she said. "Africans come into restaurants all the time. They sell fine jewelry. Fake jewelry, but cheap."

Her innocence shifted toward ignorance. Her perspective

became obvious. An absence of cultural mingling caused her ignorance. She lived in the same city as hundreds of African immigrants, but failed to interact with them. She viewed them as cheap salespeople. I grew angry, yet I understood her reasons for her thoughts. Experience would set her free.

She shifted the topic of conversation to soccer because she wanted to loosen the tension of the racial discussion. Our difference of opinion created an awkward vibe. I finished the last half of my coffee quickly. I paid at the counter. Anna paid when she ordered her drink, so I met her at the front door. We walked outside and planned to meet in a few days for more language practice.

"Well, I'm going home," she said. She pointed to the right.

"I'm walking that way too," I said.

"*Bueno*. You can walk me home," she said.

We walked a few blocks and stopped at an intersection. The park was in front of us. I reveled in the memory of the afternoon's soccer victory.

"Let's walk through the park," I suggested.

"No. We can't. It's dangerous," she said.

"Why?"

"That's where drug dealers sell their drugs," she said.

"I walk through there all the time," I said. "We're fine."

I walked across the street as the signal turned. Anna hesitated on the sidewalk, and then hustled to catch me.

"We shouldn't do this," she said. We stopped walking just before we entered the tree-covered pathway.

"I walk through here every night," I said. "I've never seen a dangerous drug dealer here. Or any drug dealer."

"They are here. Trust me," she said. "This is where all the immigrants go to sell drugs."

"Do Spanish people sell drugs here, too?" I asked with a sarcastic tone.

"No. Just immigrants," she said.

"So you're afraid of immigrants?" I asked.

"There are a lot of immigrants in Oviedo," she said. "They all hang out in the park. They play soccer at night here. They're dangerous."

"You're ridiculous," I said. I suppressed my opinion toward her second round of ignorance for the night. "Immigrants are just normal people like us. Let's go."

We walked for a few minutes in silence. *I guarantee Anna doesn't know any immigrants, either*, I thought.

She was so gorgeous, yet so uneducated in the ways of the cultural interaction. And there she was talking to me, a man from another culture. What was her deal?

The trees opened and *La Concha* appeared. It illuminated the park's center. A few people gathered around the fence and watched the pick-up game. Anna shifted toward another pathway, but I lead her straight to the fence.

"Let's watch the game for a second," I said.

"No. I have to go home," she said. Her face looked grave.

We walked closer to the fence. A few people turned to look at us as we approached. One man unhooked his fingers from the chain link and took two steps toward us. Anna clutched my hand.

"*Americano!*" shouted a familiar voice. I saw his shadowed outline. I walked closer.

"Az!" I shouted.

"*Que tal, hombre*," Az said.

We shook hands and talked about the current game on *La Concha*.

"This is my friend, Anna," I said.

"*Hola*, Anna," he said. He extended his hand.

"*Hola*," Anna said timidly.

We walked to the edge of the fence to watch the game. It ended a few minutes later with a routine shot from a short cross. A few Africans walked toward us and talked with Az.

"*Es el Americano!*" shouted the Cameroonian from our afternoon game. "You played tough."

"So did you," I said to him.

We shook hands and talked trash about a future game. He said Az had to play on the African team and we had to find an American goalie. I said we would still win. I reveled in the light-hearted, cross-cultural banter

Anna stood and watched. She said nothing.

CHAPTER 8

Marcos and I left the university at noon on Friday. The sun was out, but the temperature stayed low. I wore a scarf with my long-sleeve and jeans. I felt European in a scarf. In the States, the thought of wearing a scarf never crossed my mind. Marcos wore one occasionally in New York, but not today.

"Man, I'm glad we decided to skip our last class of the week," Marcos said.

"Me too. Getting a jump on the weekend is never a bad thing," I said.

"I bet Brad and Devon are sleeping on their desks," he said. "I can guarantee it."

"And Audrey answers every question the teacher asks," I added.

"Yeah, she does that," he said.

"Want to grab a coffee?" I asked.

"Sure. *Vamos.*"

We walked to the café and sat outside, despite the cold.

Anna saw us sit and she walked toward us. She worked Fridays at the café, so I liked to stop by and make my presence known. She pulled her hair into a high ponytail. Her leggings and boots gave her a distinct, Spanish appeal. I hadn't talked to her since we walked through the park. It seemed like weeks ago.

"*Hola*," Anna said.

"*Hola*, Anna," I said. "How are you?"

"Fine. What can I get for you, *chicos*?" she said.

"*Café con leche*," I said.

"One for me too, please," Marcos said.

Anna left to grab our coffees.

"Her shirt doesn't leave much to the imagination, does it?" Marcos whispered to me. I disagreed. My imagination exploded.

She brought our coffees a few minutes later. Two couples and one businessman left the café. One grey-haired gentleman held the door for Anna as she carried our saucers. Marcos and I were the only remaining customers.

"How long do you work today?" I asked as she placed our coffees on the table.

"Until five," she said.

"You're going out tonight, right?" Marcos asked.

"Yes, of course! It's Friday," she responded.

"What's your plan?" I asked.

"My friends and I will go to *El Serpiente*, probably," she said. "Then *Calle Mon*."

"Are your friends attractive?" Marcos asked.

"You two will have to come to *El Serpiente* and find out," Anna replied.

"See you there," Marcos said.

Marcos and I paid for our coffees and walked around town for a few hours. We cruised through the mall and bought a cheap soccer ball at a sporting goods store. We kicked the ball in a grass patch near some 1,000-year-old chapel in the middle of the city. Old couples strolled on intersecting paths through the grass. Kids ran with excitement after their release from another elementary school week.

"We have to go to *El Serpiente* tonight," Marcos said. "If Anna's friends look anything like her, I'm in for a long night."

"We should go to *Calle Mon* and dance with them after *El Serpiente* closes," I suggested.

"Yeah," he said. "Let's groove with some *chicas*."

I kicked the ball too hard and it flew over Marcos' head. He retrieved it.

"Are you going to make a move on Anna tonight or what?" he asked me.

"If the opportunity presents itself," I said, "I won't hesitate. All I want is a kiss."

"Best damn kiss you'll ever have," he said. "She's too fine."

"I bet her friends look just like her," I said. "We're in for a wild night."

"You'll get your kiss," he said. "I felt the tension between you two at the café. She likes you, *hombre*."

"I hope so," I said.

o   o   o

I did 200 push-ups for good luck while I watched *The Jungle Book* dubbed in Spanish on television. I grabbed my favorite shirt from the clothes line that hung between my window and the alley wall. I buttoned it and brushed my teeth. I felt fresh. I saw my confidence glowing as I looked in the mirror. I opened the front door and realized I forgot to put my shoes on. Nerves, I supposed. Devon opened his bedroom door.

"Where are you going, man?" he asked.

"Marcos and I are going to *El Serpiente*," I said. "Anna and her friends will be there."

"Oh boy," he said. "Good luck."

"You want to come with us?" I asked.

"No, I'm taking Roxy to dinner on *Calle Gascona*," he said. "Maybe we'll see you after we eat."

"Cool, man," I said. "Are you going to propose tonight?"

"Shut up," he replied. "You're an asshole."

"I know. Have fun, *hombre*."

I strolled past empty parks and sparse sidewalks. A digital clock on the bank edifice read *21:00*. Still early, I thought. A suave Spanish man left a nearby grocery store with two bottles of wine. I walked into the store and followed his example. I walked a few blocks and rang the buzzer for Marcos' apartment.

"Be down in a second," he said through the speaker.

He flung the doors open as he exited his building. He dressed for the occasion.

"To *El Serp* we go!" he shouted.

"Not yet," I said. "It's too early."

"We want prime seats, though," he said.

"People don't go out until midnight here, anyways," I said.

"What are we going to do, then," he said.

"Let's go to the park," I said. I lifted the wine bottles out of the paper bag.

"Now you're talking."

We walked past the cement soccer pitch in the center of the park. The lights were on. I heard a few people playing soccer, but saw no crowd gathered around the fence. No big game tonight. We strolled on a path covered by overhanging trees and lit by dim street lamps. Our path intersected with a larger artery through the park. Marcos sat on a bench next to the major path. I sat on the backrest with my feet on the bench seat.

"Damn," I said.

"What's wrong?"

"No corkscrew."

"Hmm," he said. "Time to get creative."

I pulled my house key from my left pocket and jammed it into the cork. The cork budged. I pressed with more force. It moved down the bottleneck. I pushed harder. The cork popped downwards into the wine, which caused an eruption of *vino*. Luckily, my black shirt served as a napkin.

"Here," I said as I handed the wine bottle to Marcos.

"Thanks, man."

He took a long drink and passed the bottle to me. I did the same.

"How much do I owe you for the two bottles?" he asked.

"Don't worry about it," I replied.

"Seriously, how much should I pay you?" he asked.

"Get a drink for me later," I said.

Marcos took another drink. Then me. Then him. Then me.

"What do you think of this place, man?" Marcos asked.

"What place?" I asked. "The park?"

"No. Oviedo," he said. "*Que piensas de Oviedo?*"

"I feel comfortable here," I said. "Oviedo's similar to Portland, so I feel like I'm at home. It's small, but it has all the amenities of a big city, you know? Pro soccer team. Big business. Historic sites. Friendly people, too."

"It is an awesome city," Marcos said.

"But it's still new to me, so I'm always exploring. There's always something new to do in Oviedo," I said.

"Just like New York, man," Marcos said. "Except The City is a million times bigger than little Oviedo."

"What was it like growing up in The Big Apple?" I asked.

"The Big Apple," Marcos said. "It was just that. Big. I felt lost in the shuffle, you know?"

"No, I don't know," I said. "Portland only has, like, a million people. I know the entire city."

"Come on, man. The City has, like, nine million. I loved it. I interacted with people from so many different backgrounds and life situations that my definition of a normal person or family isn't normal."

"That's awesome," I said.

"That's why I picked Oviedo instead of a huge city like Barcelona or Madrid," Marcos said. "I wanted to feel the smaller city vibe."

"Man, I picked Oviedo because I thought it would remind me of home," I said. "Now that's dull."

"At least you don't get homesick," he said.

"I really don't get homesick here," I said.

"I do," Marcos said. "All the time."

"If we keep having wild nights like the one we're about to have," I said, "home will be the last thing on your mind."

"And if we keep hanging out with Spanish girls like Anna," he said, "this place will seem less like Portland every minute."

I opened the second bottle of wine, this time with a smaller splash. Teenagers walked through the park more frequently, which meant the college crowd would emerge soon. Marcos and I drank half of the wine in the bottle quickly. I set it on the bench between my feet. Marcos punched my leg and motioned to the right.

"What, dude?" I said.

"Check it out," he whispered.

I squinted my eyes as I looked at the dark path. I saw two people sitting on a bench a few street lamps away. As my eyes adjusted to the darkness, I noticed that the girl was straddling the man.

"What the hell!" I exclaimed in a whisper.

"Exactly," whispered Marcos.

"They're really into their public displays of affection around here," I stated.

"It would appear so," he said.

I felt a small urge to laugh. The couple demonstrated passion without awareness of anyone around them. I shook from my attempts to control my laughter. The girl threw her hair back. I burst into laughter and Marcos did too. I kicked my leg reflexively and knocked the half-full wine bottle off of the bench. It shattered.

I looked at Marcos and he looked back at me with wide eyes. I looked at the couple. They heard the glass crash and stared at us. We laughed uncontrollably. The man pushed the girl off of him and rose from the bench with fury. He tripped as he attempted to jog toward us. We laughed even harder.

"Come on, man," Marcos said. "Let's get out of here!"

We ran through the park, across the street, and down an

alleyway. We took the alleyway to the plaza by the cathedral and ended our jog at the top of *Calle Gascona*. I placed my hands on my head and gasped for air, partly from exhaustion, partly from reoccurring laughter.

"What a way to start the night," I said between breathes.

"The nerve of some people," Marcos said.

"On a bench," I said. "Come on, Spain."

"Hey, at least he's getting something," he said.

We walked into *El Serpiente*. I was still breathing heavily from the run. College students from *Universidad de Oviedo* packed the bar and filled every table. Fernando saw us walk in and waved us over to the bar. He elbowed through the crowd and walked behind the bar.

"*Chicos*," he said. "How are you?"

"*Bien, Fernando*," I said. "How are you?"

"Good. I'm good," he said.

We told him about the couple on the park bench and Fernando laughed.

"*España*," he said, shrugging his shoulders.

Fernando reached below the bar and grabbed two bottles of Estrella Damm. He opened them and handed the bottles to us.

"How much?" I asked.

"*Nada*," he replied.

"Fernando, we're going to pay you for the beers," Marcos said.

"That story was worth the price of two beers," he said.

"*Gracias, amigo*," I said.

"How are the ladies looking tonight, Fernando?" Marcos asked.

"*Bonita*," he replied. "Pretty ladies everywhere."

"Jason's looking for his future wife," Marcos said. "Anna."

Fernando winked at me in support of my efforts.

"Good luck," Fernando said. "Do you boys want to sit at a table or stand at the bar?"

"A table," I said, "but they all look full. We can wait at the bar until a table opens."

"Wait here," Fernando said.

He walked through the crowd. Fernando pushed his way to a table against the wall across from the bar. Five *chicos* in their early twenties looked at him and nodded. Two stood and the other three followed their lead. The men inched through the crowd and stood against the wall near a table of middle-aged women. The women were attractive, but, judging by their age, they were already spoken for.

Fernando waived to Marcos and I. He motioned his head in the direction of the now-open table. I scouted a route to the table. I elbowed my way around a group of teenagers. Being a few inches taller than any other person in the bar had its advantages. Marcos followed. I looked behind me to make sure he was on my tail. His height measured closely to the surrounding Spaniards, but his backwards Yankees cap increased his notability in the crowd.

"Thanks, Fernando," I said as I arrived at the table.

"*No pasa nada,*" he replied. "No problem."

"What did you say to those guys?" Marcos asked.

"I told them that those ladies in the corner were talking about some sexy *chicos* at this table," he said. "I suggested that they get up and make their move on the ladies before another group of guys did."

"Crazy," I said. "It's a good thing you talked to those

ladies, then. Lucky guys."

"I haven't talked to those ladies all night," he said. "Those boys come in here every weekend and they're desperate for women. I knew they would move if I hinted at a female possibility."

"You're clever, Fernando," Marcos said.

Marcos and I drank another *cerveza*. I put my feet on one empty chair and Marcos did the same on his side of the table. I saw a gorgeous girl walk through the door. Dark hair. Red lipstick. Black dress with a leather coat. Anna walked behind her, followed by two friends.

Marcos stood up and waved. Anna saw him and nudged her three friends toward our table. We borrowed another chair from a neighboring party so the four girls could sit.

"Hello, Jason," Anna said.

"*Hola, Anna*," I replied.

"These are my friends," she said, followed by introductions.

Paloma, the babe in the black dress and red lipstick, sat next to Marcos. Cristina, a decent-looking girl, sat next to me. She had a semi-rocker groupie vibe about her. Carmen, a tall-yet-gorgeous girl from Barcelona, rounded the quartet of *chicas* at our table. Her style exemplified professionalism. Anna sat across from me. She looked just like a Spanish movie star in her tight red dress. Her olive skin showed little evidence of make-up, unlike Cristina's cake face.

"What have you ladies done all night?" I asked in English.

"Their English is not good," Anna said. "Can we speak Spanish?"

"*Sí*. How is your night going so far, ladies?" I asked *en español*.

"Good," said Paloma. "We ate dinner at a restaurant a few building away from here."

"I saw your roommate with his girlfriend," Anna said to me.

"Dev and Roxy?" I said.

"Yes. His girlfriend is white, yes?" she asked.

"Um, yeah," I said, scrambling to redirect the conversation. "This is Marcos. He's from New York City."

"I love New York City," Paloma said. "I visited with my cousin when I was fifteen."

"Oh really?" he said. "What did you do in The City?"

"Broadway and the Empire State Building," she replied. "I loved the Statue of Liberty."

"Oh, yeah?" he said. "I can see the Statue from my apartment window."

Marcos and Paloma talked about New York City for the next ten minutes, which gave me time to focus on Anna. I made her friends laugh with my thick American accent. I teased Anna about her English abilities, which made them laugh more. Anna blushed. The conversation flowed organically. I felt a strong vibe.

"What would you ladies like to drink?" Fernando asked as he approached our table.

"*Sidra, por favor*," Paloma replied.

"*Dos botellas*," Anna added.

Fernando winked at Marcos and me as he left. He returned and poured four glasses. Each girl drank her *sidra* in a few seconds. Tradition, I guess. Fernando placed two beers in front of Marcos and I, accompanies by another wink. Marcos and I bumped glasses. I caught Anna looking at me, but she shifted her gaze quickly after realizing that I saw her.

She blushed.

"Hey, Jason," Marcos shouted over the increasing crowd volume.

"What?" I said.

"Paloma wants to know if we are good guys," he said.

"Of course we're good guys, Paloma," I said. "We're the best."

"I don't believe you," Paloma said to me.

"*Que necesitas, tío?*" I said. "You have to believe good guys."

"El Jefe," Marcos shouted as Fernando strolled near our table.

Fernando walked to our table and stood behind me.

"What's up?" he said.

"Paloma, here, wants to know if Jason and I are good guys," Marcos said.

"Tell the truth," Paloma said.

Anna laughed. We locked eyes for a moment and refocused on the conversation.

"These two?" Fernando said. "Marcos and Jason are good guys. They're good friends of mine and I have known them for only two months. Treat them well, *senorita.*"

Fernando accentuated his Venezuelan charm and mystique when he spoke to women he didn't know. I noticed this within the last week and now his game became apparent to me. It worked well. He was very convincing.

"Well, if you say so," Paloma said.

"Anna thinks Jason is a good guy," Carmen told Fernando, accompanied by a slight giggle.

"Yeah she does," affirmed Paloma.

"Paloma!" Anna said as she blushed.

I smiled at Anna.

"Well, should we go to *Calle Mon*?" Anna asked the group in an attempt to escape embarrassment.

We paid Fernando for the *sidra* and a few of the beers we ordered. Fernando ensured that a few beers were on the house, so we thanked him.

"Fernando," I said, "what time do you get off work?"

"After I close the bar," he said. "Probably two."

"Come join us on *Calle Mon* after that," Marcos said.

"I will."

Marcos and I walked with Paloma and Anna, while Carmen and Cristina trailed behind us. The girls navigated the cobblestone streets with expertise in spite of their high heels. A lot of practice, I assumed. The girls led us to another bar with a small dance floor. Most large dance halls opened in an hour or two. I ordered a beer. Anna followed me to the bar and ordered a *cuba libre*. We took our drinks onto the dance floor and grooved in a group with Marcos and the other girls. Anna could dance well. She added a Spanish flare and an intoxicating hip shake along with her steps.

The rock groupie found other friends on the dance floor, so we left her with them. Now Carmen played the fifth wheel. Marcos and I ordered two more beers in bottles before we left the bar. We drank them while we walked with the girls.

"I think Funky Room opened already," Anna said.

"Let's go there later," Paloma suggested. "Want to go to iPop?"

"Yes!" Anna exclaimed.

"What's iPop?" I asked.

"A lot of singing," she said. "I think you'll like it."

We turned a corner and Anna, Paloma, and Carmen walked into a doorway littered with graffiti. The doorway led to a staircase. Marcos and I looked at each other. I shrugged my shoulders and we chugged the remainder of our Estrella Damm and we followed the girls into a basement lounge with a large dance floor. There was a projector screen on the wall with Spanish words that scrolled like a teleprompter.

"Want to sing?" Anna asked.

"What do you mean?" I asked.

"Karaoke!" she shouted. "Sign us up for a song."

A few minutes later, the DJ announced four names: Paloma, Anna, Jason, and Marcos.

"What song did you select?" I asked.

"*Con la Mano Levanta*," Paloma said.

"That sounds like a Spanish song," Marcos said.

"Of course it is," Anna said. "Can you boys handle it?"

"Of course we can," Marcos replied.

"Well, thanks," I whispered to Marcos. "Here we go."

I didn't sing a word of the song. The words scrolled too rapidly for me to follow along efficiently. I danced around the floor. Marcos followed the words for the first verse, but he was unfamiliar with the tune, so he danced next to me.

"You didn't even sing!" scolded Anna after the song ended.

"I tried really hard, though," I said.

"Sure you did," she said. She punched my shoulder.

"That was fun," Paloma said. "Let's go to Funky Room."

We walked to the main floor and onto the cobblestone street. Anna led the group through an alley and we turned left. Carmen walked with Paloma. We passed the crowded *Plaza del Sol*. The occupants of *Bar Campa* filtered onto the street. We walked into Funky Room and the temperature increased dramatically. Sweat hung in the air. A familiar hip-hop beat blasted form the speakers.

"Is that Tupac?" I asked Marcos.

"Yeah, I think so," he said.

"In Spain?" I said. "That's awesome!"

Marcos and I sang along. Anna, Paloma, and Carmen did not. The dance floor was packed with people. Hands waved and heads bounced with the beat. Fernando walked through the door while we were standing in the entryway.

"El Jefe," I said.

"*Chicos*," he said.

"Ready to dance?" I asked him.

"Always," Fernando replied.

"*Vamos*?" I said to Anna.

"*Vamos*," she replied.

Anna and I pushed our way to the middle of the dance floor. I grabbed her hand and we grooved face-to-face. Marcos and Paloma danced a few feet to my left. Fernando and Carmen danced with a Latin flare.

The tension between Anna and I grew. I anticipated an opportune moment for a well-timed kiss approaching. Another familiar hip-hop song played. We grooved effortlessly. Her hips swayed. My grip tightened on her left hand. She reached for my other hand. We stepped closer. We looked at each other sensually.

"I'm going to grab a drink," she said. "I'm thirsty."

I followed her to the bar and she requested a water glass. She took a few sips. Paloma and Marcos joined us at the bar. Marcos and I ordered two beers. Anna looked at her phone.

"Paloma!" Anna exclaimed. "He's here!"

"In Oviedo?" Paloma asked.

"Yes. He's on his way to Funky Room!" Anna said.

"Who is on his way to Funky Room?" I asked.

"Anna's boyfriend," Paloma said. "He returned home from Madrid today."

My heart sank. *She had a boyfriend the whole time? How did I miss that minor detail? Why did she let me get so close?* I attempted to suppress my rage. I hated this man and I didn't even know him. *What the hell?* Marcos looked at me. He acknowledged my anger.

"Hey, ladies," he said. "I think Jason and I are leaving. We told Devon and Roxy we would meet them in *Plaza del Sol*."

"Why are you leaving so early?" Anna asked.

"We have plans," I said coldly.

They tried to respond, but Marcos and I were already too far into the crowd. We walked outside and continued briskly on the cobblestone.

"That's ridiculous!" I shouted.

"That sucks, man," Marcos said. "I'm sorry."

I ranted for a few minutes as we slowed our pace. I calmed myself by the time we reached *Plaza del Sol*. We had no plans to meet Devon and Roxanne.

"I'm going to go back to my apartment," I told Marcos.

"And do what?" he asked. "Sulk?"

"Probably," I said.

"That's understandable," Marcos said. "Let's grab one more drink before you go."

We walked through the thinning crowd in *Plaza del Sol* and into *Bar Campa*. Marcos bought two tall *cervezas* and we walked out into the plaza crowd. I put one foot on the wall behind me and rested against it. We said nothing for a few minutes. Devon and Roxanne rounded the corner, saw us, and walked in our direction.

"How was dinner?" I asked.

"It was really good," Roxanne said.

"Where are your girls?" Devon asked.

"Don't worry about them," I replied.

"What happened?" Roxanne asked.

"Anna has a boyfriend," Marcos said.

"I'm sorry, buddy," Roxanne said.

"Don't let it bother you, my dude," Devon said.

"Easier said than done, I'm afraid," I said.

"I have an idea," Roxanne said.

"What is it?" I asked.

"Let's get out of Oviedo next weekend," she said.

"What did you have in mind?" Devon asked.

"Let's go to Barcelona," she said.

"For what?" Marcos asked.

"Because we can," she replied.

"I'm down," I said.

"So am I," said Devon.

"Let's do it," Marcos said.

CHAPTER 9

Before class on Monday, Devon and I walked to the café with Brad. We met Marcos and Roxanne at their indoor table. Thankfully, Anna wasn't working. Roxanne placed her computer on the table and opened it in preparation for our strategic Barcelona planning conference. She purchased all five plane tickets with her credit card and we paid her in cash to simplify the process.

We brainstormed Barcelona activities and decided on only one definite event: an FC Barcelona game. The soccer team played at home in Camp Nou against Sevilla on Saturday night, which was Halloween. Lionel Messi, the best soccer player in the world, and his championship team ranked first in the world. We browsed the FC Barcelona website in search of five consecutive seats. Unfortunately, only 20 seats remained in the whole stadium and each seat was alone in its section.

"Aw man," Marcos said. "Each one of us has to sit by ourselves?"

"We can wave to each other from across the stadium," I said.

"That sucks," Marcos said.

"Yeah, "Brad said, "but we have to do it. This year's Barcelona team could be the best team of all time."

"Should we buy the tickets now?" Roxanne asked.

"We could wait a few hours and see if any seats open up next to each other," Devon suggested.

"Yeah," I said. "Let's wait until after class to buy the tickets. Some family will return their tickets because of a surprise wedding or something."

"And if tickets sell out, we can scalp before the game," Devon said.

"Sounds good," said Roxanne. "We can't buy tickets online, anyways. We have to go to the travel agent in the Oviedo mall to buy them."

"Sounds complicated," Brad said. "We can figure that out after class."

"Alright," I said, "where are we going to stay while we're there?"

"I know a girl from San Francisco who's studying abroad in Barcelona," Brad said. "I can ask her if we can stay at her place. I think she lives in a small apartment, but we can crash on the floor."

"Let's do that," I said.

We discussed potential plans and tourist attractions to visit while in Barcelona. We decided to plan only the soccer game and leave the other four days to chance. Brad and Devon spent a week in the city before their tenure in Oviedo, so they would know of a few things to do once we arrived.

Roxanne closed her computer and put it in her backpack.

We paid for our coffees and walked across the café to the front door. I checked my watch as I walked through the doorway to make sure I wasn't going to be late for class. I looked up and jolted to the right. I almost walked into somebody. I turned to apologize.

"No problem," Anna replied.

I felt my face turn red with embarrassment and frustration. My animosity from the weekend returned. The lack of alcohol in my system allowed me to suppress my emotions. She looked amazing.

"How are you, Jason?" she asked.

"*Bueno*," I replied.

"Good," she said. "How was your Sunday?"

"*Bueno*," I replied again. "Hey, I'm late for class. Have a good day."

I jogged slowly across the street. My friends waited for me. We discussed that awkward moment until we reached the front stairs of the university. We split to find our respective classrooms.

Brad, Devon, and I sat in our usual seats in the middle row of the classroom. Our grammar professor was extremely attractive and appeared to be only a few years older than us. We liked to fool ourselves by pretending we had a chance with her. Naturally, we participated actively in class. She didn't know English.

"Yo, *profesora* is looking good today," Devon whispered to me as she walked into the room.

"Yeah she is," I confirmed. "Her hair is looking extra curly. I bet she knows I like curls."

"That must be it," Devon mocked.

"*Hola, clase,*" our professor said. "*La primera pregunta para nuestra tareja, por favor.*"

I raised my hand and answered successfully. I beamed. Devon answered next. He elbowed me in the rib to ensure that I heard his correct answer.

"Did you see her smile at me when I answered?" he whispered to me in English. "She liked my accent. I can tell."

"Shut up, dude," I said. "She was looking at me when you answered."

"No she wasn't," he said. "Trust me. I was staring at her eyes the whole time."

"Liar," I said. "With that tight shirt she's wearing, I know you weren't looking at her eyes."

"*Chicos,*" our professor said to Devon and I, "*silencio, por favor.*"

It was a good thing she didn't speak English.

Class ended. Devon and I met Roxanne and Brad in the hallway during our ten-minute break before our history class. We had history class with students from other Spanish levels, so we sat with Marcos and Roxanne every time. Roxanne opened her computer and sat on the floor. We watched her screen as she searched for potential FC Barcelona tickets.

"Any luck?" Devon asked.

"I'm not sure yet," she said. "This internet connection is taking forever."

"Damn," Devon said. "Class starts in a few minutes. Let's search again during our break between history and vocabulary."

"Wait!" Roxanne shouted.

"What?" I said.

"Guys, look!" she yelled. "Am I reading this correctly?"

"It looks like six seats just opened up right next to each

other," Devon said.

"That's what it says," I confirmed.

"I thought so!" Roxanne exclaimed.

"They won't be available for long," Devon said.

"They will be gone before we're out of class, for sure," I said.

"We have to go to the mall right now and buy them," Roxanne said.

"I can't skip history," Devon said. "The last two weeks have been confusing as ever. I need to pay attention if I'm going to pass my midterm."

"I can't miss it either," Roxanne said. "I skipped last class to enjoy the sunshine."

"The mall's too far away for me to go," Marcos said. "I'm lazy."

"I'll go," I said. "We need these tickets. I refuse to miss this game."

"Dude, you're wearing sandals," Marcos said. "You know the mall is a 30-minute walk from here, right?"

"Yeah, but it's only a 15-minute run," I said.

"In sandals?" Marcos said.

"It's for the tickets, man," I said.

"Alright then," Marcos said. "Good luck."

"If you buy all five tickets for us, we will pay you back tonight or something," Roxanne said.

"Have fun, *hombre*," Devon said. Ride like the wind."

"Try not to fall asleep in class this time," I said to Devon.

I ninja-kicked the front doors of the university. They swung open and I jumped down the six steps of the front staircase and turned right. I was full of energy and I refused to let my sandals slow me down. I sprinted across campus and turned left to jog along the sidewalk. A woman walking her terrier gasped in shock as I ran directly toward her. I juked right and continued my sprint. I came to a busy street. Cars sped across all four lanes. I stopped, took five deep breathes, and darted across the street at the first small window of opportunity I saw.

I jumped over a bus stop bench and landed on the sidewalk. I turned right and saw the mall in the distance. *Five more minutes*, I thought. I ran faster. As I came to an intersection, an old man turned the corner. I stopped quickly and planted my right foot in preparation to explode into another sprint. My sandal strap ripped and the entire right sandal flew into the street. I picked it up and stood on the sidewalk in desperation. *These tickets will be gone soon*, I thought.

I took off my left sandal and carried one in each hand. I sprinted barefoot as I weaved between pedestrians. I followed a path through a small park and received peculiar looks from the elderly park-goers as they noticed my bare feet. I reached the mall parking lot and darted toward the front door. I flung the door open and burst through the opening. I checked the map at the entrance and found the travel agency. *Downstairs.*

The elevator was too slow, so I walked briskly to the escalator and jogged. A man moved quickly to the side to avoid my juggernaut approach. I saw the travel agency sign and darted for the door. The two people in line found travel agents after a few minutes. A woman at a desk called for me to sit at her station.

"Where are your shoes?" she asked me in Spanish.

I held them above the desk for her to see.

"My sandal broke and I wanted my tickets," I replied.

She laughed and told the travel agent next to her. He laughed. I told her I saw six available tickets next to each other on the FC Barcelona website about 15 minutes ago and I wanted them.

"Well," she said, "let's see if we can get your tickets, then."

She browsed silently on the computer for a moment.

"These tickets?" she asked as she turned her monitor toward me.

"*Sí*," I replied.

"All six tickets?" she asked.

"Only five," I said.

"These tickets are in the highest row of the stadium," she said. "We can find better seats for you, but you will have to sit alone."

"I want the five tickets next to each other, please," I said.

She typed on her keyboard, clicked the mouse, and the printer made noise.

"Here you are, sir," she said as she handed me five tickets.

"Thank you so much," I said, attempting to hold back my excitement.

I paid, stood up, and walked across the room. As I reached the door, the travel agent called to me.

"Sir!" she shouted. "There's a shoe store upstairs."

o   o   o

Devon and I met Brad in front of his apartment on Friday morning. We walked to a kebab restaurant and order three kebabs to go. I watched the chef carve thin slices of lamb from the rotisserie with his electric cutting device. He tossed them onto three pieces of pita bread and covered each piece with vegetables and two sauces. He folded each pita in half and wrapped them into three delicious kebabs. We paid and walked with our weighted backpacks to meet Roxanne and Marcos at the bus station.

After a short bus ride, the five of us walked into the airport, through the security checkpoint, and into the terminal. Devon was selected for a random security check and had to throw his new toothpaste tube in the trash can. We boarded the plane and attempted to contain our excitement as the engines propelled the plane into the air. The plane touched Barcelona airstrip after 30 minutes and we cruised through the huge airport in search of a taxi.

We squeezed four people into the back of the cab, while Brad sat alone in the front seat.

"*Passeig de Gracia, por favor*," Brad told the taxi driver.

"What building?" the driver asked,

"*Casa Gracia*," Brad said.

Brad's friend in Barcelona already had houseguests for the long weekend, so we made plans to stay four nights in an inexpensive hostel where Brad and Devon stayed a few months ago.

"I hope Irena still works at the front desk at *Casa Gracia*," Brad told Devon.

"Yeah, she was fine," Devon said.

Roxanne punched him in the arm. The cab driver weaved in and out of traffic at alarming speed, which caused an uncontrollable game of corners between the four of us in the back seat.

The sun was setting as we stepped onto the sidewalk in front of *Casa Gracia*. I grabbed my backpack from the trunk and followed Devon up the stairs to the first floor.

"*Hola*," Devon said to the man working at the front desk. "Checking in."

"How many?" the man asked.

"Five," Devon said.

The man handed Devon five keys and five city maps.

"Hey, we stayed here a few months ago," Brad told the man. "Does Irena work today?"

"No, Irena left Barcelona for Rome two weeks ago," the man said. "The major tourist season ended, so we had to let her go."

We dropped our bags off in our room and left the hostel to find dinner. We walked around aimlessly for a half hour until we found a restaurant with a soccer game. Real Madrid played Valencia. We sat at a table and watched. The game only made me more excited for tomorrow's late night game between Barcelona and Sevilla.

CHAPTER 10

I woke up early Saturday morning. The sun snuck through the window blinds and hit my eyelids. I wanted to shut the blinds badly. I hopped to the floor from the top bunk and landed without much stealth. I looked outside at the busy street in central Barcelona and a sudden burst of energy hit me.

"You're up early," Brad said from the bunk below mine.

"Yeah. I'm excited to be in Barcelona, I guess," I said.

"I can't sleep either," he said. "Let's go get some food."

I put my shoes on and we walked down two flights of stairs to *Passeig de Gracia*.

The sun was beginning to warm the air, but I still felt the crispness of morning. An old couple walked slowly along the sidewalk. A few men in suits walked briskly. Some crossed the street at a major crosswalk. With no destination in mind, Brad and I cruised.

We found a market that had opened a few minutes ago. We walked in. I bought a bottle of orange juice and three large baguettes. Brad bought cheese and meat. I stood in a short line. Brad chose a longer line, but the line moved quickly and he beat me to the front door. We strolled toward our hostel down *Passeig de Gracia* with our groceries. As we neared the *Casa Gracia* front door, it opened from the inside and out walked Audrey Reigert.

"Look who it is," Audrey said coldly.

"Good morning, Audrey," I said.

"Are you staying at *Casa Gracia* too?" Brad asked.

"No, I'm just walking out of its front door," she said.

"Good one," Brad said.

"What are your plans for Barcelona?" I asked. I'm sure my insincerity sliced through the formality.

"Well," she said, "Stanley and I are going to some museums today. We're going on a Gaudi architecture tour tomorrow morning at nine."

"Sounds like fun," Brad said monotonously.

"And I suppose you two are going to the beach today to drink beer? Club-hopping tonight?" she said.

"That's the plan!" I said.

"How cultural of you," Audrey said.

"We're going to the FC Barcelona game tonight, also," I said.

"Stanley suggested that last month when we made our plans, but I wasn't interested," she said. "Grown men getting drunk and yelling at other grown men while they kick a ball around on grass. I don't see the value."

"Well I can't wait," I said. "Soccer is the most popular sport in the world and we're going to see the best player in the world play for the best team in the world. I'm psyched."

"If soccer was the most popular sport in the world, it

would be America's Favorite Pastime," she said.

"Now that's an ignorant comment if I've ever heard one," I said.

"Read a book, Jason," Audrey said.

"Watch T.V., Audrey," I replied.

Stan Johnson came out of the building.

"Hey, guys," he said. "Funny seeing you here."

"Likewise," Brad said.

"Come on, Stanley," Audrey said. "Let's go intelligently enjoy the cultural asphyxiations of Barcelona."

She grabbed Stan's arm, turned, and walked away. Brad and I strolled into the hostel and climbed the stairs.

"Can you define 'asphyxiation' for me?" I said to Brad.

"And give me the etymology," Brad added.

"Use it in a sentence," I said.

"I bet she was the fifth grade spelling bee champion of her suburban elementary school," Brad said.

"I heard 'asphyxiation' on one of those police shows once," I said.

"What does it mean?" Brad asked.

"I can't give you the Oxford definition, but the victim was 'asphyxiated' to death," I said.

"So she didn't use that word correctly at all, did she?" he said.

"We should tell her," I said.

"No way," Brad said. "She might 'asphyxiate' us."

Roxanne and Devon were out of bed when we returned to the room. Marcos was awake, but still under his blankets. I took my shoes off and jumped onto my top bunk and let my feet hang from the bedside. The sun flickered on the wall as a draft of wind from the open window made the blinds dance.

"We bought breakfast," I said.

"Thanks, guys," Roxanne said. "How was the stroll to the store?"

Brad and I reenacted the conversation with Audrey, which featured exaggeration and achieved laughter from the whole room. We ripped the baguettes and made simple sandwiches with our other ingredients.

"Well, what should we do today?" Roxanne asked.

Her chipper attitude suggested that she was a morning person.

"What did we do all day when we were here last time?" Brad asked Devon.

"We hit the beach," Devon replied.

"Hell yeah!" Roxanne shouted.

"To da beach, mon," I said in a butchered Jamaican accent.

We wore our swimsuits and bought cheap towels at a local market. We submerged into the Barcelona subway tunnel near our hostel and bought tickets. In front of us, locals jumped over the turnstiles, so we decided to save our tickets for the return trip and we followed the locals' example.

The train to Barceloneta was packed with people. On a warm October day like this, everybody wanted to enjoy the sun at the beach. Every seat was filled with passengers, so we stood near the door. I carried my wallet and cell phone in my hand instead of the cargo pocket on the side of my board shorts.

My board shorts were new. They were black with a University of Oregon graphic on the left side. The pocket on the right had a bottle opener attached to the inside by a thick elastic band. I couldn't wait to use it on a beach bottle of Estrella Damm.

"Only two more stops," Devon said.

"Then a five block walk and we're there," Brad added.

A few people entered the subway car, which forced a group to shift our direction. A short man with a leather jacket draped over his right arm inched closer to me to allow room for the new passengers. His dark complexion suggested South American immigrant.

I turned my head to say something to Devon when I felt my pocket move upwards. I whipped my head toward my pocket to find the bottle opener dangling next to the short man's hand that was covered by his leather jacket.

"Watch your hands, man," I said in Spanish.

He unleashed Spanish verbal abuse; his speed quickened with every word and I couldn't keep up. Everyone in our train car looked our direction. He spoke with such ferocity that I had no opportunity to interject. He tried to pick my pocket, undoubtedly, and I wanted to accuse him officially. Devon and Brad stood behind me and folded their arms. We glared at the professional pickpocket as he scrambled to escape persecution.

The train stopped. The doors opened. He burst through the crowd of people entering the train and he disappeared into the depths of the Barcelona underworld.

"What the hell was that?" Marcos asked.

"That dude tried to rob me!" I shouted.

I flicked the dangling bottle opener and wondered what my pickpocket thought he was grabbing.

Two stops later, we exited the train and walked to the surface. I grumbled about the pickpocket with every step I took on the staircase. *At least he didn't steal anything*, I thought.

The sun hit my eyes as my head emerged from the subway tunnel. It warmed my face, then my entire body. I forgot about the pickpocket. The environment was too perfect to remain agitated, anyway.

Brad and Devon led our group toward the beach. We passed rustic beach apartments. Yellow, blue, orange, green, and pink walls, doors, and roofs. Palm trees lined the sidewalk. The atmosphere felt nearly tropical.

We arrived at a short wall that separated the cement from the sand. Though summertime had passed, the beach was crowded. We weaved between chairs connected to a beachfront restaurant patio.

I took my shoes off and wiggled my toes in the sand with each step. We strolled for a few minutes and searched for an ideal location to establish our sandy post for the day. The tide rolled along the beach. Calm water.

Roxanne flung her towel on an open area and the guys did the same. I took my shirt off and sprinted into the water. I dove headfirst into the water. The clear Mediterranean Sea refreshed my body. I held my breath and swam underwater for ten seconds and propelled myself with a dolphin kick. I emerged, feeling revitalized.

Marcos swam near me. We returned to our beach territory and sat on towels by Brad, Devon, and Roxanne.

"Man, this is the life," Devon said.

"Yeah it is," Roxanne confirmed.

An Indian man walked toward us in the sand. He dragged a cooler behind him.

"*Cerveza.* Beer. Cold beer," he said to us.

"*No gracias,*" Devon said.

The man continued down the beach and asked our neighbors the same question.

"They will do that all day," Devon said.

"Do what?" I asked.

"Solicit cold beer to us," he said. "Just wait."

Five minutes later, two Asian women walked over to us.

"*Quieres masaje*? Massage, massage?" one Asian woman asked us.

"*No gracias*," Devon replied.

The women continued to the next potential customer.

"We'll get that all day, too," Devon said.

"Cold beer, massages, and the beach," I said. "Looks like we're in for a rough day."

Roxanne asked pointed toward perfectly squared stones piled a football-field away in the sea.

"What are those?" she asked.

"Wave breakers," Brad said.

"Well let's check them out!" Roxanne shouted.

"I just went swimming," Marcos said. "I'm going to stay here and work on my tan."

"Yeah, that looks too far away for me to swim at this point in my day," Brad said.

Devon, Roxanne, and I ran into the water and swam. I opened my eyes underwater. It was so clear that I could see the bottom. It was a long way down and the thought of killer sea monsters crept into my mind, so I emerged and kept my head above water for a while. We swam for a long time. The breakers looked a lot closer from our onshore viewpoint on the shore.

Roxanne reached the closest square boulder and climbed it. She used nearby boulders for support. I followed. With bare feet, I almost stepped on a sea urchin. *That would have been a day-ruiner*, I thought.

"This is awesome!" Roxanne shouted from atop a breaker.

I looked toward the beach. Brad and Marcos appeared to be the size of my thumbnail. We hoped from boulder to boulder and explored the marine life between crevasses and gaps. After admiring the starfish that clung to the wave breakers, we sprawled on the hot rocks for a while.

"This is too perfect," Roxanne said. "I don't want to leave Spain."

"I know," Devon said. "Too bad we have to go back to the States in a few months."

"Yeah, what do we have to go back to?" I asked.

"Rainy West Coast winters," Devon said.

"Intense school work," Roxanne said.

"Loans and tuition payments," I said.

"Family problems," Devon said.

"It's nice being away from all that drama," I said.

"We have to find a career next year," Roxanne said.

"Yeah, and in this economy, too," I said.

"I don't want to," Devon said.

"Let's just stay here in paradise forever," Roxanne said.

"I wish stuff was as cheap in the States as it was here," I said.

"That's what I'm saying," Roxanne said. "Let's just stay."

We sat in silence for a while. I looked across the open ocean, away from the beach. The ocean met the sky and faded into abyss, tranquil and continuous.

We swam to the beach and sun-dried on our towels. Brad awoke and sprang to his feet.

"I have an idea," he said. "Is it noon yet?"

"Almost," I said.

"Come on, Jason," he said. "Let's take a walk. Bring your wallet."

"Where are we going?" I asked.

"Just come with me," he said. "Guys, watch our stuff while we're gone."

"I'm coming, too," Devon said.

Brad grabbed his backpack. I put my shirt on and grabbed my shoes. Devon did the same. We walked along the beach and jumped over the dividing wall. I landed on the cement and put my shoes on. We strolled on the sidewalk and came to a convenience store.

"I figured since the Barcelona game starts in ten hours, we should start preparing ourselves," Brad said.

"What did you have in mind?" Devon asked.

"Well, we have five people in our group," Brad said. "So, five bottle of wine should do the job for now."

"Yeah, buddy," I said. "You're thinking big. I like it."

We walked to the back of the store. The Arabian man behind the counter followed us. He pretended to organize the shelf to our backs, but he eyes locked onto us and never wavered. Our backpack probably drew suspicion. We picked out five bottles of cheap red wine and carried them to the counter.

We passed the employee and he followed us to the register. He seemed relieved that we planned to pay for our beverages.

"*Tienes un sacacorchos?*" I asked.

"*Si,*" the clerk responded.

He handed me a corkscrew and we paid for it, along with the five wine bottles. We put the bottles in the backpack and returned to the beach.

"I think it's illegal to drink on the beach," Brad said, "but I'm not sure."

"Good call on the backpack, then," I said.

We sat on our towels and Brad handed me a wine bottle. I opened it with my new *sacacorchos*. Roxanne slept on her towel.

"Roxy!" I shouted.

"Ah! What?" she said, startled.

"Look alive," I said.

I passed the wine bottle to her.

"Oh boy," she said. "Already?"

"Yes ma'am," I said. "It's game day. Time to start tail-gating."

I opened the next bottle and gave it to Devon. I handed the next to Marcos, the next to Brad, and I took the last one.

"Cheers," I said. We slammed our bottles together and drank.

I jammed the cork into my bottle and buried half of it in the sand.

"Sneaky, Jason," Marcos said. "Very sneaky."

We developed a rotation. A few people swam and a few stayed with our things and drank wine. When the swimming group returned, the other group swam. Sometimes, our whole group stayed on the beach and drank wine.

"Hey, Jason," Roxanne said. "What's the deal with you and Anna?"

"At this point," I said, "I don't know. I thought I knew, but now I don't."

"Come on," she said. "What do you think?"

"She has a boyfriend, I guess," I said. "I thought I felt a

vibe between us, but I guess I was wrong."

"I thought there was a vibe between you two also," Devon added.

"There was a vibe," Roxanne said. "Want to know what I think?"

"Hit me with the female perspective," I said.

"I think," she continued, "that Anna likes you. Her boyfriend lives in Madrid and she liked him a lot. Now, she found you, the exotic American who treats her well."

"But that still leaves me with the boyfriend problem," I said.

"For now," Roxanne said. "Wait until he goes back to Madrid. I bet she will realize that she likes you more."

"Thanks for the words of encouragement, Roxy," I said, "but I don't know if that's going to happen."

"Hey, man," Devon said. "If the vibe's there, the vibe's there. You can't fight the feeling."

"You sound like an R&B singer," I said.

"I am an R&B singer," Devon replied.

"Shut up, dude," I said.

"*You can't fight the feelin','*" Devon sang to me.

"We'll see what happens back in Oviedo, I guess," I said. "I'm not too worried about it at this particular juncture in my life."

"Yeah," Brad added, "especially with all these Barcelona babes walking around the beach."

We took another gulp from our wine bottles.

"Guys," Roxanne said, "I have a problem. My wine's gone"

"The worst kind of problem," Brad said. "We can fix that."

Marcos waved to an Indian man with a cooler. The man wobbled toward us and stopped near Marcos.

"*Cerveza*. Beer. Cold beer," the man said.

"*Cinco cervezas, por favor*," Marcos said.

The Indian man reached into his cooler and grabbed five cans. Marcos paid and thanked him. The man looked at me.

"*Cerveza*. Beer. Hasheesh?" he asked me.

"No, I don't want any of your hasheesh," I said. "But thanks for the beers, sir."

The man continued down the beach and asked another group the same question.

"You can get it all on the beach in Barcelona," Brad said with a laugh.

I sipped my beer and looked at the horizon. *Why should I leave Spain?* The sea seemed to rest and roll simultaneously. It crashed into the square boulders in the distance. I envisioned myself in an apartment that overlooked this beach view. My exotic Spanish wife brought me a *café con leche*. She stood next to me as we gazed at the sea...

"*Quieres masaje?* Massage, massage?" asked an Asian woman.

Her question startled me and I jolted from my trance. I looked at Brad.

"Dude," I said. "Let's get a massage."

"How much?" he asked the woman.

"Three Euros for feet," she replied.

"That's it?" I said to Brad.

"Hell yeah," he said. "Are you guys going to get a massage, too?"

"For three Euros?" Marcos said. "Absolutely."

The woman called two other women to assist her. One

woman massaged my feet, while the other two worked on Brad and Marcos.

The three masseuses moved from China to Barcelona four months prior because they heard that work was easier to find in Spain. The women connected with a recruiter who sent them to Barcelona. Once in Barcelona, they connected with an overseer who controlled a team of wandering beach masseuses. In exchange for giving cheap massages and paying the overseer, the women received housing and food from their boss.

"Ah!" I shouted as the woman dug into the ball of my right foot.

"Hurt?" she asked me.

"No," I said with a wince. "It feels great."

"Turn over," she told me.

I turned onto my stomach and she massaged my calves. I looked to my right and Brad received the same calf treatment.

"You boys are very strong," Brad's masseuse said.

"Thanks," Brad said.

"You have fun in Barcelona?" my masseuse asked.

"Yes," I said.

"Go to football game?"

"Yes," I said. "We're going to the game tonight."

"Be careful if you take the train," she said. "There are thieves."

CHAPTER 11

We left *Casa Gracia* just as the sun sank behind the hostel building. I wore a red shirt and blue hat in support of the red-and-blue stripes adorned by FC Barcelona. In our Spanish history course, I learned that the FC Barcelona jersey nearly matches the Catalonian flag.

The soccer club represents pride for Catalonia, the Spanish province that contains Barcelona, which has pushed for total independence for centuries. During Francisco Franco's dictatorship of Spain during the middle of the 1900s, FC Barcelona symbolized a free Spain. Franco's government operated from Madrid and, as a result, Franco professed unwavering support for Barcelona's archrival, Real Madrid.

We ran across *Passieg de Gracia* and submerged into the familiar subway station. We passed the ticket-purchasing machine and I jumped over the turnstile. A liter of San Miguel *cerveza* fueled my courage to act like a local. Devon, Brad, Roxanne, and Marcos followed.

Our group entered the subway train and we pushed our

way into the middle of the overcrowded car. The morning's Barceloneta beach crowd seemed sparse compared to the night's soccer game swarm. The train moved. I remained immobile as I wedged myself between Roxanne and Brad, among other travelers. With six stops until the famed Camp Nou soccer palace, I couldn't imagine how more people could fit into our subway car.

More fans packed the train with each stop. I contorted my body to allow more room for other passengers. I felt hands dart in and out of my pockets. With my inability to turn my head or move any limb on my body, I had no power to accuse any potential thief. Thanks to the morning's run-in with the South American pickpocket, I carried my wallet and game ticket in my hand and under my shirt.

"Dude," I said to Devon. "These sneaky pickpockets are everywhere."

"I know man," he said. "People keep grazing my pockets. Someone's hand would be broken if I could move mine."

"You boys are so tough," Roxanne jested.

"Whatever, Roxy," I said. "You know you're lucky to have strapping young lads like us on your side."

"Knights in shining armor," she said.

"Does that make me the Black Knight?" Devon asked.

I felt a sly set of hands graze my pockets each time the train jostled. A man next to me inspected the safety of the chain connecting his belt loop and wallet. *Local wisdom*, I thought.

"Guys, I'm getting way too excited," I said.

"Take a lap," Brad suggested.

"Yeah, I'm juiced," Devon said. "This is going to be crazy."

"I went to the Rose Bowl in Los Angeles when the Ducks played Ohio State last year," I said. "That was the most intense sporting event I've ever been to. I bet this tops it."

"I think it will," Brad said. "I go to almost every Giants baseball game, but nothing beats a European soccer game from what I hear."

"I don't know," Marcos said. "When the Knicks play in Madison Square Garden…"

"The Knicks haven't been good since Patrick Ewing was in *Space Jam*," I interrupted.

"Tell that to Spike Lee," Marcos said.

The train stopped. Every person on the train rushed through the doors as they slid open. We followed the mob. I shouted with excitement as we passed the subway sign that pointed upwards to Camp Nou. Fans chanted Barcelona fight songs and soccer cheers as we climbed the steps.

"Where do we go from here?" Roxanne asked.

"Follow the noise," I said.

Tall buildings blocked any potential view of the stadium, but I heard the sounds of pregame electricity. We passed bar after bar, each one full of red-and-blue-clad fans.

Kickoff commenced in two hours.

"What should we do?" Brad asked the group.

"Go to a bar, of course," Marcos said.

"We won't be able to get a drink," Devon said. "These places are too packed."

"We have to drink before the game, though," Marcos said.

We discussed the idea of buying beer at the game until we realized that alcohol wasn't allowed in the stadium. We heard rumors of rowdiness and soccer hooligans, so we attributed the stadium's no alcohol policy to the truth behind these rumors.

"So we should drink before the game, then," Roxanne said.

"We could pull a *Parque San Francisco*," Devon suggested.

"Good plan, Dev," I said. "Let's find a store, buy something to drink, and find a park."

"Then let's get to work, Team Fun," Devon added.

We roamed the sidewalk on the major avenue and looked for a convenience store. Overcrowd bars allowed fans to use the sidewalk to drink in order to allow more space for customers. As we passed a bar, we weaved through the overflow. A drunk man stumbled into his buddy and they slapped each other on the back. I aimed to pass him on the left side, but he swayed into me.

"*Lo siento,*" I said.

The man looked at me for a few seconds. His demeanor suggested confrontation.

"What team are you for?" he asked me in slurred Spanish.

"Barcelona, of course," I answered.

"*Bueno!*" he shouted. He told his friends of my team allegiance and his group allowed us to pass. We high-fived bar customers as we passed through the tunnel of fans. I turned and approached the drunk man.

"Excuse me, sir," I said. "Where can we find a store that sells liquor?"

"Around the corner!" he shouted.

"Thank you," I said.

"*Viva Barcelona!*" he replied.

"Come one, people," I said to Brad, "I thought my red and blue gear would make it clear that I'm a Barcelona fan."

"You might have to buy a jersey or something, then," he

said.

Not a bad idea, I thought.

We turned the corner and found the liquor store. Marcos and I walked in and bought a bottle of rum and a bottle of cola. We wandered for a few minutes and found a small grass patch and Roxanne sat on a short cement wall. Brad sat next to her. Devon and I sat on an opposing bench that faced the wall. Marcos stood for a minute and sat next to Roxanne. To our right, we saw Camp Nou. The soccer shrine illuminated the sky and the noise from its pilgrims reverberated around the city.

"Woof, this rum is harsh," Devon said. He shivered after he drank from the bottle.

"And the cola's almost empty," Roxanne added as she handed the bottle to him.

"At least we still have a lot of rum," Marcos said.

"Enough drinks of this stuff and you won't care if we have cola or not," Devon said.

A group of Barcelona fans shouted to us in support as they walked by the grass patch. Roxanne shouted back with affirmation. A group of Sevilla fans walked by a few minutes later. We shouted in unwavering support of Barcelona. They retaliated with Sevilla chants.

"Forget those guys," Marcos said.

"I love getting riled up like this for a Spanish soccer game," I said.

"It's exciting, man," Devon said.

I took a drink from the rum bottle. The cola bottle was empty. I passed the bottle to Devon, who took a drink.

"Roxy, guess what?" Devon said.

"What?" Roxanne replied.

"Your turn," Devon said and handed her the rum bottle.

"Brad, what time is it?" I asked.

"9:30," he said.

"Half hour until game time," Marcos said.

"Let's finish this bottle and cruise," I said.

We passed the rum around in a circle and finished quickly. I felt warm inside. I stood and stumbled as the rum hit me. We walked toward the stadium and merged with an increasingly large mass of fans.

"Guys," I shouted, "let's check out these kiosks for a minute."

"Good plan," Devon said.

I bought a Barcelona scarf to show my allegiance. Roxanne and Marcos bought jerseys and Brad bought a flag. I attempted to barter with the clerk, but his price didn't budge.

We merged with the crowd and entered the gate that surrounded the stadium. I asked a man with two boys to take our picture. I gave my camera to him and he captured our group with Camp Nou as the backdrop. I thanked him and shouted Barcelona support. His boys shouted back.

I gave my ticket to the woman at the entrance and she scanned it. My excitement increased with every step. I felt the energy rise as each new fan entered the stadium. Spectators shouted. Opposing fans retaliated. I looked for signs of potential hooliganism, but I didn't see any yet.

We walked in the tunnels underneath the seats and climbed the stairs. The cement walls and winding metal structure gave the inner-workings of the stadium a raw feel. We came to the first level. I looked through the tunnel and saw rows of fans shouting with anticipation. The upper decks shadowed their sections. It looked like a sea of red and blue; the rows of fans met the vibrant green field. The sea met the horizon.

We kept walking. We climbed more stairs and the mass of fans thinned as we passed entrances to the second and third levels. We climb more stairs and the staircase ended. We walked through the tunnel and emerged into the open air of the top level.

We climbed the stairs between sections and found our seats at the highest row in the entire stadium. I looked over the edge of the wall and saw the ground below me. *Talk about the nose-bleed section.* A tingling feeling crept up my spine and I turned quickly toward the field. The view inspired me to shout. One hundred thousand fans looked on as both teams warmed up on pristine grass. Flags waved behind each goal. The scoreboard clock counted down the seconds until kickoff. Five minutes.

"This is unreal!" Roxanne shouted.

"Barcelona!" I yelled.

"Look at this dude in front of us," Devon said to me.

A teenage boy and his father shouted wildly. They told us that they had attended nearly every game for the last six seasons. They said the city owns the team, so the team belongs to its fans. I felt a true sense of Catalan pride in the father's statement. Four middle-aged women sat to our left. Marcos talked to them about the game. This was their first Camp Nou experience.

The countdown on the scoreboard ended. Both teams entered the field through the tunnel at the midfield line. Each team walked in single-file formation. Each player held a child's hand as they walked onto the field. They lined up and a small ceremony occurred.

The teams gathered on the sideline for a quick pregame meeting and hustled to their respective field positions; Lionel Messi and David Villa lined up as forwards for Barcelona, while Carles Puyol, Barcelona's veteran long-haired enforcer, lined up on defense. Sevilla approached the ball and Barcelona awaited the first touch on the outer edge of the circle. The stadium erupted with noise. Even the noise at record-setting Autzen Stadium couldn't compare to the volume at Camp Nou seconds before kickoff. I bounced with anticipation. Devon said something to me, but I couldn't hear him. Our seats shook.

Sevilla kicked off. The forward passed to his left and the receiver passed behind him to a midfielder. Barcelona attacked the ball and engulfed the midfielder. He scrambled to pass and the ball rolled behind him and a Sevilla defender possessed it. The defender passed to his right and shifted the action to the opposite side of the field. Barcelona compressed their defense and swarmed both potential outlet passes for the nervous Sevilla midfielder who now possessed the ball. A Barcelona defender stole the ball after a pathetic juke attempt by Sevilla. The red-and-blue jersey sprinted with precise control in his dribble. He crossed the midfield line and passed to his right. Barcelona had the ball on the right side of the 18-yard box.

The attacker waited. He scanned the field. He passed to David Villa at the top of the box. He shot, but a Sevilla defender blocked it with his body. The ball ricocheted and another striped jersey found it. He ripped a shot that bent into a diving Sevilla keeper. Another ricochet. Messi waited patiently in front of the goal. The ball rolled slowly by a sliding Sevilla defender and Messi took control. He dribbled slightly to his left and fired the ball into the goal. The game clock read *3:40*.

The crowd erupted in unison. Every fan bowed in their seats as the crowd shouted *Me-ssi, Me-ssi,* in perfectly synchronized Gregorian chant. The on-field celebration ensued. Sevilla kicked off a few seconds later, but the crowd maintained the chant for minutes. The father-and-son duo in front of us high-fived each and hugged.

"Hell yeah!" I shouted.

"Messi's the man!" Brad shouted back.

A few nonchalant possessions occurred. Barcelona out-hustled the entire Sevilla team. The early goal asserted the Catalan team's dominance on the field. The game clock read *23:00*. Messi sprinted down the center of the field with the ball. David Villa kept pace to Messi's right side. Five Sevilla defenders stood between Messi and the goalie. Four defenders collapsed on the Argentine and Messi kicked the ball to Villa. Messi sprinted toward the goal, keeping parallel to Villa. All four defenders anticipated the cross to Messi in the center. One defender approached Villa, the pride of Asturias.

Villa cocked his leg back for the cross to Messi and the defender flinched. Villa knocked the ball behind his left leg and dribble around the defender. He stumbled. With one step, he recovered and fired a left-footed shot into the top corner of the goal. *Vi-lla, Vi-lla, Vi-lla!* The crowd resumed the Gregorian chant.

"Let's go, Asturias!" Marcos yelled.

"*Villa!*" shouted the boy in front of us.

I high-fived him. His father turned and looked at me. I

high-fived him, too.

One minute remained in the first half. A loose ball rolled to the corner of the field and Barcelona threatened to score again. A Sevilla player contested the Catalan. Jersey-grabbing ensued, followed by a swift Sevilla elbow. The Barcelona player fell and the referee blew his whistle. He pulled a yellow card from his shirt, which gave the Sevilla player his second yellow card of the game. The crowd cheered as he left the field and left Sevilla with one less player for the duration of the match.

"What a first half," I told Devon.

"Hell yeah, man," he said.

"I can't believe Messi scored," Brad said. "We saw a goal by the best player ever."

"How long's halftime?" Roxanne asked.

"I don't know," Devon said. "Check the scoreboard."

"Good thinking, punk," she said with a laugh. "I'll be back. I'm going to buy some food. Does anybody want anything?"

"No, thanks."

"I'm good."

"Alright, see you guys soon," Roxanne said as she stood and merged into the hungry crowd.

The second half started sooner than expected. Roxanne wasn't back yet. Barcelona started with the ball, but a rare errant pass gave Sevilla possession. Eight minutes passed on the game clock and little excitement occurred. Sevilla controlled the ball near its own goal. A defender lofted the ball to a teammate near the top of the box. He jump and headed the ball back to his own goalie.

A Barcelona attacker appear from outside his field of

vision. The goalie panicked. He ran toward the ball as it dropped from the air. The Barcelona midfielder jumped and curled his left leg inwards and propelled his right leg forwards. His spikes hit the ball and pushed it beyond the airborne goalie who flailed like a falling spider. The crowd shouted wildly at the ninja-like goal by Alves.

Roxanne appeared and carried three bags of popcorn and one bag of peanuts.

"You missed the goal!" I shouted.

"No I didn't," she shouted, "I saw it! I was standing on the platform about to come up the stairs and the crowd started yelling, so I turned around."

"It was awesome!" Devon shouted.

"Yeah, that was one acrobatic goal," she said.

Roxanne handed Marcos a bag of popcorn as she passed. She handed the bag of peanuts to me and another popcorn bag to Brad. She sat next to Devon and they shared the last bag.

"Thanks, Roxy," I said.

"Yeah, thanks a lot," Brad said.

"I knew you guys were hungry," she said

"You know us so well," Devon added.

I took a few handfuls from Brad's popcorn bag. The substance curbed my hunger and eased the effects of the rum. I shared a few peanuts as I passed the bag from left to right. I cracked a shell. I ate two peanuts and dropped the shell to the floor.

I watched a Sevilla midfielder launch the ball across the field. A teammate awaited the pass near the center of the midfield line. Messi sprinted from behind the receiver and startled him. The Sevilla midfielder's first touch sent the ball toward Barcelona's offensive front. Messi and the Sevilla player sprinted toward the ball and collided. The white jersey fell to the ground and Messi stood with possession. He dribbled quickly down the middle of the field toward the goal and five defenders awaited his arrival and anticipated every juke.

Messi didn't juke. He ran past every defender and fired a shot from the top of the 18-yard box. The ball flew by the goalie and hit the back of the net. A familiar *Me-ssi* chant ensued.

"There he goes again!" Brad shouted.

"He's the man!" I shouted.

Roxanne kissed Devon on the lips. I hugged the middle-aged woman next to us and high-fived the father-son duo. I offered the boy some peanuts and he took a handful. The Sevilla defensive line hung their heads.

The game clock read *88:30*. Since a few minutes remained in the one-sided game, we decided to follow the crowd and leave. Our lofted seats created a lengthy decline. I stood in a human traffic jam midway down the staircase. I watched the on-field action.

Messi darted toward the goal and received a well-placed through-ball from a teammate. The defense collapsed and surrounded Messi. He pushed the ball to Villa who stood alone at the top of the 18-yard box. Villa took one dribble to his left to evade an oncoming defender. He fired with his left foot. The ball reflected off of the defender's foot and escaped the goalie's outstretched gloves.

Yet again, the crowd erupted. I jumped and shouted. Marcos propelled himself into the air, using Brad's shoulders as a springboard. He slipped on the cement stairs, but continued to shout in support of the Catalan football club. The boy in front of me turned and we yelled at each other in pure fanaticism. Devon rubbed my head and I retaliated with the same gesture. Barcelona routed Sevilla in a 5-0 victory. The clock struck midnight as the game clock expired.

CHAPTER 12

I looked at my watch. It read *9:30*. I rolled over in my small hostel bed and buried myself in the sheets. My head throbbed and my joints ached from dehydration. I closed my eyes. I didn't feel sick, but I definitely had a hangover from the rum and postgame beers. I checked my watch again. *9:31*. I rolled off of my top bunk. Clumsily, I put a shirt on and looked out the window. The sun was bright.

"Dude. How are you out of bed right now?" Devon asked from the depths of his covers.

"I was asking myself the same thing," I replied.

"What time is it?" he asked.

"Early," I said.

"Gah," Devon said, "I can't sleep. My head hurts."

"Want to hit a café?" I asked.

"Now?" he said.

"Yeah, I guess," I said.

"Sure," Devon said. "Let me pull myself together."

Devon staggered to his backpack and unzipped it. He

grabbed a shirt and basketball shorts and put them on. I found my wallet under my pillow and put it in my pocket. We looked around the room to see if our three roommates were awake, but they slept peacefully, so we left. Devon closed the door slowly behind him. I asked the girl at the front desk if she had any café recommendations. She directed us toward the market that Brad and I visited earlier in the trip.

"What a game last night," I said as Devon and we walked along *Passeig de Gracia*.

"Yeah it was," he said. "Messi is the man."

"We're going to hear about him on some soccer documentary in 50 years and tell our grandkids that we saw the greatest soccer player that ever played," I said.

"You can't put a price on that," Devon said.

We rounded the corner in accordance with the concierge's directions. Devon noticed the café sign above the door and nudged me toward it. We sat outside. Our seats faced the cobblestone road that intersected with the busy *Passeig de Gracia*. A few people occupied three tables around ours. The metropolis seemed vacant aside from a few elderly men who strolled by us from time to time. They seemed to have no destination in mind.

"*Café con leche, por favor*," I told the waiter as he approached our table.

"*El mismo para mi*," Devon said.

He brought two coffees with milk in small ceramic cups. We thanked him. I looked at my coffee and decided to wait before I took my first sip. Devon drank half of his coffee in one gulp.

"What are we going to do today?" I asked Devon.

"We should visit all the tourist sites," he said. "If we move fast, we can get to all the important ones in a few hours."

"Sounds like a plan," I said. "We'll see how our other roommates feel about moving fast this morning."

"I think Roxy will be feeling the rum this morning," he said.

"She drank it like champ, though," I said.

"She does like to have fun," he said.

"How are things with Roxy going, anyways?" I asked.

"We're good, man. We're good," he said. "It's hard to get alone time on a group vacation like this, though. You know?"

"I bet it is," I said, "especially with the three of us in the room."

"Yeah, but it's cool," he said. "We're having fun."

"You say the word and I'll make sure Brad, Marcos, and I take an extended walk around the block or something," I said.

"Well, I just might have to take you up on that," Devon said.

"Let me know," I said.

I took my first sip of coffee. Neither Devon nor I spoke for a while. An old man walked down the middle of the cobblestone street, away from *Passieg de Gracia*. He clasped his hands behind his back. His right hand clutched three fingers from his left hand gently. His posture slouched, but his head remained proud and observant.

"Look at that old guy," Devon said. "He's probably out for his weekly Sunday cruise through the city."

"I bet he's content," I said.

"Yeah," Devon said, "only a guy who's content with his life can walk with that attitude."

"I want to be like that guy when I'm old," I said. "I want my happy, content Sunday cruise."

"I'm going to walk with my hands behind my back like him, too," Devon said. "Or walk with a badass cane."

"And a thick mustache like him," I said.

"That's a necessity," he said, "but only if it's in style when we're old, though."

I finished my coffee. We paid and returned to *Casa Gracia*. Devon thanked the girl at the front desk for her suggestion. I told her the coffee was very good. I opened the door to our room and found Brad leaving the bathroom. Marcos sat upright on his bed with a blank expression that suggested he just woke up. Roxanne mumbled from her bed, but I didn't understand a word.

"Big plans today, team," I said.

"What are we doing?" Brad asked.

"Hitting the town," Devon said. "Let's do the tourist thing today."

"*Sagrada Familia*, *Las Ramblas*, and all of that stuff?" Brad asked.

"Yeah," Devon said. "Good plan?"

"I'm down," Brad said.

"When?" Marcos asked.

"Sooner than later," I said.

"But, like, how soon?" Marcos asked.

"Whenever you're ready, princess," I said.

"Thanks, your highness," Marcos replied.

"How's Roxy doing?" Devon asked.

"I'm good," Roxanne said as she revealed her face from underneath her covers. "I'm just tired."

"At least you're smiling," I said.

Devon looked at me and we made eye contact. He motioned his head toward the door. I looked at him while my brain attempted to decipher the meaning of his non-verbal communication. Then, I understood. I nodded with affirmation.

"Hey dudes," I said loudly, "let's go get food at the market. I'm hungry."

"Me too," Brad said. "Marcos looks like he needs a muffin."

"Or a hug," Devon added.

Brad and I moved toward the door.

"Come on, Marcos," I said. "Let's go."

"I don't want to go anywhere, man," Marcos said.

"I'll buy you an orange juice," I offered.

"Alright, fine," Marcos said. "Let me find my shoes."

Brad, Marcos, and I left our room and walked past the concierge's desk. Marcos waved to her and she returned the acknowledgement. We walked to the market that Brad and I found the day before on *Passeig de Gracia*. I bought Marcos an orange juice and one for myself. Brad bought some bread and cheese. Marcos didn't say a word or make much of an effort to do anything. The rum effect was making his morning very rough. The checkout line was short, so we were back on the street quickly. I slowed our walking pace in an effort to give Devon and Roxanne more time.

We entered the hostel doors and climbed the stairs. I stopped at the front desk and asked the concierge about popular clubs in town. I told her that we wanted to go out tonight and dance at a *discoteca*. She suggested three clubs near the beach. She said that the clubs were popular with both tourists and local people in our age group. After a long conversation between the four of us, Marcos walked down the hall toward our room. Brad and I followed. I reached the door first and knocked forcefully.

"We have keys, man," Marcos said.

He put his key in the door and opened it. Devon sat on the bed with a smile.

"Where's Roxy?" I asked.

"She's in the shower," he said.

"Cool," I said, relieved.

Devon looked at me with an appreciative expression. Devon claimed his place in line for the shower and Marcos secured his spot after Devon. Brad and I exercised in the center of the room while we waited for the line to dwindle. We played a game to encourage our efforts in fitness. I grabbed a deck of cards from my backpack and flipped one over. It was an eight of hearts. Brad and I each did eight push-ups. Brad flipped the next one and it was a two of diamonds, so we did two push-ups. We continued this game until we flipped all 52 cards. Coincidentally, Marcos finished his shower as Brad flipped the last card.

After the five of us were ready for the day, we walked outside and strolled to the subway station near our hostel. We hopped over the turnstiles and found the train that led us to the old section of downtown Barcelona. The short train ride gave me enough time to forget my headache and build excitement for the unknown adventure that awaited me. The doors opened and I burst out of the train.

We strolled down six hundred-year-old cobblestone streets and in between sturdy medieval apartments. Brad found a small ice cream shop and bought chocolate gelato. The four of us admired his necessary gluttony and bought some for ourselves. After wandering through alleys and former major thoroughfares, we entered a large plaza. The

Barcelona cathedral stood at the plaza's main focal point.

"Let's check it out," Roxanne said.

"Do you think they will let us in with ice cream?" Marcos asked.

"You haven't eaten yours yet?" Roxanne said.

"No. It's too cold," Marcos replied.

"Don't be a baby," Roxanne said. "It's delicious."

We strolled across the vacant plaza and walked up the short staircase. We stood at the front entrance to the cathedral. I looked through the towering open doors and that the inside of the cathedral was dimly lit. My eyes needed time to adjust to the thick darkness. I saw a few candles flicker from somewhere deep within the medieval place of worship. Brad entered first. I followed and walked by his right side. My eyes adjusted quickly.

"Dude, we just walked into Sunday morning mass," I whispered to Brad.

"We couldn't have planned this any better," he whispered back to me.

Thousands of people filled the rows of pews in front of us. They faced the bishop of Barcelona who stood behind the altar. He spoke in rapid Spanish. The five of us walked quietly toward the back pew. I wanted to sit and listen to an authentic Spanish Catholic mass.

Halfway to the bench, the bishop ended mass and the crowd dispersed. A line of churchgoers walked between our group and Brad and I were separated from Marcos, Roxanne, and Devon. The line thickened and I lost sight of those three as they merged with the growing crowd.

I turned around toward Brad, but another line shuffled me to the right. I had no choice but to move with the crowd. The line behind me grew and pushed more forcefully. I saw Brad move in the opposite direction of me as he merged with another crowd wave. My line moved down the center isle toward the altar. I reached the front row of pews and another line swept me to the right.

I turned to look for my friends, but I couldn't distinguish any familiar face in the swarm of Spaniards that flocked toward the cathedrals' multiple exits. After five minutes of shuffling along with the crowd, I found an exit located in a sidewall of the side of the church. I followed the line out the door and merged with another line that seemed to be at a standstill. I swiveled my head in desperate attempts to find my friends, but I realized that they likely exited through opposing ends of the cathedral.

As I looked around in my stationary line, I found myself in a Muslim-influenced courtyard surrounded by high stone walls. Surrounded by a black metal gate in the center of the courtyard was an oasis. Geese shaded themselves underneath low palm trees. Active birds jumped near small pools. I took my camera from my pocket and took a picture. My line moved gradually through the stiff crowd. The oasis seduced my attention. The line shifted forward. I turned to see where I was going and flung my head back in surprise.

The bishop of Barcelona stood in front of me. He wore ornate green robes that signified Ordinary Time on the church calendar. His tall bishop's hat matched the ornamentation of his robes. The man in front of me kissed the ceremonial bishop's ring on the bishop's outstretched hand. Though the clergyman was shorter than me, his demeanor commanded respect. He looked at me with a warm expression. He extended his hand. His ring faced skyward. I shook his hand.

"Nice to meet you," he said to me in Spanish. "Thank you for your attendance this morning."

"Nice to meet you, too," I said. "And thank you for your attendance."

He slowed his handshake and raised one eyebrow as he pondered my response.

"Where are you from?" he asked.

"*Los estados unidos*," I replied.

"I could tell by your accent," he said.

"It was that obvious?" I asked.

He smiled.

"Welcome to Barcelona," the bishop said. "Enjoy this beautiful city."

"Thank you, sir," I said. "I will."

The woman behind me nudged against me. She wanted her turn to meet the bishop. He held his hand out and she kissed his ring.

I weaved through the remaining crowd. I found a small doorway without a door in the stone wall that surrounded the courtyard. I went through it and found myself in a narrow cobblestone street. Tall stone apartments rose above me. I followed the outer wall of the cathedral and rounded the corner. The crowd of churchgoers hadn't moved too far. It seemed like most of them went from the pews to the plaza. I pushed my way through the crowd and climbed the staircase that led to the front doors of the cathedral. I stood on a short wall and scanned the crowd for my friends.

"Jason!" shouted a female voice behind me.

I turned and saw Roxanne waving her hands wildly. I walked toward her and saw Brad, Marcos, and Devon sitting on the top step of the cathedral's main staircase.

"Where have you been, man?" Devon asked.

"We thought we lost you," Marcos said. "You were gone for, like, 15 minutes."

"I was just blending in with the crowd," I said.

We sat on the steps and watched as the crowd formed a wide circle in the center of the plaza. Dancers linked hands and preformed a traditional Barcelona dance while a band played behind them.

We walked back to the subway station and took the train to *Sagrada Familia*, the iconic cathedral built by Gaudi, Barcelona's heroic architect. The unfinished cathedral looked like a melting sandcastle. We cruised to the base of a long hill. Devon led us to an outdoor escalator. We rode the escalator to the top, which took about five minutes. Another escalator awaited us, then, another, then another. We reached the base of *Parque Guell*, a park designed by Gaudi in 1900. We walked by statues, houses, and walls designed with Gaudi's trademark absence of 90-degree angles.

We climbed the narrow stairway to the park's peak. We sat on the cliff's edge and overlooked Barcelona. The park provided a panoramic view. I could see the entire city sprawling in front of me. The beach spanned the horizon from North to South. Towering hotels and ramshackle houses lined the miniature streets that intersected far below me. I captured the view with memory in an endless instant.

The decline on the series of escalators provided ample time for us to determine our next move. We decided to take the train to *Las Ramblas*, the wide artery that links West Barcelona to the Eastern ports. We arrived at the subway stop and emerged from the tunnel. Precise palm trees lined the street. Cars drove on either side of the wide center walkway. A man painted entirely in silver stood motionless. A little girl threw a coin into the box in front him and the silver man jerked his body around like a robot and stopped instantly, frozen again. A fat man in a Mickey Mouse costume stood on the opposite side of the walkway from the silver robot man. He waved and anticipated tips in his box.

I strolled next to Devon and Brad. We stopped at a kiosk that sold pet rabbits and turtles. I almost bought one, but Roxanne brought me back to reality when she asked me how I was going to walk onto a plane on Tuesday morning with a rabbit. Devon, Roxanne, and Marcos cruised across the walkway and browsed through artistic pictures of Barcelona. Brad and I decided to ask the kiosk owner about the cost of the rabbit. Every impractical thought escaped us.

"Brad!" shouted a female voice behind us.

We turned and saw two girls move briskly toward us from the other side of the walkway.

"Angie!" Brad shouted. "How are you?"

Brad gave her a hug.

"Angela, this is my friend, Jason," he said.

I shook her hand.

"Angie goes to U of O, too," Brad said. "She's my friend who's studying abroad here in Barcelona."

"Yeah," Angela said, "I'm sorry you guys couldn't stay with me this weekend. I have a few friends from U of O staying with me until Tuesday. It's a group of girls who are studying abroad in Sevilla. They decided to visit me this weekend since Monday is a holiday."

"Hey, no worries," Brad said. "We're living large at *Casa Gracia.*"

"Oh, this is my friend, Grace," Angela said.

"Hi," Grace said, "I'm one of the friends from Sevilla."

Angela and Grace were both very pretty girls. Angela was taller with brown hair and a naturally athletic figure. She had round facial features that accentuated her dimples. Her yoga pants displayed her musculature. Grace was shorter than Angela. She had a cute face with a little nose and light, cropped hair. Her wide eyes thinned when she smiled. Angela's figure was well-endowed, but Grace's petite frame supported an equally appealing physique.

"What are you guys doing tonight?" Angela asked.

"I want to go to a *discoteca* and groove," I said.

"That's the plan," Brad added.

"We're going to some clubs by the beach," Angela said. "We're drinking at my apartment before we go out. You guys should come over and drink with us and we can all go out together."

"Let's do it," Brad said. "Where's your place?"

"It's only about ten blocks from *Casa Gracia*," Angela said.

She wrote her address on a piece of paper and gave it to Brad.

"We won't leave until one in the morning," Angela said. "Clubs around here open at two or three. Come over at eleven"

"We'll be there," Brad said.

"Wait," Angela said, "I'll write my home phone number on that piece of paper in case you get lost."

Brad gave her the paper. She wrote her phone number on it and gave it back to Brad. He put it safely in his pocket.

"Alright, we need to find our friends," Angela said, "but we'll see you tonight."

"Nice to meet you girls," I said.

"Nice to meet you, too," Grace said.

Angela and Grace turned and walked down the middle of the walkway. An elevated statue of Christopher Columbus stood behind them. His finger pointed toward the Mediterranean Sea. Brad and I walked the opposite direction toward our three compatriots. We bumped knuckles silently.

CHAPTER 13

I turned off the shower and dried myself with the towel I bought near the beach. Some sand was still imbedded in the fibers. It scraped my face, so I shook the towel and tried again. I wrapped the towel around my waist and left the bathroom. Devon's computer rested on the windowsill and old school rap song thumped through his laptop speakers. The room lights were bright against the dark windowpane and we could see our reflections as we got ready for the night. I put my clothes on, buttoned my shirt, and used the reflection in the window to fix my collar.

"I'm so glad we have tomorrow off," Devon said.

"Me too," Brad said. "You have to love a Monday holiday."

"Like school on Monday has ever stopped us from drinking on a Sunday night," Marcos added.

Marcos combed his hair and shifted his head side-to-side while he checked his reflection.

"Where are we going?" Roxanne asked.

"We're going to Angela's apartment," I said. "It's only a few blocks from here, I think."

"Is she having a huge apartment party?" Roxanne asked.

"No," Brad said. "There will be a few girls there, but we're just having a few drinks before we go to the *discotecas*."

"At least I'll have some female company for once," Roxanne said.

"Come on, Roxy," I said. "You know you love hanging out with us dudes."

"Of course I do," she said.

Roxanne stood in the center of the room and checked her reflection. She hadn't decided on a shirt to wear, so she stood in her jeans and bra while she brushed her hair. She was attractive, but we all knew she was Devon's.

"Damn," Brad said, "it's still early."

"Yeah it is," I said. "We're not supposed to be there for another two hours."

"What should we do until then?" Marcos asked.

"Let's buy some beer and drink on the patio by the lobby," I suggested.

"I'm down," Devon said.

Devon and Roxanne went to the market and returned with a twelve-pack of Estrella Damm. We passed the front desk on our way to the patio. The middle-aged concierge looked bored as he sat behind the desk.

"Slow night?" Devon asked the concierge in Spanish.

"Very slow," he said. "Do you have big plans for tonight?"

"We're going to drink this box of beer on the patio and see where it takes us," Marcos said.

"Come join us," I said.

"Thank you for the offer," the concierge said, "but I have

to watch the lobby."

"Come on," Marcos said. "You can see the lobby from the patio."

"Let's sit in the lobby," the concierge said.

"If you drink with us, we'll sit in the lobby," I said.

The lobby was open with an eclectic collection of tables, chairs, and cupboards. Well-used card decks and unread magazines were scattered throughout the room. A massive portrait of an unknown aristocratic family stared at us from on wall, while small photos of past tenants littered the opposing edifice. The lobby red carpet created a pathway to an open glass door that led to a small deck overlooking *Passieg de Gracia*.

He stood up and walked with us toward a round table surrounded by eight chairs. Roxanne put the box of beer in the center and passed one can to each of us, including the concierge. The concierge's name was Israel. That's what his friends called him, at least. His real name was long with a complicated Israeli pronunciation, so he went by his country of origin. He told us that he spoke five languages: Arabic, Spanish, English, Russian, and French. He learned Spanish in four months after he moved to Barcelona. Israel had lived in a few countries along the Mediterranean Sea and had traveled to dozens. He was born in Tel Aviv and said it was the greatest city in the world. He explained the roots of the eternal conflict in the Middle East, but said he still didn't understand why people fight each other.

Israel finished his beer. I passed him another one from the box. He thanked us and opened the can. He encouraged us to learn as many languages as we could because he believed that language was the key to understanding the way the world works. I babbled about my desire to continue my travels after my academic tenure in Oviedo ended. No person entered the lobby.

"Damn," Marcos said as he reached into the beer box and discovered it was empty.

"Nice work team," I said.

"Where are you going now that your beer box is empty?" Israel asked.

"We're going to a girl's apartment to have another drink," Roxanne said.

"Then we're going to some clubs by the beach," I said.

"What clubs?" Israel asked.

"Opium and Razzmatazz," Brad said.

"Razzmatazz?" Israel said. "Tonight, that club has a 20 Euro cover charge just to get through the door."

"Yikes," Devon said, "maybe we're not going there anymore."

"It's the best *discoteca* in Barcelona," Israel said.

"It better be the best for 20 Euros," Devon said.

"Wait here for one minute," Israel said.

Israel stood and walked to the front desk. He sat and picked up the phone and dialed a phone number. He spoke quietly for a moment, hung up the phone, and returned to the round table.

"When you go to Razzmatazz," Israel said, "ask for Pedro. Tell Pedro that Israel sent you."

"Who's Pedro?" Brad asked.

"A friend," Israel said.

"Why should we ask for Pedro?" Brad asked.

"Consider it my repayment for the Estrella Damm," Israel said. "Now, go get your girls and have fun tonight."

We said goodbye to Israel and left *Casa Gracia*. We stopped at the market to buy more beer for the small apartment gathering. The market closed in five minutes, so we hustled. Brad and I bought six bottles and put them in a box. Each bottle contained one liter of San Miguel *cerveza*. We passed a Gaudi-designed building and turned right. Brad handed the box to me because his arms were exhausted.

We found Angela's apartment building and she buzzed us in. She lived on the seventh floor. My arms grew tired, so I handed the box to Brad as we reached the fourth floor. We were sweating by the time we reached the seventh floor. Roxanne knocked on room 702 and Angela opened it.

"Come in, guys!" Angela said.

I walked through the door and looked into the living room. Twelve girls stared back at me. Each girl was gorgeous and dressed in fine club attire. High heels. Short, tight dresses. Time-invested hair-dos. The girls looked seductive, yet classy. The girls had a regal appeal.

"So much for a small pre-game *fiesta*," I whispered to Brad.

"Damn," he said, "they're drinking fine wine and we brought 40s. Damn."

"And we're all sweaty," I whispered.

"We really are, aren't we," Brad said.

Devon overheard us and laughed.

"Shut up, dude," I said. "Drink your San Miguel."

Brad set the box of San Miguel in the kitchen and we grabbed our individual liters. I looked through the doorway into the well-lit living room. Girls crowded around the dinner table and a few sat on the couch. I lifted my chin and puffed my chest in an attempt to make myself feel confident. My hand shook from nervousness. I clutched my San Miguel bottle tightly and walked through the doorway into the living room.

I saw Angela talking with three girls. She held her glass of red wine loosely, as if she was comfortable with the action. She dominated the conversation and had the three girls laughing. I approached the group as they stood by the dinner table.

"Hey, Angela," I said. "Nice apartment."

"Thanks, Jason," she said. "Jason, these are my some of my friends who are visiting from Sevilla. They go to Oregon also."

She introduced the three girls, but their names escaped my memory as soon as they entered. They were pretty girls, but seemed to lack Angela's confidence. Natural familiarity with her environment gave Angela an aura of assuredness. I talked with the girls about superficial subjects and inquired about mutual connections. We shared similar Spanish travel stories. Angela remained quiet and stood poised with her wine glass. She appeared content with her introduction and simply observed our interactions. Grace left her conversation with two girls near the couch and approached me.

"Jason, I'm glad you made it!" Grace shouted.

"It took a while to find the place," I said, "but we got here."

"What are you drinking?" she asked.

"Beer," I said. I showed her the liter bottle of San Miguel.

"Perfect," Grace said. "The girls want to play a drinking game on the coffee table. Come play with us."

I followed her and we sat on the couch. Two girls sat on chairs on the other side of the coffee table. Their seductive class inhibited my usual flowing chatter. For some reason, I felt nervous and uncomfortable. I shouted to Devon and approached the coffee table. He took a casual sip of his San Miguel.

"Sit down and play a drinking game with us," I suggested.

"Alright," Devon said. "What are we playing?"

"I don't know," Grace said. "Do you know any fun drinking games?"

I suggested a few involving cards. The girls were unfamiliar with the games I offered, so Devon and I explained the rules to a game called "Ride the Bus" that we played at *El Serpiente* occasionally. Devon spread the necessary cards on the table and we all drank soon enough. We abandoned the game after the conversation grew more exciting and my San Miguel bottle emptied. The shrinking bottle contents enhanced my social courage. I talked with another group of girls that I recognized from school. They said they knew me, but didn't say anything when I walked into the apartment because they were afraid I didn't know them. This may have been true, but it made for good drunken conversation either way.

Angela entered the living room from the kitchen. She carried a full bottle of tequila and announced that cabs would arrive soon. She poured shots for everyone and dispersed them across the table. She led a toast and the entire group drank.

"Where are the cabs taking us?" I asked Grace.

"To Javier's house," she said.

"Who's Javier?" I asked.

"Some Spanish guy that Angela knows," Grace said. "He lives near the beach clubs, I guess."

"I hope he's cool with having some random guys like us

show up," I said.

"With this many girls, he won't even notice," Grace said. She winked.

"Good point," I said. "It is an attractive group of girls."

She smiled. After that comment escaped, I knew the San Miguel was working. I took a long drink and finished the bottle. I found Brad and his bottle was empty. Devon and Marcos had some work to do, but Roxanne's liter was gone. Brad opened the last liter bottle and we passed it between the three of us until it was gone. The cabs arrived and I hopped in one with Brad, Marcos, and Grace.

The cab took us through an elaborate part of town. High-rise apartments intertwined with Gaudi buildings and fine dining establishments. The driver stopped and we waited on the sidewalk until Angela's cab arrived. She led us to the apartment building front door and Javier unlocked it from his apartment. We climbed to the top of the building. Angela knocked on the door of 1813 and a short Spaniard with perfectly sculpted hair opened the door and he let 17 drunken Americans into his home.

Javier's apartment was more of a penthouse suite than a modest personal living space. Gold ornamentation lined the high ceiling. Deep red walls and portraits expressed luxury. Elongated mirrors with elaborate frames enhanced the richness of the living room and kitchen. This was his parents' apartment and Javier's father was a prominent Barcelona banker. Javier's parents were in France on vacation this weekend. *Lucky us*, I thought.

Javier introduced himself to everyone and his two male friends sat on the couch wide-eyed at the mass of beauty that walked through the door. The girls sat on couches and moved chairs to form a social circle around a glass coffee table. Javier opened the sliding glass door. I walked onto the deck and marveled at his view of the Barcelona cityscape and the major street below us. Devon, Marcos, and I talked with Javier on the deck. A few stars managed to overpower Barcelona's heavy light pollution. A cloud sliver moved in the breeze and revealed a bright three-quarter moon.

"Thanks for letting us drink at your house," I said to Javier in Spanish.

"You're welcome," he said.

"Sorry for showing up unannounced," Devon said.

"No problem," Javier said. "You brought the girls."

"Yes we did," Marcos said.

"How do you know Angela?" Devon asked.

"I studied abroad in the United States when I was fifteen," Javier said. "I stayed with her family."

"Cool."

Javier looked diminutive standing next to Devon.

"Do you guys smoke?" Javier asked.

"Smoke what?" Devon replied.

"Tobacco. Cigars," Javier said.

"Yeah, sometimes," I said.

"I enjoy a good cigar," Devon said.

"I smoke cigarettes every once in a while," Marcos added.

"Do you want to smoke some cigars out here?" Javier asked.

"Sure," I said, "but we didn't bring any with us."

"My dad has a large collection," Javier said. "I'll bring some for you."

Javier walked inside, through the living room, and into an adjoining office. He returned carrying four cigars, a cutter, and a butane lighter. He cut a stubby cigar and handed it to Marcos. He cut a medium-length cigar and gave it to me. Devon took a light Churchill, and Javier saved the cigar with the most ornate label for himself. He lit his cigar and coughed from smoke inhalation. I lit mine and puffed six times. A passed the lighter to Devon. Only half of my cigar tip lit, so Devon lit the rest while I puffed twice more. Devon and Marcos lit their cigars with precision. Javier closed the sliding glass door to keep the smoke outside.

"Do your two buddies want to join us?" Marcos asked.

"I doubt it," Javier said. "They haven't moved since the girls sat down."

We looked at the wide-eyed Spaniards inside and laughed.

"So," Javier began, "how do you like my city?"

"It's awesome," Devon said. "We did all the tourist stuff today. We went to the Barcelona game last night."

"I did, too" Javier said. "Where did you sit?"

"The top row," Devon said. He raised his hand above his head to add to the effect.

"I sit in the first level near midfield," Javier said.

"Ouch," Marcos said. "How much did that cost you?"

"I don't know," Javier said. "My family has had season tickets since I can remember."

I peered over the edge of the balcony. Cars sped along the street and consistently honked. The height made me shiver, so I stepped back.

"That must be nice," I said.

"It's alright," Javier said. "Sometimes the games bore us, so we don't go."

"What!" Devon and I shouted in unison.

"How can you get bored watching the best soccer team in

the world?" Marcos asked.

"It becomes routine around midseason," Javier said.

"Routine?" Marcos exclaimed. "Routine?"

"*Hermano*, Messi is the best player in the world and you get to see him play every week," I said. "How can that be routine?"

"My parents fly us around Europe all the time on our private jet to see good *fútbol*," Javier said.

He dragged his cigar.

"We flew to the World Cup last summer and saw the final match between Spain and Netherlands," Javier continued.

"Is your dad the king of Spain or what?" Devon asked.

"No, but he owns the most prominent bank in the Iberian Peninsula," Javier said. "What do your parents do for work?"

"Both of my parents are teachers," I said.

"My dad's a mechanic and my mom's a nurse," Devon said.

Marcos started to say something, but the sliding glass door opened. Grace and Roxanne walked onto the deck.

"Hey guys," Roxanne said.

"We wanted to come out here and see what you boys were doing," Grace said.

"We're just jaw-boning and smoking stogies," Devon said.

"Can we join you?" Roxanne asked.

"I suppose," I said.

"Can a try your cigar?" Grace asked me.

"Absolutely," I said.

I gave my cigar to her. She wrapped her pointer finger around the tobacco stick and secured it with her thumb and took two dainty puffs.

"You're a cigar fan, eh?" I asked.

"A little," Grace said. "I've smoked a few with my dad before and I like them."

"That's cool," Devon said.

"How's it going in there, Roxy?" Marcos asked.

"We're having a great time in there," Roxanne said. "You boys are missing out."

"We still have a few hours until the *discotecas* become fun," Javier said.

We listened to Javier tell wild stories about his lavish lifestyle as we finished our cigars. I pressed the end of mine against the railing until it stopped glowing. I tossed it off the balcony and watched it fall 18 stories to the sidewalk. Marcos dropped his on the deck floor and snuffed it with his left foot. Javier looked at him with restrained alarm. Javier kept silent, probably to avoid an inevitable argument with short-fused Marcos. I walked inside. Ten girls sat around the coffee table. High-pitched chatter filled the room. Javier's two male counterparts looked more comfortable on the couch, but remained silent and observed the ricochet of conversation. I felt more confident as I compared my comfort level with theirs.

I sat in an open chair next to a recognizable girl from Oregon and entered the conversation. Her low-cut dress drew my eyes away from hers. My hands shook from the building tobacco buzz and I felt beads of sweat form on my scalp. I felt my heart beat quicken. I stood and opened the sliding glass door and closed it behind me and moved to the left to avoid the girls' view.

I placed my hands on my head and breathed deeply through my nose. I looked over the railing and thought about vomiting, but the immediate sense of vertigo brought me back to reality, somehow. The tobacco buzz left as quickly as it arrived. I entered the living room with less confidence than my entrance moments ago. I sat in the same open chair and prepared my excuse for stepping outside, but the girl never questioned my departure.

Angela moved to the portable sound system and selected a popular American hip-hop song and increased the volume. Javier moved toward her and motioned frantically for her to lower the volume. Every girl stood and started dancing. The seductiveness of their attire influenced their dance moves and Javier forgot about his panic. Devon danced in front of Roxanne and she wrapped her arms around him. He danced well.

Brad and I stood in the middle of the wheel of girls. I put my arms in the air and grooved. The San Miguel aided my rhythm. Grace and a tall red-head danced in front of me. I smiled at Grace. She looked at me and turned. She returned the glance seconds later.

The Spaniards stood uncomfortably. The taller of the men started dancing first. Timidly, he moved one foot forward and the other back, then reversed the motion, followed by a slight hip movement. He gained confidence quickly and emboldened his steps. By the time the chorus hit, he was grooving fluidly. Grace swayed his direction. He grabbed her hand and he led her in a samba. The other Spaniard followed suite and reached for the nearest girl paw he could find. It worked well for him. Javier danced with Angela near the sound system and I was left with the red-head. She was pretty, but Grace had an extra spark that attracted me. Seeing her dance with the Spaniard brewed jealousy. I suppressed it, but it simmered.

The song ended and the volume lowered. Everyone sat and beer bottles appeared in every hand. Shots appeared in front of each person. We drank. We laughed. In what seemed like five minutes later, we stumbled out of the apartment and walked down the 18 flights of stairs to the sidewalk. The shorter Spaniard weaved to a motorcycle and pulled a set of keys from his pocket. He asked if any *chicas* wanted a ride to the *discoteca* and no volunteer stepped forward. He straddled the motorcycle seat and put the keys in the ignition. Brad ran to him and persuaded him to walk with us instead, and the Spaniard obliged.

Somewhere along the walk, Marcos and I found ourselves alone with Angela, Grace, and three other girls. We found a *discoteca* called Opium and stood in line. The line was long. I grew impatient. The velvet rope held the line in place and the bouncer only let a few people in as an equal number left the club. Finally, we reached the front of the line. It was almost our turn to enter the massive dance hall. The bouncer lifted the velvet rope. The three girls in our group passed through. Angela followed.

"Ladies first," I said to Grace. I nudged her gently forward.

Marcos stood behind me as I prepared to pass through the opening. The bouncer let Grace through and dropped the velvet rope in front of me, dividing me from Grace. I didn't notice, or didn't care, and I stepped over the low velvet rope.

The bouncer stood swiftly and punched me hard in the nose. I flew to the ground. The bouncer pounced and wrestled on top of me while the other bouncer kicked me twice in the ribs. Marcos hit the kicking bouncer in the ear, but the massive Serbian bouncer's elbow dropped Marcos to the ground. He received two kicks to the ribs. The girls in our group didn't notice and continued to walk into the club.

The bouncers laughed and returned to their posts. Marcos and I remained still on the cobblestone for a minute. I was flat on my back. Not a single thought ran through my brain. I collected myself and realized what had happened. A couple waiting in line helped me to my feet and another helped Marcos stand.

"Go to hell!" Marcos shouted to the nonchalant bouncers.

"I bet you feel real cool hitting some drunk guys with a rabbit-punch," I yelled. "Stupid cowards!"

"Come over here and fight us for real, tough guy!" Marcos shouted.

He pounded his chest twice.

One bouncer looked at us and said something in a language I didn't recognize. He turned and continued his casual conversation with the other rope guard.

"Club Opium? What kind of name is that?" I yelled toward the entrance line. "Let's get out of here, Marcos."

Marcos and I walked silently toward the beach. I was fuming. My left cheek twitched and my clenched fists vibrated as pure anger pulsated through my body. Marcos walked bowlegged with determination. We didn't know where we were going, but we knew we needed to go. We walked on the sand near the boardwalk, sat on a low cement wall, and looked at the ocean.

We verbally belittled the bouncers to make ourselves feel better. I thanked Marcos for his support in the brawl. An Indian man with a backpack approached us and asked us if we wanted to buy beer from him for one Euro per can. We bought six. I opened mine and we dedicated our first drink to the bouncers.

I looked around and saw a line forming by a building on the other side of the boardwalk. It was extending quickly.

"Dude, I think that's Razzmatazz," Marcos said.

"No way," I said. "That building is way too small to be the best club in Barcelona."

"Maybe you're right," he said.

We finished our beers and each opened another.

"*Hombres*," Brad shouted from the end of the line by the small building.

He ran to us and sat on the wall. We told him about the brawl with the bouncers and Marcos handed him a beer.

"Let's drink these while we wait in line at Razzmatazz," Brad said.

"Where is it?" I asked.

"Right there," he said and pointed to the small building with the line.

"Told you," Marcos said.

"Devon and Roxy are saving our spots in line," Brad said. "Some of the Sevilla girls are with us. I don't know where the Spanish dudes are. Where are Grace and Angela?"

"They went into Opium," I said.

"Well that's unfortunate," Brad said.

I put the last beer in my pocket and handed it to Devon when we found him in line. He opened it and drank it discretely. Brad told Devon, Roxanne, and the Sevilla girls about the brawl and embellished a few details that made Marcos and I appear more tough and noble. I didn't mind.

The line moved quickly. When we reached the front of the line, Roxanne asked the bouncer for Pedro. He said something into his radio and told us to wait behind the velvet rope. Marcos and I looked at each other and laughed. *Velvet ropes.* A short, tan old man with slick grey hair opened the door and walked outside.

"*Soy Pedro,*" the man said. "Who wants to see me?"

"We're Israel's friends," Roxanne said.

"Israel?" Pedro said.

"Yes, sir. He told us to ask for you when we got here," Roxanne said.

"Well," the old man said, "a friend of Israel is a friend of mine."

He motioned for us to follow. The bouncer lifted the velvet rope and we followed Pedro into Razzmatazz. A blue light illuminated the entryway, which consisted of a closet and a staircase. Pedro thanked us for coming and commanded us to have fun. He gave us each a ticket for a free drink and I was excited, not because I needed another one, but because it was free.

We climbed the staircase, which widened as it rose. The music grew louder with each step. I used the railing to aid my climb and I felt the vibration from the bass on my hand. The staircase twisted three times and stopped. I saw a wide double-door in front of me. I couldn't see what was behind them because its windows were tinted. Two men dressed in black suits and Secret Service earpieces opened each door simultaneously.

Red laser lights danced across the room and mingled with green and blue pulsing light beams. Smoke machines thickened the air. Disco balls spun on the ceiling. Girls in bikinis danced on poles near the DJ booth. Towering speakers hung from the ceiling and vibrated every nerve in my body. A mass of people danced in the center of the warehouse-sized room. Hands waved and hips shook from side to side. I shouted to Devon, but the heavy bass wafted through the room and stole my words.

We walked to the bar and used our free drink tickets. I ordered a whiskey-and-cola. Devon and I leaned against the bar and watched the mob dance wildly to the bass-infused music.

"Where did you guys go after we left Javier's apartment?" I shouted to Devon.

"We got lost," he shouted. "Some girl we were with told us she knew where to go. Obviously, she didn't. We ended up walking in a circle and we strolled by Javier's apartment again. Roxanne took the lead from there and then we saw you."

"You missed a great brawl," I said.

"Sounds like it," he said. "You alright?"

"Yeah," I said, "I'm fine. My ribs hurt a little, but enough whiskey should cure that. I'll worry about it tomorrow."

"Marcos said you were pretty mad," Devon said. "I've never seen you mad before. What were you doing?"

"I was just yelling at the bouncers after the fight," I said. "I was pissed off. So was Marcos."

"You cooled off pretty quick," he said.

"I guess," I said. "I kind of forgot about it once I saw you guys."

"Well, let's have some fun and forget about it some more," Devon said.

He motioned to the bartender and ordered another round for the two of us. Grace and Angela appeared at the bar and saw Devon and I. They walked to us.

"That Opium *discoteca* wasn't very fun," Grace said to me.

"When did you leave?" Angela asked.

Devon looked at me with a smirk.

"I didn't go into Opium," I said. "I didn't like the crowd."

"Neither did I," Grace said. "There were a lot of creepy guys in there."

"That's what I was thinking," I said.

Devon turned away to contain his brewing laughter about the girls' obliviousness. Roxanne shuffled through the bar crowd and grabbed Devon and I by the arms.

"Let's go dance, guys!" she shouted.

"Let's do it," I affirmed.

Grace followed, but Angela stayed at the bar. I saw Angela touch Brad on the shoulder as I turned to grab Graces hand and lead her through the crowd. I carried my second whiskey-and-cola in my other hand. We stopped somewhere in the middle of the dance floor. I held Grace's hand as we grooved to the fast-paced, bass-heavy thump. Roxanne and Devon danced next to us. Grace danced as if nothing else in the world existed except the rhythm. The DJ played different songs, but they blended together as I entered Grace's world. We danced. I sweated from the heat. I waved my hands in the air. I spun Grace in circles. She danced around me. She moved seductively. We faced each other and I kissed her. She pushed me away, then pulled me toward her and she kissed me. We danced intensely.

Devon punched me on the shoulder.

"Jason, we're all leaving," he shouted.

"Why?" I yelled.

"It's 5:30 in the morning. The club closes soon," he shouted.

We walked to the double-door entrance and walked down the staircase. Devon, Roxanne, Grace, and I waited for the rest of our large group to emerge.

"We should go swimming," Grace suggested.

"When?" I asked.

"Right now," she said. "Let's run into the Mediterranean as the sun rises."

Devon's eyes widened at the abruptness of her comment, or the thought of actually having to follow through with her suggestion. Brad and Marcos walked down the stairs with the rest of the girls.

"We're going swimming," Devon said.

"When?" Brad asked.

"Right now," Roxanne said.

"Alright," Brad said.

"I'm not," Marcos said. "I'll watch your clothes or something."

The entire group left the club. I thought Javier and his friends were still in Razzmatazz, but the more I thought about it, the less confident I was that they even went to Razzmatazz. We walked on the boardwalk and stopped when we reached the sand. The beach was empty and dark. I heard the tide, but I couldn't see the Sea from the boardwalk. I took my shoes off and continued toward the resounding waves. All 17 of us stood on the sand and looked at the water, which became more apparent as our eyes adjusted to the moonlight. I sensed tension between the group members. No one wanted to be the first person to take their clothes off and run into the Mediterranean. I looked at Brad. Brad looked at Devon, Devon looked at me.

With an unspoken agreement, the three of us took our shirts off, then our pants, and stood in our boxers. The girls giggled. Grace undressed and so did Roxanne. Angela followed their actions, which inspired three more girls to undress. We placed our clothes at the feet of the landlocked group-mates and sprinted into the water.

I dove over an oncoming wave and glided through the warm night Sea. I lifted my head above water and saw Grace's half-clothed body rolling inside the tumultuous wave. She wasn't a graceful diver. She stood and flopped into the Sea. We swam freely. Our friends shouted onshore, but there words were nondescript as they cut through the sea breeze. We were silent in the water.

Brad emerged onto the beach first. He walked to our group as they whistled and shouted at him and his half-nakedness. Grace emerged next; I followed shortly after that. The moonlight illuminated the entire crew of swimmers. I put my clothes on even though I was dripping.

Brad looked for his pants, but he couldn't find them. He assumed a girl moved his clothes when he found his pants a few paces away from the group, but no one admitted to moving his pants. Brad put his pants on and shouted. His shout carried an angry tone.

"Where's my wallet?" he said as he felt his pockets.

"I don't know," the red-head girl said.

"Your pants were right behind us the whole time," another girl said. "No one moved them."

"Everyone look on the sand," Brad commanded.

A 17-person search party commenced. After a few minutes, Brad declared his wallet stolen.

"Someone must have snatched my pants when we were watching you guys swim," one girl said.

"Jason, let's go get my wallet," he asserted.

We strode along the beach and saw two dark men standing

inconspicuously against the low wall.

"I know you stole my wallet," Brad said to the African men.

"We didn't steal anything," the shorter African said.

"You're the only other people on this beach. I know you stole it," Brad said intently.

"You should leave," the taller African said.

"Give me my wallet and I will," Brad said.

Three well-dressed Africans emerged from the darkness of the beach and walked toward us briskly. His face expressed determination and experience in these matters.

"These are my employees," said the well-dressed man in the middle of the three new arrivals. "Your wallet is ours now."

He pulled a knife from his pocket and flipped it between his fingers with casual precision. Brad and I looked at each other and backed up slowly. We knew that, whether they stole Brad's wallet or not, our lives were more important.

"Goodbye, gentlemen," said the man with the knife.

We turned and walked quickly toward the group.

"Did you find your wallet?" Roxanne asked.

"Nope," Brad said. "Let's go. Now."

"We can keep looking for your wallet if you want," Angela suggested. "Maybe it's buried beneath the sand somewhere. Want to look with me?

"He wants to buy a new wallet," I said.

Our group stood on the beach in hesitant confusion. Brad and I put our shoes on quickly and moved onto the boardwalk. The group followed us from a distance because Brad and I moved with intent. We stood on the street and waved at a passing taxi. It stopped.

We waited for Marcos, Devon, and Roxanne. I squeezed into the back seat with them and Brad sat in front. The girls stood on the corner in confusion as another cab stopped for them. I looked through the rear window and saw Grace. She watched our taxi leave. I hoped she was thinking about me.

CHAPTER 14

I woke up around four in the afternoon after a long post-class nap on Tuesday. It was comforting to be back in my own bed in Oviedo. Earlier that day, my grammar and vocabulary classes seemed never-ending. As soon as the bell rang, I hustled home and my head melted into my own pillow while my brain and body recovered from our romp in Barcelona. I slept longer than I wanted to, but not as long as I needed to.

I walked into the kitchen and opened the window. Steady, homogenized cloud cover made Oviedo overcast and brisk, but our apartment was stuffy from our weekend absence and I wanted to let some air in. I flipped the page of the wall calendar from October to November. The accompanying November picture showed an old University of Oregon running back diving into the end zone. Devon's mom sent the calendar to him so he wouldn't feel homesick.

I made some coffee on the stove and poured it into my cup. I added some milk and set my cup on the table to let the coffee cool off. I turned on the radio and listened to a soccer game. The announcer commentated in rapid Spanish, which I deciphered after I made the unconscious decision to concentrate.

Devon emerged from his room and walked into the kitchen. His eyes were dark and he squinted while his eyes adjusted to the light from the window. His budding afro was flat on one side from his pillow. He sat across from me and rested his elbows on the kitchen table. He buried his face in his hands and groaned.

"I'm too tired, *hombre*," Devon said.

"I'm wiped out, too," I said.

"What a weekend, though," he said.

"It was wild," I said. "Thankfully we don't have much work to do in school this week."

"What should we do all week, then?" I asked.

"Besides nap every day after class?" Devon replied.

"No way," I said, "we can't nap. There's too much to do out there."

"I know, I know," he said. "I'm down to do something, but nothing that involves too much effort. The weekend wore me out."

"I would be down for a hike to *El Cristo*, but that entails more effort than either of us wants to expend," I said.

"I wish we had a little weed so we could just hang out here and chill for a night or two," Devon said.

"Do they even have weed here?" I asked.

"Spaniards have to have some, right?" Devon said.

"I'm sure the Oviedo black market has some," I said.

Devon leaned back in his chair and stared at the coffee pot. He seemed to slip into a state of deep thought

"My goodness, I'm hungry," Devon said. "Do you want to get some food somewhere?"

"Sure," I said. "What should we get? Kebabs?"

"Or we could go to *El Serpiente* and eat," Devon said.

We left our apartment and entered the elevator. We dropped and the door opened when we reached the ground floor. An elderly woman waited for us to exit before see walked into the elevator. Devon held the sliding door for her as she used her cane for balance.

The sun had ducked behind the taller buildings in downtown Oviedo by the time we reached *El Serpiente*. Fernando was working alone in the empty restaurant and was organizing menus when we walked through the front door. He turned and shouted to us.

"*Chicos!*" he yelled.

"Hey, Fernando," I said.

"What's new?" Devon asked.

"*Nada*," Fernando replied. "How was Barcelona?"

"Too much fun," I said.

Good, *chicos*," Fernando said. "What can I get for you?"

"I'll have some water and a sandwich," Devon said.

"I'll have the same," I said.

"Good," Fernando said. "I'll tell our chef."

Fernando strolled into the kitchen and returned. We told him about our adventures in Barcelona. He laughed at my potential pickpocket story, but showed genuine empathy when Devon told him about Brad's stolen wallet. He lightened the mood with crude innuendos about our skinny dipping escapades.

"What will you *chicos* do this week?" Fernando asked.

"Nothing much," Devon said.

"Yeah," I added, "we're tired from our adventure."

"You should be," Fernando said.

"We want to sit on our couch, watch a soccer game, and smoke a little *marijuana*," Devon said.

"*Tienes mota?*" Fernando asked. "Do you have weed?"

"No," I said, "do they even have that here."

"Do you know where we could get some?" Devon asked.

"No," Fernando said, "but my brother does. Wait here. I'll go ask him. He works at the bar across the street."

Fernando walked out of his restaurant and returned five minutes later with his brother, Carlos. We introduced ourselves. Carlos looked similar to Fernando, except he was much taller and younger. Both projected an aura of Venezuelan pride in their demeanor.

"How much do you want?" Carlos asked.

We told him that we wanted four grams, or enough for a few joints. We gave him our colorful Euros and he left. Fernando carried our food to us. Devon ate his sandwich without saying anything. His only focus was his sandwich. I sat and sipped my water. I was foggy from my nap. I didn't take my first bite until Devon finished his entire sandwich. Carlos returned by the time I finished my meal. Nobody entered the restaurant, so he took the plastic bag of marijuana and handed it to Devon. Devon put it in his pocket.

"Thanks, man," Devon said.

"Yeah, thanks," I added. "I hope this wasn't too much trouble for you."

"No," Carlos said, "another waiter at my restaurant sells it."

"Tell him 'thanks' for us," Devon said.

Carlos left and we talked to Fernando for a while. He told

us that *El Serpiente* didn't see many customers on Sundays. Most Spaniards hosted large family meals in their homes. We paid for our meals and said goodbye to Fernando and thanked him for his help with our new acquisition. I took an *El Serpiente* matchbook on my way out the door. The matchbook depicted a green snake eating an apple with a figure resembling the biblical Eve in the background. We stopped at a tobacco shop on the way home and bought a pack of rolling papers.

When we reached the front door of our apartment building, we saw a sign that said the elevator was broken. We walked up the stairs to our fifth floor apartment and sat at our kitchen table. The wall clock read *6:27*. Devon pulled the bag of weed from his pocket and placed it on the table. He opened it and smelled the contents. He took a nugget from the bag and held it up to the light.

"It smells weak and it looks less potent than Oregon weed," he said, "but I bet it will work just fine."

He handed the bag to me and I inspected our new purchase. The leaves were stringy. Each bud lacked the orange and purple fibers that I was accustomed to seeing in my Eugene strands.

"He gave us a lot for what we paid," I said.

"Yeah," Devon said, "he was generous with his portions."

"Can you roll a joint?" Devon asked me.

"No, I can't," I replied. "I've tried once, but it didn't turn out well."

"I'll show you how it's done," he said.

He pulled the rolling papers from his pocket and placed them on the table next to the weed bag. Devon grabbed the scissors from the table and chopped three weed nuggets into fine powder. He pulled a business card from his wallet and tore an elongated rectangular piece off and rolled it and made a crutch. He placed the crutch at the end of an open rolling paper, then sprinkled a pinch of weed into the paper. Devon used his thumbs and forefingers gently and rolled the substance into one long herbal mass. He rolled the paper around the crutch first. He twisted the paper around the weed and licked the sides carefully and pinched the open end of the emerging joint. He shook it and twisted the tip. Devon flipped the completed joint between his fingers and tossed it to the middle of the table. I picked it up and inspected his handiwork.

"Nice job, dude," I said.

"Yeah," Devon said, "I think that will work."

"It looks like we have enough left in the bag for two more," I said.

"I think we do," he said. "This was some dense stuff."

"Where should we smoke it?" I asked.

"We could smoke it in the living room and watch soccer," Devon suggested.

"Sounds good to me," I said.

We walked into the living room and sat on the couch. Devon turned on the TV and searched through each channel. We found no soccer game. FC Barcelona played in three hours, but that was our only soccer-watching option for the night.

"Let's smoke it on the deck since there's no soccer on," I said.

"I like that," Devon said.

We walked through the kitchen and sat in two rickety wooden chairs. Our deck was small. Devon and I had plenty of room, but if we added a third person, we would be compact. The ceiling hung low. Vines grew on the brick walls that encased the deck on both sides. We saw *El Cristo* from our vantage point. It stood high above the other apartment buildings and mountain homes we saw in the distance. The statue was glowing as the sky grew dark. Oviedo's street lamps illuminated gradually. Devon pulled the matchbook from his pocket and gave it to me along with the joint.

"You do the honors, man," he said.

"If you insist," I replied.

I sparked the match. I put the end of the joint near the flame and burned the twisted paper wing tip. It blazed, then crumbled to ash in seconds. The ash blew away in the slight breeze. I put the crutch to my lips and lit another match and brought the flame to the charred tip. I puffed twice to aid the smolder. The end lit into a nearly perfect glow of orange. The smolder spread evenly across the width of the rolled weed. I inhaled the smoke and held it in my lungs until I needed to breathe. The smoke bellowed from my nose.

I pinched the crutch with two fingers and passed it to Devon. He took one deep breath in preparation. Devon smoked. He took the smoke into his cheeks and opened his mouth slightly. The smoke funneled toward his nose. He inhaled through his nostrils as the thick smoke hung in front of him. He smoked again and passed the joint to me.

"This Spanish weed isn't too bad, man," Devon said.

I smoked.

"It does the job," I said.

Smoke accompanied my voice.

"What a view," Devon said.

I smoked and passed it to Devon.

"It is pretty awesome," I said. "The view front that Gaudi park in Barcelona was intense, but the view front the balcony might take second place."

"Gaudi knew what he was doing," Devon said.

He smoked.

"Barcelona kept me entertained," Devon said. "I dug that city."

"I would pay to see another soccer game like that," I said.

"Yeah," Devon said, "Messi destroyed Sevilla. What an opportunity to see him play. Halloween weekend. Are you kidding me?"

He smoked and passed it to me.

"That was crazy," I said. "I spent way more money than I thought I would, though."

"Yeah, me too," Devon said.

"We still have two months here," I said. "I need a short-term loan or something."

"You should get a job," Devon suggested.

"I don't have a work visa, *hombre*," I said with a smoke-joined voice.

"Under the table? Tax free?" Devon suggested. "You could join the mafia."

"Maybe I will," I said. "I need a cool mafia name, then."

"San Miguel," Devon said.

"And I'll only drink liter bottles of San Miguel," I said. "Perfect."

"I know what you can do. At school," Devon said, and smoked, and continued, "I saw flyers asking for English tutors."

He exhaled with his voice.

"I do speak English pretty well," I said.

"Yeah, we each have 21 years of experience on our resume," Devon said.

"Let's make some phone calls and get jobs," I said. "Not right now, but, like, later."

"Good call," he said.

He inhaled deeply and exhaled with a thick mass of smoke. The air turned more pungent. The sun was behind the mountains, but the sky glowed. *El Cristo* became more visible. Houselights dotted the mountainsides and apartment lights flickered down the street. The corner streetlight flickered and immersed the intersection in an orange glow. The joint had burned halfway.

"Look at that statue of *El Cristo*, man," Devon said. "That's some big-city stuff. I'm talking Rio, you know?"

"That is pretty crazy," I said. "I wonder how they got that statue up there."

"A big crane probably," Devon said.

"No way," I said. "They don't make cranes that can reach mountains. They used a helicopter to fly it up there."

"Not possible," Devon said. "That statue's too heavy for a helicopter."

"Maybe the same aliens that built the pyramids in Egypt built this statue," I said.

"No," Devon said, "those aliens were too old and this statue is too new. Construction workers built it on top of the hill," Devon said.

"Good call," I said.

We both smoked and looked at the view.

"That's crazy that the Muslims controlled all of Spain except for Oviedo," Devon said and pointed at *El Cristo*.

"I wonder what we would see in Spain now if the

Christians didn't win that 700-year battle for the peninsula," I said.

"That would be crazy," Devon said. "And possible, right? They only had to destroy Oviedo, then they would have ruled the whole peninsula."

"For sure, dude," I said. "The ideas of the Crusade helped, I think. Catholic kings wanted to beat the Muslim expansion."

I smoked and passed it to Devon. He smoked.

"Muslims and Christians will always be fighting, dude," Devon said.

"Yeah," I said. "How can religions fight each other? Isn't that against their religion?"

"I feel you, man," Devon said.

"What is religion, anyways?" I said. "Religion is man's imposition on spirituality."

"Religion is just a governing body for spirituality, that's all," Devon said.

"Islam and Christianity are the same," I said. "They both started from Judaism. They grew and matured in different parts of the world and blended with that culture."

"Yeah, forget all that violence business," Devon said. "Every group should be happy and it will make the world better."

"We just solved the World Peace issue," I said.

"I agree with all that," Devon said, "and I'm Catholic."

"Me too, man," I said. "The church made some bad moves back in the day."

"So did the government," Devon said. "I mean, so *does* the government."

"Nixon with Watergate," I said. "Reagan with Iran-Contra. Clinton and his secretary."

"Prohibition," Devon said. "Not to mention slavery. If I was born 200 years ago, I would have picked cotton for some old lazy dude and I wouldn't have gotten a paycheck. I mean, you would get your ass kicked for talking to me."

"People would gasp at you and Roxy," I said.

He laughed and smoked.

"People were dumb back then, man," Devon said.

"We still have some dumb people in this world, though," I said.

"Yeah we do, unfortunately," Devon said.

"People in Spain look at any African dude like a potential thief or drug dealer," I said.

"Yeah, you told me about Anna and her comment about the immigrants in the park," Devon said. "That's ignorance, man. Pure ignorance."

"Any immigrant needs to make money," I said. "Look at Fernando. He's a Venezuelan immigrant and needs money, so he opens a restaurant. And his brother sells pot."

"No, his brother's *amigo* sells pot," Devon said.

"Good call."

"Or that picketpocket on the Barcelona subway, or the knife-wielding thief on the beach who stole Brad's wallet," I said.

"Good call," Devon said. "But you'll find native thieves wherever you go, too. Some dude robbed me in middle school at the bus station. They're everywhere."

"They really are," I said. "Someone robbed me in Portland when I was a freshman in high school. Desperate people everywhere."

"With all this wealth our government has," Devon said, "we shouldn't have desperate people. People should, you know, receive money for being people."

"Man," I said, "all that government corruption and religious squabble needs to stop. It's all dumb."

"Let's do something about it," Devon suggested.

"Let's run for President and Pope and run this world the right way," I said.

"How do we get there?" Devon said. "I don't go to Harvard. I'm not becoming a priest."

"Fair enough," I said. "Back in the day, the Pope didn't have to be a priest. He just had to be rich."

"You have to be rich to run for President, too," Devon said.

"Good point," I said. "Kings of European countries, then."

"That's the way to go," Devon said. "Let's just live in Europe."

"We should," I said. "Let's stay in Spain."

"I'm down," Devon said.

"I have more fun in Spain that I do at home," I said. "And I'm happier."

"Me too," Devon added. "Let's push this forward. Call the Spanish government and tell them we're staying here."

"If we become Spanish citizens, we should get knighted by the queen," I said.

"That's England, dude," Devon said.

"Oh, yeah," I said.

Devon crushed the decaying joint against the flower pot and flicked it over the balcony. It dropped five stories. Devon suggested that we walk to a restaurant for dinner. Cooking seemed like too much work at this point in my day, so I agreed.

"We should smoke another joint before we leave, though," Devon said.

"I'm down," I said.

He walked into his room and rolled another joint quickly. I grabbed a cup form the cabinet and filled it with water. I drank half of the water in the glass, so I refilled it. Devon entered the kitchen and pointed at my water glass. He grabbed a cup and filled it with water and we walked onto the deck. I set my water glass beneath my chair. Devon handed the joint to me, but I refused and insisted that he light our second of the night. He sparked the lighter and lit the joint. It burned crookedly at first, then evened.

We smoked it and talked about our dinner destination. I spoke adamantly in favor of a kebab shop — or two if possible. Devon favored *El Serpiente* because we might receive free food or a beer on the house. Devon won. He thought seeing Fernando was a good idea. I agreed. We finished the joint and Devon stomped it with his foot and pitched it over the balcony. I stood and watched it fall. We walked into the house and I locked the door to our cubby-hole deck. I had forgotten that elevator was broken, so we took the stairs and emerged onto the streets of Oviedo.

It was dark, but the streetlights gave a comfortable feeling to the brisk walk through town. The sidewalk tinted orange from the streetlamp's glare. I heard a woman singing from her open apartment window. She wasn't a good singer, but she sounded happy. A middle-aged woman walked her dog on the other side of the street. She didn't notice us, but her little dog barked in our direction. I marveled at the Cathedral tower. It was illuminated and towered over apartments.

We reached *El Serpiente* and walked in. Fernando was

talking with a family seated in the corner, but he saw us and greeted us at the door. He sat us near the bar. After we sat, he looked at us and held his stare. His mouth curled into a smile and he laughed loudly.

"*Chicos*," he said between hearty laughs, "you're high."

"*Si, Fernando*," Devon said.

"We are. We are," I said. I nodded in overexcited affirmation.

"Wait here," Fernando said.

He walked across the restaurant floor and into the kitchen. He returned with a plate of potato wedges and four styles of dipping sauce. Fernando placed the platter in the middle of our table. He laughed.

"Enjoy, *chicos*," Fernando said. "A gift from our chef, *Carmen*."

"Tell Carmen we said '*gracias*'," I said.

"Yeah tell her that," Devon said with his mouth full of potatoes.

"Bring her out so we can tell her," I said.

"*Uno momento*," Fernando said.

He returned from the kitchen with a short, round woman in a chef's hat. We thanked her. She shook our hands and retraced her steps through the kitchen door. I had a beer and we stood to leave. We left Fernando a gracious tip for the free plate of potatoes. We walked out of the restaurant and Fernando's brother was leaning against a wall with a cigarette. We waved to him and he waved back. We all laughed with mutual understanding. Devon and I stopped at the market near our apartment building. I bought candy and a loaf of bread and orange juice. Devon bought an apple and a banana and a soda.

We left the store. Stars hung above us as we walked across the street to our building. I saw Az and his wife. Devon and I waved to him and walked into our apartment building and climbed the stairs.

PART 3

CHAPTER 15

I stood behind a Swedish student while I waited in line for the water fountain. He took a quick drink and stepped to the left. He muttered something in Swedish and I nodded in agreement, although I didn't understand him. I pulled my steel water bottle from the side pouch of my backpack and unscrewed the cap and filled it with cold water.

I took my time. I made a conscious effort to absorb the environment around me. Class was over for the day and I had no plans for the remainder of my Wednesday afternoon. Devon waited for me on the top step. We walked from the third floor to the first and discussed potential afternoon plans.

"You want to grab a beer?" Devon asked.

"Not yet," I said.

"Why not? Too tired?" he asked.

"Yeah," I said, "I am tired. I don't want to take a nap though."

"Coffee, then," Devon said.

"Good plan," I said.

We strolled on the brick pathway and crossed the main campus plaza. Brad waved to us from the other side. He quickened his pace and met us near the library.

"Come get a coffee with us, *hombre*," Devon said.

"I'm down," he said. "I'm done with class for the day. My professor held us for, like, ten minutes after class because some girl kept asking questions."

"Rough day," I said.

"Tell me about it!" Brad shouted.

We neared the crosswalk.

"Wait for a second, guys," I said. "I want to pop into the library real quick."

"For what?" Brad asked.

"To check the advertisement corkboard," I said.

"For what?" Brad asked again.

I didn't answer. I jogged to the library's front door and opened it. A student holding a pile of books evaded me as he turned the corner hastily. I held the door for him and he walked out of the library. He thanked me. No one was working behind the front desk, so I stepped behind it and looked at the crowded corkboard carefully. I saw advertisements on colorful paper for roommates, pets, and Spanish tutors. I didn't see any that asked for English tutors and felt discouraged.

I moved a few flyers and found a small white piece of paper with handwritten blue ink. The advertisement asked for a native English speaker and asked the reader to call the listed phone number. I put the paper in my pocket. A library employee strolled down the hall and saw me behind the desk. She yelled at me, so I moved in front of the desk and left the library expediently.

"Did you find any good books?" Devon asked.

"No, but I found an ad for an English tutor," I said. "At least I think it's for an English tutor."

"Nice work," Devon said.

"I'll call the phone number tomorrow morning," I said. "Now it's coffee time."

"Actually," Brad said, "while you were being studious in the library, Devon and I masterminded a plan."

"Oh really?" I said. "What is it?"

"Since the sun is shining and it's the beginning of November," Brad said, "we should hike to *El Cristo*."

"Sounds like a plan," I said.

"I know it's chilly, but I bet we can see for miles in this clear weather," Brad said.

o   o   o

Devon and I changed our clothes and Brad met us in front of our apartment building. We strolled on the sidewalk toward the mountain. The road forked and we started down the familiar right-flanking path.

"I wonder where this left fork goes," I asked.

"It looks like it winds around the mountain the other way," Devon said.

"We've never taken the left path before," I said. "Let's do it."

We decided to forego familiarity. We banked left on the skinnier road without a sidewalk. The sun hung low in the sky as it does every year during late autumn along the 45th parellel. As we walked closer to the mountain, clouds intruded upon the clear blue sky. They aimed for the mountain and left the city sky clear. The road led us to the forest and we took a narrow offshoot into the woods. The dirt path was dry and cold. The sun disappeared behind the clouds.

I caught my sleeve on a thorn bush and unhooked myself and we continued. The path zigzagged across the flat face of the hill. We traversed three switchbacks and turned to look at the city, which was still sunlit. We were halfway up the mountain when Devon shouted.

"Did you guys feel that?" Devon yelled.

"Feel what?" I said.

"It felt like a raindrop on my face," Devon said.

"No I didn't feel anything," Brad said.

We pushed forward. The forest grew thicker and thorn bushes became more prevalent. Vines and dense under-growth vegetation impeded our path.

Soon, I began to doubt that a path even existed. We followed the path of least resistance, but it seemed to be more of a deer trail than an actual route to our usual viewpoint. The forest appeared as if it would never lead us to our destination and we contemplated turning around and abandoning our route.

We pushed through a thick section of forest and, suddenly, the forest stopped.

We emerged from the tree line and found ourselves on a wide walking path surrounded by tall grass. We were on the opposite side of the mountain from our usual hiking route. I saw the base of *El Cristo*'s platform, but we still had a hefty walk ahead of us. Devon shouted again.

"I think the clouds are opening, dudes!" he yelled.

"No way," I said, "I didn't feel a raindrop."

I looked up. A moist drop hit my left eyeball. I closed my eyes tightly. When I opened them, a flurry of snow dumped from the low clouds and we found ourselves in a November snowstorm. The snow piled on the cold grass and tried to accumulate on our asphalt walking path. We pushed forward.

"This is awesome!" I shouted.

"Hell yeah it is!" Devon shouted back.

The road flattened and we approached the base of *El Cristo*. A herd of ten cattle roamed the grass in front of us. Two stood in the middle of the road. We walked past them, too close for my comfort level.

I looked at one cow as I sauntered next to it. Its sheer mass intimidated me. Frosty breathe funneled from its nose. We touched the base of *El Cristo* and I place my hands on my head to catch my breath.

The cold air awakened my lungs. Each exhale felt warm. We stood at the edge of the mountain and looked at Oviedo. The dimming sunlight from Oviedo's cloudless sky illuminated the city. Deep shadows from buildings sprawled across town. Business people were probably leaving work and nonchalantly enjoying the crisp sun. And here we were: immersed in a snowstorm with a herd of cattle underneath *El Cristo*.

CHAPTER 16

History class ended. I had an hour before grammar class, so Devon and I walked to the café. Anna brought us two coffees with milk as we sat inside. We talked with Anna because the café traffic was light. I told her about our adventures in Barcelona and she marveled at our fortunate survival and our ability to grasp opportunity. An elderly woman entered the café, so Anna left to assist her. She promised to return soon.

"That girl," Devon said. "She's playing games with you, man."

"What do you mean?" I said.

"She's flirting with you like crazy, but she has boyfriend," he said. "She's playing with your heart. Bouncing it like a basketball."

"She really is," I said.

I drank my coffee.

"I'm going to call this English tutor phone number that I got from the library yesterday," I said.

"Good luck," Devon said. "You know what you're going to say?"

"Not at all," I said.

"My man," he said.

I walked to the counter and asked Anna for the café's phone. She placed it on the counter. She poured coffee into a small cup and brought it to the elderly woman. I pulled the advertisement from my pocket. The paper was wrinkled, so I flattened it and dialed the blue-inked phone number.

"*Hola*," said a woman's voice on the other end of the line.

"*Hola*," I said.

"*Quien es?*" asked the woman.

"I'm Jason," I said in Spanish. "I saw your advertisement for an English tutor in the University library."

The woman paused.

"Oh, yes, yes," she said. "My sons need help with English. Are you an English tutor?"

"Yes, I am," I said.

My conscience nagged at the slight dishonesty.

"Good," the woman said. "I would like to meet with you before I hire you. Can you meet today?"

"I can," I said.

"When?"

"I finish class at two," I said.

"I can meet at two," she said. "Do you go to *Universidad de Oviedo*?"

"I do."

"I will meet you there at two," she said.

I walked back to the table and sat. I sipped the rest of my coffee.

"How did it go?" Devon asked.

"She wants to meet with me at school after class," I said.

"Who is she?" he asked.

"I have no idea," I said.

We laughed and paid for our coffees. Anna waved to us as we walked through the door into the cold sunlight.

"Hey!" Brad shouted.

Devon and I jogged across the street to meet him.

"Cologne, are you still trying to hang out with that Anna girl?" Brad asked.

"Yeah he is," Devon said.

"She's all looks, no substance," Brad said.

Devon grimaced at the harsh reality. I ignored the comment, but recognized the growing truth in Brad's analysis. We walked into the University and entered grammar class. Our grammar professor entered shortly after we did. She was punctual as usual. And attractive. Her fashion and exotic ambiance aroused me during every class period. *Profesora* called on me to answer a question and I answered with excitement. Brad and Devon did the same when she asked them. The ladies in our class didn't possess the same affinity for grammar class as the three of us did.

Class ended and I strolled to the University's main entrance. I sat on a low step and waited for the woman to appear. Then I realized that I didn't know who I was looking for. I didn't know the woman's name. I didn't know anything about this rendezvous. I thought about walking to the café and calling the blue-inked phone number from Anna's café, but I decided to wait. It wasn't 2:00 yet.

A middle-aged woman in a felt hat and scarf wandered through the University plaza. She strolled from one end to the other, then retraced her steps. The woman looked around passively. I assumed she was the woman who I spoke with on the phone, so I stood and walked to her.

"*Hola*," I said to the woman.

"*Hola, eres Jason?*" the woman said.

"Yes, I am," I said.

I extended my hand and she grasped it and kissed me on both cheeks. This was a typical Spanish greeting between a male and female. It still caught me off guard. The woman's name was Paloma. She had two boys: Jorge, 12, and Paulo, 14. They studied English in school, but they struggled with applying their knowledge outside of the classroom. She wanted and authentic English speaker to coach them through their missteps. She would pay 15 Euros per hour for my services. Paloma suggested that my first tutoring session should serve as a tryout. From there, we could discuss a weekly schedule.

o   o   o

The streetlights illuminated the otherwise damp darkness. I strolled past the cathedral. A neon pharmacy clock read *18:56*. I had four minutes to find Paloma's apartment building. I wrote her address on a piece of paper, but I didn't know where the street was. I walked into *El Serpiente* and asked Fernando. He pointed toward the cathedral plaza and told me I was only a few blocks away. I quickened my walking pace.

At *19:04*, I found the building and pressed the button for apartment 614. A man's voice answered.

"*Quien es?*" the man asked.

"Jason Cologne," I said.

"Why are you here?" the man asked.

I panicked. *Was I at the right building?* I stepped back and looked at the building number. It matched the address on my piece of paper.

"To tutor Jorge and Paulo," I said.

The door buzzed and swung open. I waited for the man's response. The man said nothing. I walked through the open door and climbed the stairs to the sixth floor. I found apartment 614 and knocked on the door. The hallway was dark and the apartment door had no exterior light. The door opened and a tall, imposing man stood in the doorway. He was bald with a thick, black beard. He wore a tight, black t-shirt with a rock band graphic emblazoned on the front, and jeans and sturdy workers' boots. I stood wide-eyed as this intimidating man eye-balled me from head to toe.

"I am Chema," the man said in English. "Paloma is my wife and Jorge and Paulo are my sons."

"Nice to meet you, Chema," I said awkwardly.

I shook his hand and followed him inside. The entryway was dark, aside from two small candles on a corner stand. I followed Chema's thick shadow as he walked down the hallway and toward the lighted kitchen. We entered and Jorge and Paulo stood from the kitchen table to greet me.

"Paulo knows French very well," Chema said. "He can write good English, but he doesn't speak it."

"That will change very soon," I said. "What about Jorge?"

"Jorge tries," Chema said with a touch of embellishment. "He is shy about speaking English, too. His written English is so-so."

"They will be fluent in no time," I said.

"I'm fluent in French and Romanian," Chema said, "but I

take English classes on Monday nights at the University. I may listen to your lessons, also."

"That's fine," I said.

"So," Chema continued, shifting to Spanish, "how do you usually begin your lessons?"

The question surprised me. I had never given and English lesson in my life. *He caught me*, I thought. *He knows I'm a fake tutor. I'm done. Finished.* I stalled my Spanish translation to give myself more time to think about my answer.

"Well," I said, "*como se dice?*"

I hadn't given any thought to my approach to an English lesson. I called Paloma on a whim. I arrived at their apartment with no lesson plan, no thought as to how I would teach my language to someone.

"I like to get to know my students on a personal level on the first day," I said. "I like to gauge their English skills through natural conversation. After that, I can craft my lesson plans for the individual student for the following lessons."

"I like that very much," Chema said boldly. "Where should we sit? The living room?"

"Yes, we have couches in there," Jorge said. "It's more comfortable than the kitchen table."

I agreed. We walked into the living room, which was decorated with ornately framed mirrors and oversized picture frames. Multicolored china sets and old books filled the shelves and counter spaces. The woodwork around the fireplace gave the room an aura of medieval nobility. I sat on a pink couch next to Jorge. Paulo sat in a padded, wooden armchair and propped his feet on top of the ottoman. Chema folded his arms and leaned against the doorway. He cocked his head sideways and prepared to observe a professional tutor at work.

I spoke to Jorge and Paulo in simple English. We talked about sports. I told the boys about my adventure at the FC Barcelona game.

"We like Real Madrid, not Barcelona," Jorge told me.

I told them to ask me questions in English. Both boys spoke slowly, but their grammar was nearly perfect. I maintained a slow speaking pace, but enhanced my vocabulary level. Chema chimed in twice, but remained silently observant for most of the tutoring session. After an hour of English speaking, the boys looked exhausted. Chema unfolded his arms and strolled to the center of the room.

"That's enough for today, boys," Chema said.

He pulled money from his pocket and gave the bills to me.

"Thank you," Chema continued. "Boys, what do you say?"

"Thank you," Jorge and Paulo said in unison.

"You're welcome," I said.

I stood next to Chema. I was unsure of my next move, so I stood awkwardly.

"Can you teach the boys three days next week?" Chema asked me.

"Of course I can," I said.

"Monday, Wednesday, and Friday?" Chema asked.

"19:00? Just like today?" I asked.

"Yes. Monday, Wednesday, Friday at 19:00," Chema confirmed.

"*Bueno*," I said. "*Adios, chicos.*"

I shook Chema's hand and Jorge and Paulo walked me to the door. I stood in front of the elevator and pressed the button. I heard the machinery working behind the closed elevator doors. I waited. I turned and saw Chema. He hustled down the hall toward me.

"Jason!" he shouted.

"*Sí*?"

"I forgot to ask you something," Chema said, breathing heavily. "I have a niece. She needs an English tutor as well. Can you teach her?"

The elevator doors opened. Chema thrust his arm in the doorway to prevent them from closing.

"Yes I can," I said. "How should I connect with her?"

Chema wrote his niece's phone number on a piece of paper and gave it to me. He thanked me and retraced his steps toward his front door. I stepped into the elevator. The doors closed and I looked at the piece of paper that Chema gave me. Above the phone number, he wrote "Maria", followed by an illegible last name.

I walked home in the dark. The street lamps provided a warm light, but the air was chilled. Spaniards roamed the quiet cobblestone roads in scarves. I put my sweatshirt hood over my head because my ears were cold. The kebab shop near the Pumarin *barrio* was closing, so I snuck in before the owner flipped the lights off. I ordered one kebab and ate it while I walked home.

Devon was gone when I opened our fifth floor apartment door. He was with Roxanne, I assumed. I opened the kitchen window and made coffee on the stove. The coffee steamed. I poured some into my petite cup and dribbled milk into the remaining space. I sat at the kitchen table and placed Maria's phone number in front of me. I looked at it blankly. I picked up the phone and dialed the phone number.

"*Hola*?" said a female voice.

"Hello," I said in Spanish, "is this Maria?"

"*Sí*," Maria responded.

"I'm Jason. I tutor your cousins in English. Your uncle, Chema, told me that you needed a tutor."

"*Sí, sí, sí,*" Maria said. Her tone shifted from guarded inquiry to genuine excitement.

"Good," I said. "Would you like to meet with me this week?"

"Yes," Maria said. "I don't have class tomorrow. Can you meet me in the afternoon?"

"I can," I said.

She gave me her address and hung up the phone. I stared at my steaming coffee and turned on the radio. A soccer game was playing. The announcer rambled excitedly. I drank my coffee and fell asleep early.

I awoke the next morning and felt revitalized. I exercised in my room. I showered and drank coffee and listened to the radio. Devon's bedroom door was open and his bed was empty. I assumed he slept at Roxanne's house. I grabbed my backpack and walked to class. A familiar old woman waved to me as I left the apartment building. She carried two grocery bags. A small boy, probably her grandson, walked next to her. He carried a stick and pretended it was a sword. He swung the stick and hit a tree and his grandmother scolded him.

"What's up, dude?" Devon said as I walked into class.

"How was your night, *hombre*?" I asked.

"Good," Devon said. "I stayed at Roxy's after dinner."

"That's what I figured," I said.

"How did the teaching session go yesterday?" Devon asked.

"It went well," I said. "I have another job today. I'm

tutoring this dude's niece."

"Bring on the money," Devon said.

After class finished, I walked with Devon toward Maria's house. She lived near the center of town. Devon said he would walk around for an hour and meet me at a café when my tutoring session ended. I found Maria's building and pressed the button for her apartment. Maria answered and buzzed the door open. I climbed the stairs instead of taking the elevator. I found her apartment on the top floor and knocked.

"*Uno momento*," shouted a female voice behind the closed door.

I heard frantic footsteps. I stood in the empty hallway and watched the apartment door with anticipation. The door wiggled. I heard locks jostling on the other side. The doorknob turned and door opened.

"*Hola. Soy Maria.*"

Maria stood awkwardly, yet seductively in the well-lit doorway. Her olive skin hid behind a baggy sweatshirt, which draped over her black tights. Her hair was tied into a bun and her glasses magnified her already-large eyes. Even with the sweatshirt, I could tell that Maria had an exotic figure. Her small mouth curled into a nervous smile. She had a freckle on one cheek; a beauty mark as far as I could tell. She was gorgeous and attractive and casual.

"*Hola,*" I replied. "I'm Jason."

Maria shook my hand. Her face turned slightly red. She led me into the house. We took a tour and stopped in the kitchen.

"I'm embarrassed to be dressed this way," Maria said. "When Uncle Chema told me about you, he forgot to mention that you were my age."

"Yeah," I said, "he didn't tell me that either."

We walked into the dining room and sat at the table. I followed the same makeshift strategy from Jorge's and Paulo's lesson. I spoke with Maria in basic, slow English. I enhanced the vocabulary after realizing that Maria spoke precisely. She lacked confidence in her ability, but she made few mistakes.

"What do you study?" I asked.

"I study biology at *Universidad de*," Maria said, "University of Oviedo."

"What do you do for fun?" I asked.

"I go out with friends," she said. "We go to bars and restaurants and stores."

"Do you play sports?" I asked.

"No," she said with a laugh. "I played basketball as a child, but I was no good."

I laughed at her pronunciation of "basketball" and she scowled at me playfully.

"Do you like soccer?" I asked.

"Soccer?" she replied.

"*Fútbol*," I said.

"Ah, soccer," Maria said. "I do. I like Real Madrid. Cristiano Ronaldo is good."

I gave a disapproving look and mentioned my affinity for FC Barcelona. We talked for a full hour. I stood to leave and she walked me to the door. We scheduled another tutoring session for Monday morning before our classes started.

"What are you doing on Friday night?" Maria asked.

"I don't know yet," I said. "Probably going to a bar with some friends."

"You should go out with *mi amigas y yo*," she said.

"I would like that," I said. "Where should I meet you?"

"A bar on *Calle Gascona*," Maria said. "It's called *El Serpiente*."

CHAPTER 17

I stepped out of the shower and heard a rapid knock on my apartment front door. I wrapped a towel around myself and hustled down the hallway. The knocking speed increased. I was nervous. I looked through the peephole, but it was covered and I couldn't see the hurried knocker. I opened the door slowly. Devon greeted me with a hug and told me that he forgot his keys when he went to the store. He carried a box of beer and placed it in the refrigerator. I stood in front of the mirror in my apartment hallway and buttoned my shirt. Devon laughed at me from the kitchen.

"You've spent all that time looking in the mirror and you still haven't realized it," Devon said.

"Realized what?" I asked.

"You can't look as good as me," Devon said.

"Shut up, dude. I look good in this shirt," I said.

"I'm just kidding, man," Devon said. "Are you ready to show this Maria girl how we own *El Serpiente*?"

"You know it," I said.

He threw a beer can to me. I cracked it and took a sip. I sat at the kitchen table with Devon and we finished our beers and listened to a soccer game on the radio. I brushed my teeth, tied my shoes, and flipped my jeans over my shoelaces. I grabbed a light jacket from the closet to cut the brisk Oviedo winter night. Devon stood from his kitchen chair and we left.

Marcos was sitting at a table in the back of *El Serpiente* when Devon and I arrived. We greeted Fernando and sat at Marcos' table. Fernando brought an Estrella Damm for me and Devon.

"You're early tonight," Fernando said in Spanish.

"We wanted to get a good table," I said.

"You know I always make room for you," Fernando said.

"We know, we know," Marcos said.

"Jason's meeting a girl here later," Devon said.

"*Que chica?*" Fernando asked.

"Jason tutors her in English," Devon said. "Her name's Maria and she comes to *El Serpiente* with her friends every weekend, she says."

"I don't know her," Fernando said, "but I might recognize her when she walks in."

A group of students walked in and sat at a table near the front, so Fernando left to serve them. He returned after he brought drinks to the new arrivals.

"I have an idea," Fernando said. "Do you *chicos* want to be my DJs tonight?"

"Yes!" Marcos exclaimed.

"You can only play American music, though," Fernando said, "and it needs to be upbeat."

"Don't worry, *jefe*," Devon said. "We've got you covered."

Marcos strolled to the music control station and plugged his personal music player into the sound system. A familiar American hip-hop beat filled the bar. The group sitting in the front of the restaurant looked around the room with unfamiliarity, while Devon and I sang every word to the first verse of the song. We continued to sing and drink as more people filled the restaurant. Our table had three open seats, but nearly every other table was occupied. Spain's Friday night prime time was in full swing.

Maria and three friends walked through the door. Fernando looked at me from across the room and pointed. I motioned in agreement and he approached the girls and brought them to our table. I stood.

"Maria, how are you?" I asked after a double-cheeked kiss greeting.

"I'm good. And you?" Maria asked in heavily accented English.

Fernando brought another chair to our table and all four girls sat. Maria introduced her friends to me and I introduced my friends to her. Maria's *amigas* didn't speak English well, so our conversation proceeded in Spanish. Marcos flirted incessantly with Maria's petite friend, while Devon occupied the other two on his side of the table.

"We should speak in English," I said to Maria. "It will make you better."

"We spoke English during our tutoring session," Maria said. "Now, it's your turn to speak Spanish."

"She told you, Jase!" Devon shouted.

"Whatever, Dev!" I shouted back.

"So," Maria continued in Spanish, "you live with Devon?"

"*Sí.*"

"And Marcos is your friend from school?" she asked.

"He is," I said. "How do you know your friends?"

"The two girls talking with Devon are from biology classes. And I know Loreto, the girl talking to Marcos, from childhood," Maria said.

I heard Fernando whistle from behind the bar. I looked and saw Anna walk into *El Serpiente* with a few friends. Maria's back was to the door, but she turned and looked. She was unaware that I knew her.

"I don't like that girl who just walked in," Maria said.

Loreto turned and nodded in agreement.

"Why don't you like her?" I asked nonchalantly.

"She dated my brother," Maria said.

"Which girl?" I asked.

"The girl dressed in red. Her name is Anna," Maria said. "She dated my brother last year, but she cheated on him with another boy."

Devon heard our conversation and looked at me. Our eyes connected in mutual understanding. I felt my heartbeat quicken.

"I'm sorry to hear that," I said.

"I yelled at her on campus the day after it happened," Maria said. "Now, she doesn't like me."

"Why did you yell at her?" I asked.

"No one messes with my brother except for me," she said proudly.

I guided the conversation away from the subject. We talked about Maria's family, and then Devon and I teased Marcos about his basketball skills and all the girls laughed. Marcos acted embarrassed, but he thrived in the attention.

I heard another whistle from behind the bar. I looked and

Fernando motioned for the *chicos* to come to him. Devon, Marcos, and I stood and maneuvered our way through the growing crowd. I leaned on the bar with both elbows.

"*Que necesitas*, Fernando?" Devon asked.

"I need your help," Fernando said.

"What do you need?" I asked.

"There are three drunken men at the front table," Fernando said. "They're being rude to the girls next to them. I asked them to leave *El Serpiente*, but they won't go. They just sit there and yell at the girls."

"Ask them again and we'll be right next to you, *hombre*," Devon said.

Fernando walked around the bar and we followed. He stood in front of the drunken men's table and we stood next to him. I folded my arms in an attempt to toughen my appearance. I saw Maria and her friends watching from our table, and then I notice that Anna had turned to look.

"*Chicos*," Fernando said to the drunken men, "it's time for you to leave."

"No," slurred a short man. "We want more beer."

"No." Marcos said. "You want to leave."

"Who are you?" another man slurred.

"These are my bouncers," Fernando said.

I waved. The short man's eyes widened, but he sat still in his chair.

"*Americanos*?" the short man slurred. "Where is my beer, *hombre*?"

"Leave, or we'll make you leave," Marcos said.

"We're not leaving," the short man said, focusing on Fernando. "No South American bartender can tell me what to do in my country."

Fernando looked sideways at us with affirmation and nodded his head toward the drunken men. Devon, Marcos, and I moved. We each stood behind one drunken man. I grabbed the short man's shirt, lifted him upwards, and pushed him through the crowd toward the front door. He made frantic efforts to evade my grasp, but I held firmly until the short man was outside.

He turned a swung his right arm slowly. I dodged his telegraphed punch. Devon laughed behind me and pushed his target outside. The short man swung at Devon, who dodged the slow punch. I kicked the short man's knee and it buckled and he fell. His two friends helped him to his feet and cursed at us. Devon, Marcos, and I stood in the doorway and smiled.

We walked into the restaurant and Fernando high-fived us. I saw Maria watching us from our table. Anna stood and walked toward me. She tapped me on the elbow. Devon stood with me to ease the potential awkwardness. Marcos continued through the crowd and sat at our table with Maria and her friends.

"What happened outside?" Anna asked.

"We were just helping Fernando with something," I said.

"I haven't seen you in a few days," she said. "How are you?"

"I'm good," I said.

I felt Maria watching me and I felt myself shifting with nervous energy.

"Yeah, we're good," Devon added.

"Who are you here with?" Anna asked with a hint of premonition.

"Devon and Marcos," I said.

"*Bueno*. Who are the girls at your table?" she asked.

"I'm tutoring one girl in English. We met her friends here," I said.

"Is one girl named Maria?" Anna asked.

"Yeah," I said.

"Oh," Anna said. "Well, have fun. If you get bored, come and sit by me."

Anna winked and touched my upper arm as she walked back to her table. Devon and I pushed through the crowd and returned to our table. Maria's friends laughed at her as I sat in my chair.

"I was just telling Maria about your courage and strength out there," Marcos said.

"You fought that bad man outside?" Loreto asked me.

"Jason's the man!" Devon shouted.

Maria looked at me. I sensed a vibe of adoration from her glance. I felt my face turn red. Fernando brought more Estrealla Damm for our table. He returned ten minutes later with two bottles of *sidra*. He lifted the open bottle above his head and poured. The *sidra* cascaded into the cup he held below his waist. Maria drank the first cup. He repeated his pouring scheme, and Loreto drank the second cup quicker than Maria did. We each drank a cup as Fernando poured it. Fernando drank the last cup.

At midnight, Maria and her friends stood to leave.

"Why are you leaving?" I asked.

"I have to wake up early tomorrow," Maria said. "My cousin is getting married in Santander and I have to drive there in the morning."

"I'm going to the wedding, too," Loreto said.

"But we had fun with you *chicos*," Maria said.

"We had fun, too" I said. "Enjoy the wedding."

Maria turned and led her friends toward the front door. After her first step, Maria turned.

"I'll see you Monday," Maria said in perfect English.

Her friends giggled as they left. Five minutes later, Anna stood and walked to our table with another girl. Anna and her friend sat across from us.

"What are you boys doing tomorrow?" Anna asked.

"I don't know," I said.

"My parents are in France for the weekend," Anna said.

"Good to know," Devon said.

"You three should come to my house tomorrow afternoon. Some *amigas* will be there and we can drink and swim in my pool," Anna said.

"I'm down!" Marcos shouted.

"Uh, sure," I said. "Where's your house?"

She wrote the address on a napkin and handed it to me. She leaned forward. Anna licked her lips quickly. I sensed an aura of seduction, but I dismissed it.

"We'll be there," I said.

CHAPTER 18

The early afternoon sun began to extinguish the fog. I walked to my kitchen window to close it, but I stopped because I heard a man shout. I put my head out the window and looked to the street below me.

"Hurry up, dudes!" Brad shouted from the street.

"We're on our way down!" I shouted back.

Devon and I walked downstairs. Brad sat on a bench and stood to meet us when we exited our apartment building.

"Are you guys ready to see this Spanish babe's pool?" Brad said.

"You know it," I said.

I draped my backpack over my shoulders. It carried my swimsuit and towel. Devon carried his own supplies in his backpack, while Brad held his in-hand.

"Are we walking by Marcos' apartment to get him?" Brad asked.

"No," Devon said, "he's meeting us at the bus stop on *Calle Uria* with Roxy."

We strolled through downtown Oviedo. Tourists roamed the plaza and took pictures. A Portuguese family stood in front of the cathedral and posed for a picture. A group of teenage girls walked out of a café and they bundled their coats and tightened their scarves to block the chill. As we strolled down *Calle Uria*, picturesque families wandered in and out of stores and window shopped for expensive, designer products.

"Hey guys!" Roxanne shouted as she leapt from the bus stop bench.

"What's up, Roxy?" I said.

"I'm just waiting patiently for you guys to get here so we can go to Anna's house," Roxanne said. "When does our bus get here?"

"In a few minutes," I said.

"Where is Anna's house, anyways?" Marcos asked.

He reclined on the wooden bench and stretched his arms across the backrest.

"It's up in the hills," I said. "Devon and I mapped our bus route. It should be a half-hour ride. She lives in the hills on the opposite side of Oviedo from *El Cristo*."

"Woah," Marcos said, "that neighborhood has huge houses. Anna must live in a mansion."

"If she has a pool, her house has to be big," Roxanne said.

"Yeah, you don't see many pools around Oviedo," Devon said. "Her family must have dodged the economic crisis."

"Anna's family owns a small café, though," I said. "I doubt the café brings in enough money for a hilltop mansion with a pool. Maybe her house is smaller than we think."

"Maybe her dad is a black market kingpin," Devon said.

"Yeah, I bet he runs a casino in the back of his café," Brad said.

"No way," Marcos said, "you need more than an underground casino to buy a mansion."

"Good point. He's probably the leader of the Spanish mafia," Devon said.

"That's the only logical explanation," Brad said.

"You guys are ridiculous," I said. "Anna's dad probably made smart investments, and then pulled his money out of the stock market before the crisis hit."

"I guess we'll find out when we see this house," Marcos said.

The bus turned the corner on *Calle Uria* and stopped in front of us. We paid the driver and sat near the back of the bus. Two women sat near the middle. They looked out the window and seemed mystified by the bustling Saturday crowd.

The bus cruised through Oviedo. It stopped five times and the occasional traveler joined our journey. The cityscape thinned and tall buildings became sparse. Immaculately paved roads morphed gradually into gravel. The road inclined. Buildings and plazas were replaced by trees and fields. I looked through the window and saw a stone farmhouse. Smoke spiraled from its chimney. The bus climbed. Farmhouses became more luxurious. Single-level homes shifted to double. Simple entryways became lavish.

"Look at that house," I said to Devon. "It has marble columns!"

"Check out that one!" he shouted, pointing to the other side of the bus. "It has a stone wall around it."

For the next five minutes, we pointed at every mansion we saw. The bus stopped and we exited. The bus looped and retraced its route down the mountain. Apparently, we stood at the last stop on its route. The five of us looked at Oviedo from our altitudinous viewpoint. I hadn't seen the city from the perspective. *El Cristo* faced us from its pedestal on the other side of the city.

"Alright, Cologne," Brad said, "where do we go from here?"

I looked around. I took three steps to the left and looked at Anna's address on the piece of paper in my hand. I stopped, pondered, and turned.

"This way," I said.

My voice echoed with total confidence, but I was unsure. We walked past five elaborate homes with expensive gates, some ancient, some modernized. Fine automobiles graced each driveway. The addresses increased in number as we continued. Since we hadn't passed Anna's address, I gained confidence in my directional decision.

"Here it is," I said.

I pointed to the numbers on a high stone wall. They matched the address I held in my hand. The wall was so tall that I couldn't see anything beyond it.

"I'll ring the doorbell," Roxanne said.

She pressed a button to the right of the gate.

"*Quien es?*" a female voice asked through the speaker in the wall.

"Jason and his friends," Roxanne said.

The gate crept open. We stood in awe of the lavish home that unveiled before us. High, marble columns lifted the entryway. The house was made of pure, massive stone. Giant windows and an impeccable garden. We followed the elongated driveway to the columns and knocked on the door. It swung open. Anna stood in the doorway wearing a bikini top and tiny shorts. Her outfit left little for the imagination. Brad gasped quietly; only I heard him.

"*Bienvenidos a mi casa,*" Anna said.

She motioned for us to come in. I greeted her with a double-cheeked kiss and entered her house. Anna led the five Americans into her living room. My eyes gazed upward at her high-vaulted ceilings. The home's large windows illuminated the room. I stared at Anna's shorts as she bounced into the center of the room. I looked at Marcos and his eyes focused on Anna's shorts as well. Two girls in bikinis walked into the living room from the backyard. They each carried an Estrella Damm and wore wide sunglasses.

"Do you remember Paloma and Carmen from *El Serpiente?*" Anna asked, pointing to the bikini-clad girls.

"Yes, I do," Marcos said.

"How are you, *chicas?*" Brad asked.

"*Bien,*" Carmen replied, lifting her beer bottle.

"I'm good," Paloma said.

"You can put your things by the chair," Anna said. "Do you want anything to drink?"

"*Una cerveza, por favor,*" Devon said.

"I'll take a beer, too," Marcos said.

Roxanne and Anna went into the kitchen and returned with beers for everyone, including Paloma and Carmen. Anna led us outside to the pool. Two girls sat by the pool and three Spanish *chicos* were in the water. One of the men dated one of the poolside girls. The other two men were tagalongs.

The sun warmed the air and the pool looked refreshing. I introduced myself to the five new Spaniards and went inside with Devon, Brad, and Marcos. We changed into our swimsuits and returned to the pool. I drank half of my

Estrella Damm and sat in a chair next to Paloma.

"Anna has one of the most beautiful homes in the area," Paloma said.

"I'm not surprised," I said.

"I live five houses away from here," Paloma said.

"Which house is yours?" I asked.

"It has columns like Anna's," Paloma said.

"I think we rode by it on the bus," I said.

"You took the bus here?" Paloma said

"*Sí*," I said.

"Why didn't you take a taxi?" Paloma asked.

"Taxis are expensive," I said.

She looked at me with a disconcerting expression.

"Jason Cologne, let's test this diving board, *hombre*," Brad shouted from the other side of the pool.

"I'm down!" I shouted back.

I walked along the pool's edge. Brad approached the diving board and bounced lightly when he reached the end of the plank. He slammed his weight into the board and exploded upwards. Brad flipped once and hit the pool with a splash. Water reached Paloma's toes and she shrieked. I walked to the edge of the diving board and bounced twice and shot upwards. I flipped once and continued into a dive before I hit the water. The water pressure pushed my shorts to my knees, but the splash clouded the water and gave me enough time to pull my shorts up before anyone noticed. My nerves shook momentarily from the potential embarrassment.

Devon found a soccer ball in the grass and threw it to me while I was in the pool. He jumped off of the diving board and I threw the ball to him and he caught it in midair. Brad jumped out of the pool and off of the diving board and Devon threw him the ball. Brad missed the ball and it hit Roxanne in the leg.

"Watch it, Dev!" Roxanne shouted.

"I was throwing it to you, Roxy!" Devon joked. "Be ready next time."

"Yeah, be alert, Roxy," I said.

"Don't encourage him, Jason," Roxanne said.

We threw the soccer ball to each other for a while. I exited the pool and sat on the edge with my feet in the water. I drank another beer. Anna sat next to me and we talked. I felt a spark between us, but the thought of her boyfriend still nagged me. We talked for twenty minutes. We talked as if nothing in the world existed except our conversation.

The doorbell rang. Anna stood and walked inside to answer the door and I heard Anna scream with joy. She ran outside holding the hand of a tall, good-looking Spanish man. I felt a jealous rage smolder in my core. Devon looked at me with an empathetic expression. Marcos took two discreet steps toward me.

"Should we kick his ass?" Marcos whispered to me.

"No," I said, "let's see how this plays out."

My composure remained calm and confident, but my soul burned with jealousy. Anna walked toward me, dragging the man behind her.

"Jason," Anna said, "this is my boyfriend, Alfonso."

I reached out my hand and shook his. I gripped his hand tightly in a subconscious attempt to assert dominance. He equaled my force.

"Alfonso," I said, "*me llamo* Jason."

"Nice to meet you," Alfonso said passively.

Alfonso dismissed me and walked to Paloma and greeted her with a double-cheeked kiss. Anna followed him. She glanced at me as she passed. I thought that I sensed an apologetic vibe in her gaze, but maybe I imagined it.

I swam for a while and drank a few more *cervezas* by the pool. The sun began to set and the temperature dropped. Anna told us that more people were coming to her house at night for a party. She asked us to stay and join the *fiesta*. The five Americans held a semi-private team meeting in the living room to discuss our plans.

"What do you want to do, dude?" Devon asked me.

"Let's stay and party," I said.

"Are you sure?" Roxanne said. "I don't want you to be upset about Alfonso."

"If we leave, he wins," I said.

"There we go, Cologne!" Brad said.

"Let's show these Spaniards how to *fiesta*," Marcos said.

I smiled.

"Are you guys down to stay?" I asked.

"That's been established," Roxanne said.

"Alright, then," I said, "let's *fiesta*."

Anna told us that we could shower upstairs. Roxanne claimed the first shower and climbed the staircase.

"The bus stops running in an hour," Anna told us. "You can sleep here if you want. We have guest bedrooms and couches and blankets. Make yourselves comfortable."

Anna walked outside and joined her friends by the poolside.

"Let's show Alfonso how it's done, my dude," Devon said to me.

We bumped knuckles.

I heard a toilet flush and the bathroom door opened. Alfonso walked out of the bathroom and averted eye contact with Devon and I as we stood in the living room. I looked at Devon and a mischievous grin appeared on his face.

"Alfonso!" Devon shouted.

Alfonso turned quickly. He seemed startled.

"*Quieres un chupito de ron?*" Devon asked.

"*Que?*" Alfonso said.

"Do you want a shot of rum?" Devon repeated.

"No," Alfonso said.

"Come into the kitchen and take a shot of rum with us, *hombre*," I said.

Alfonso hesitated. He looked outside, and then walked toward us.

"Good decision, Fonz," Devon said.

We walked into the kitchen and found three shot glasses in Anna's cupboard. I grabbed a half-full bottle of clear rum from the counter and filled each shot glass. Devon raised his glass and I raised mine. Alfonso followed suit. Our glasses clinked.

"Go Ducks," I said.

"Go Ducks," Devon repeated.

Alfonso raised one eyebrow in slight confusion. He hesitated. We drank our rum shots and I winced. The rum was strong. Alfonso turned to leave.

"Hold on, Fonz," Devon said.

"*Porque?*" Alfonso said.

"Because we're taking another shot of rum before you go outside," Devon continued.

"No, no," Alfonso said.

"*Para España*," Devon said.

"Fine," Alfosnso said, "I'll do it for Spain."

I jumped and sat on the counter. Devon leaned against the sink. Alfonso stood in the center of the kitchen in an awkwardly dominant stance. He seemed intimidated by the two *americanos* in the room, yet confident in his familiar domain.

From the corner of my eye, I saw Alfonso sizing me up. The more I noticed this, the more insecure I began to feel. I puffed my chest subconsciously and placed my hands on my hips to make me seem more dominant, but I felt my insecurities building. I turned toward Alfonso and sized him up. I noticed that Devon did the same, which gave me more confidence. *Two against one, if that's what it comes to.* With every silent second, I felt the tension rise.

"Alfonso," Devon said, "do you play *fútbol?*"

"*Sí,*" Alfonso replied. "When I can. I'm so busy with work."

"You should play with us in *Parque San Francisco* sometime," Devon said.

"No, I cannot do that," Alfonso said. "That's where all the Africans and South Americans play."

"Yeah," I said. "They're probably way better than you, so that's understandable."

"I would destroy those stupid immigrants," Alfonso said. "They play dirty and they don't belong on a Spanish pitch."

"We play there all the time," Devon said. "Those African guys are good."

"They're African," Alfonso said. "They don't belong on the same court with me. They don't even belong in Europe."

I looked at Devon. His eyes widened and he bit his lip in an attempt to stop himself from spewing his current thoughts with blunt honesty.

"That makes sense that you two *americanos* play at *Parque San Francisco*," Alfonso continued. "You aren't from Spain either. I suppose you all have to stick together. And I'm sure playing with people more your skill level makes it more fun."

I stood slowly from my counter seat. I looked down and bit my lower lip as I pondered my next sentence while trying to calm myself down. I felt my face rise with heat. My left fist clenched by my side and I looked up, directly into Alfonso's eyes. In my peripheral vision field, I noticed that Devon was watching my anger progression.

"Guess what?" Devon blurted.

"What?"

"Rum time," Devon said.

He filled three shot glasses quickly with clear rum and we raised our glasses and drank. I tightened my face and felt the rum warm my body. I breathed and felt loose. Anna walked into the kitchen.

"*Chicos*," she said, "Roxanne finished her shower. There are two showers upstairs. You can use them now if you want."

Devon and I grabbed our backpacks from the living room and climbed the elaborate staircase. We reached the top level and turned left and walked down the hallway.

"Where are the showers?" I asked.

"I don't know, dude," Devon said.

"I guess we have to wander aimlessly through this big ass mansion then," I said.

"Yeah," Devon said, "we're going to get lost."

"I hope they don't have trapdoors or guard dogs," I said.

"Or some haunted suit of armor around the corner,"

Devon said.

I opened a door on the left side of the hallway. I saw a bed and no adjoining bathroom, so I closed it and continued to walk. Devon opened a door to the right. He closed it immediately.

"Coat closet," he said.

Devon opened the door to another small bedroom. We turned left and continued down the hallway. A large portrait of Anna's family hung on the wall. A mirror with a gold frame hung across from it, giving the illusion of two portraits. We passed the mirror and portrait and Devon opened a door on the right.

"Damn!" he exclaimed.

"What?" I asked.

"Check out this office," Devon whispered.

He opened the door and walked into the office and I followed. The office was huge. I stood in the center of the room and looked around. I saw a massive wooden desk with a leather chair, a wall-to-wall bookshelf, and a wide window. I gazed through it and saw an illuminated *El Cristo* statue. It seemed to float in the middle of the black sky. A portrait of a man hung from the wall. I assumed the man was Anna's father, which led me to assume that we were in his office. I walked to the desk. Devon sat in the leather chair.

"I mean, this guy knows how to live," Devon said.

"We should get into the café business," I said.

The desktop was impeccably organized aside from a somewhat disrupted stack of papers. Devon opened a desk drawer.

"What are you doing?" I asked.

"Nothing," Devon said. "I've had just enough rum to be

curious."

"And mischievous," I added.

I flipped through the unkempt stack of papers on the desk. I saw checks and handwritten records. I saw a café bank statement. I saw a few spreadsheets with names and numbers and monetary values.

"Jason, look at this," Devon whispered.

I walked around the desk and looked into a drawer that Devon opened.

"This guy has a gun in his drawer," Devon continued.

"The café business is rough these days," I said.

"I guess," Devon said. "I'll close this one."

I heard footsteps coming up the stairs rapidly. Devon and I looked at each other and sped through the doorway and closed the office door behind us. Anna turned the corner, so we acted lost and pretended to admire the wall paintings and family portraits. She pointed down the hallway toward the showers and then she turned and went downstairs.

I walked into the bathroom and closed the door and locked it. I took my swimsuit off and looked in the mirror. *How did I get here? What am I doing?* I turned the shower on and let the water heat before entering. The warm water electrified my skin and brought me out of the numbness of rum. I was in the shower for three minutes, but it felt like ten. My thoughts were moving from Anna to beating up Alfonso to Maria. Then, I could only think of Maria.

I turned the shower off and put my clothes on and went downstairs. The post-pool party commenced. Spanish pop music blared from the invisible-yet-powerful speakers in the living room. The Spanish girls were dancing in the middle of the room as my *americanos* stood back and drank more rum.

The rum encouraged us to join the dancing. The girls attempted to teach us the newest Spanish pop dance. Marcos seemed to catch on, while the rest of us made the girls laugh.

Anna and Alfonso moved to sit on the couch. Her legs were intertwined with his. Devon he stood in the corner with an unopened beer in his hand and talked to Roxanne. *Couple bubble*, I thought. I walked toward Marcos, who was in an intense conversation with Paloma. Marcos touched Paloma's arm and kissed her, so I flanked to the right before I interrupted their moment.

"Jason," Anna said, standing from the couch. "How was your shower?"

"Refreshing," I replied.

Anna touched my upper arm. Alfonso stood and walked toward us.

"You have a really nice house," I said.

"Thank you," Anna replied.

I felt her gaze through my eyes and into my soul. The rum fueled her innuendo. Alfonso approached and put his arm around Anna.

"So, *Americano*," Alfonso said, "you should call a taxi so it arrives in time to pick you up to go home."

Anna playfully pushed away from Alfonso.

"You don't need to call a taxi, Jason," Anna said. "I told you that you and your friends can stay here for the night."

I looked straight at Alfonso and smirked.

"Isn't she great?" I said to Alfonso.

"Come on, Anna," Alfonso said. "Let's go to bed."

"Goodnight, Jason," Anna said.

She kissed me on both cheeks and turned to walk upstairs. Alfonso looked at me and smirked.

"Where's Brad?" I asked Devon.

"He went upstairs with Carmen," Devon said.

"He did?" Roxanne asked. "Smooth, Brad."

Devon and Roxanne went upstairs to find a bed. Marcos was on the couch and Paloma was all over him. I walked into the kitchen a grabbed a beer. With no one to talk to, I walked outside and sat in a pool chair.

Stupid couples. I wish Maria was here. Anna's taste in guys is terrible. Maria should be here.

I opened my beer, but didn't take a drink. I thought about my short time left in Spain.

I didn't want to go back to the States. Not yet, anyways. But how could I stay in Spain? I had to finish college. My parents would kill me if I didn't come back home. But am I in love with Maria? Maybe? Do I even know what love is?

I turned my head and looked through the glass doors. Marcos and Paloma were asleep. I saw a light turn off upstairs. I felt drunk and frustrated. An impulse overtook me and I stood and threw my full beer bottle over the fence as hard as I could. I didn't hear it land, but the act of throwing the bottle made me feel better temporarily, until I realized that my dilemmas were present still. I didn't want to leave Spain, but there was no way I could rationalize staying here. *And why wasn't Maria here?*

o   o   o

I woke up on a couch in Anna's living room. Marcos was still asleep on the floor and Brad was sitting upright on another couch. He held his head in pain. I sat up and held my head too. *Damn rum,* I thought.

"What a night," Brad said.

I walked into the kitchen and filled a glass with water and drank it quickly. I walked back into the living room as Roxanne and Devon were walking down the stairs. We resurrected Marcos and left Anna's house. It was a cold, cloudy, damp morning. We stepped onto the bus and sat silently for most of the way home. The quiet hum of the bus engine soothed my hangover.

CHAPTER 19

I woke up and opened my bedroom window. The air in my room tasted stale and I was craving freshness. Rain fell from thin clouds. The sun hadn't risen fully yet, so the sky glowed with pre-dawn twilight. I stuck my hand out the window to feel the rain. It was cold. Water collected in my palm and I wiped my face. *Refreshing.*

"Yo, Jason!" Devon shouted from the kitchen.

"What's up, Dev?" I shouted back.

"You want some coffee?" he asked.

"Sure," I replied.

"Cool," Devon said. "I just made some. It's on the stove. I poured myself some already so the rest of the coffee's yours."

"Thanks, *hombre*," I said as I walked into the kitchen.

I sat at the kitchen table and turned on the radio. Commentators rambled in Spanish about the current soccer game between Real Madrid and Espanyol. Devon sat across from me. The coffee aroma inspired me to stand and pour a cup for myself, so I did and returned to my seat.

"Happy Thanksgiving," I said.

"Yeah, Happy Thanksgiving to you, too," Devon said.

"It's too bad that Spaniards don't celebrate Thanksgiving," I said.

"They should," Devon said, "Columbus sailed for the Spanish."

"But he landed in the Caribbean," I said. "Thanksgiving celebrates pilgrims landing at Plymouth Rock."

"Good point," Devon said. "Another reason why I admire Abe Lincoln."

"What's the first reason?" I asked.

"He abolished slavery," Devon said.

"Solid reason," I said.

"And the second reason," Devon continued, "is that Abe Lincoln made Thanksgiving an official national holiday."

"Did he?" I asked.

"Come on, history major," Devon said. "Read a book."

Devon threw his hands in the air in exaggeration and laughed. I took a sip of my coffee and caught a commentator glorifying Real Madrid's Cristiano Ronaldo, per usual.

"Whatever, dude," I said. "I'm into Thanksgiving for the mashed potatoes and gravy and turkey."

"I can't wait to munch on some turkey tonight," Devon said. "My mom makes the best turkey."

"Where are you eating turkey?" I asked.

"Good question," Devon replied. "I don't know. I guess I'm not eating Thanksgiving dinner this year. Damn."

Devon's face shifted from an expression of excitement to devastation upon this realization. I felt my face reflect my mood shift as well. I felt homesick for the first time.

"Do Spaniards sell turkeys?" I asked.

"I haven't seen one in any *carneceria*," Devon said.

"Neither have I," I said.

"Uh huh."

Devon stood quickly. His eyes widened. He walked briskly into the hallway and stopped and walked back into the kitchen.

"What are we doing in history class today?" Devon asked.

"I don't know," I said. "I think we're listening to another lecture from *profesora*. Why?"

"I'll be right back," he said.

Devon hustled into his room and reappeared a few seconds later. He grinned with anticipation. I sat in my chair anxiously; I was jittery with uncertainty and I had no idea why Devon looked so excited. He reached over the kitchen table with a closed fist and opened it and a thick joint dropped in front of me.

"A little morning marijuana?" Devon asked.

"I mean, why not?" I said.

I stood and followed Devon onto our small deck. The clouds became brighter as the sun rose behind them. Rain fell harder.

Workers walked with umbrellas five levels below us as Devon lit the joint and smoked. He passed it to me and I smoked. We finished the joint and Devon flicked it off of the deck. I watched it fall until it landed in a puddle on the sidewalk. We returned to the kitchen.

I put on jeans and an Oregon Ducks sweatshirt. My hair was longer than normal and I thought it looked unkempt, so I put on a baseball hat and turned it backwards. Devon and I walked out of our apartment and I locked the door.

"Oh no," Devon said, "the elevator's out of order."

"To the stairs, then," I said.

We descended five levels. A familiar old woman was climbing the stairs and we greeted her. She replied with the attitude of someone who enjoyed every morning's ambiance.

"I'm hungry," Devon said.

"So am I, Dev. So am I," I said.

"Market?"

"Market."

We were ahead of schedule. History class started in thirty minutes and we needed ten minutes to stroll to campus, so we entered the market near the entrance of our apartment building. Employees bustled around the small store, which opened twenty minutes ago. I waved to the girl at the register. She recognized us from our frequent trips to the store. She worked the night shift, usually, so we bought *cervezas* from her often.

Devon and I cruised through the middle aisle and grabbed bottles of orange juice. I laughed. *Zumo de narjana.* I replayed my first encounter with Spain three months ago in the Madrid airport: I was incredibly hungover when I walked off the plane and I asked for *jugo* instead of *zumo*. I was a rookie then.

"It's crazy how much we've learned since we've been here, dude," I said to Devon.

"It really is," Devon said. "Imagine how much more we could learn in another three months."

I smiled and my eyes squinted. We walked to the bread aisle and I grabbed a small loaf. The baker made it earlier that morning. It smelled fresh.

I picked up an apple and a milk chocolate bar and walked to the register and paid. While Devon was paying for his food,

I continued my friendly-yet-topical conversation with the girl at the register.

Rain fell lightly as we strolled toward campus. I opened my chocolate bar, which I regretted instantly when a raindrop hit it, so I ate the whole bar in three bites.

"Columbus was an ass," Devon said.

"Yeah," I said. "He sent slaves into the jungle to find gold and he chopped off their hands if they came back empty-handed."

"So what did we do?" Devon said. "We made a nation holiday in his honor: Columbus Day. What a joke."

We entered the classroom and I sat next to Brad and Devon. Roxanne sat behind us with a few girls. Our professor walked into the room and stood in front of the class and the murmuring stopped. The day's history lesson dealt with Francisco Franco and the Spanish Civil War; plots and betrayals; values and resistance.

I listened intently. I hung on every word our professor spoke. I focused solely on the content of the lecture; I was wrapped in curiosity.

I felt the classroom fade away. It was only me and the story of Franco and the Spanish resistance. I visualized myself as the main character of the story of an Asturian resistance fighter. My mind wandered again. I made connections to prior lessons about World War Two.

This is why Spain didn't fight in World War Two, I thought. *They would have joined the Axis Powers with Hitler and Mussolini! Franco was a Fascist just like them, but Spain was demolished from their own Civil War, so they didn't have the resources to join World War Two on either side.*

"This is awesome," Devon whispered to me.

"Yeah," I whispered back, "we should hang out on the deck before class more often."

"I don't see why not," Devon said. "I bet we would focus on..."

"*Chicos!*" our professor said as she pointed to Devon and me.

"*Lo siento*," Devon said.

I laughed silently. Our professor saw my giggle and she smiled.

History class ended. We had an hour-long break until grammar class began, so we went to the café. People crowded the counter and most tables were occupied. Roxanne and Devon walked to the back and sat at a table with four chairs. Brad and I stood at the counter. We ordered four *cafés*: Two *con leche* and two without milk. The woman behind the counter was a new employee. She appeared overwhelmed by the crowd and I didn't recognize her. We grabbed the four drinks and sat by Roxanne and Devon.

"Thanks, boys," Roxanne said.

"Any time, Roxy," I said.

Anna walked out of a backroom door with a heavy cardboard box in her arms. She placed it on the floor behind the counter and walked to our table.

"*Hola, chicos*," Anna said.

"Anna, how are you?" Brad asked.

"*Estoy bien*," she replied.

"The café seems busy today," Devon said.

"*Sí*," Anna said.

"Does your dad ever come into the café and help on busy days like this?" I asked.

"No," Anna said, "he owns the café, but he never works

here. My mother works here sometimes. She manages the day-to-day stuff."

"Interesting," Devon said. "What does your father do during the day?"

"He focuses on his other investments," Anna said.

"*Interesante*," Devon said.

Anna turned and reentered the back room to work on restocking the café.

"I wonder why Anna's dad has a gun in his office," Devon whispered to us.

"He has a gun in his office?" Roxanne asked. "How do you know?"

"Jason and I did a little investigating during Anna's pool party," Devon said.

"Good work!" Brad shouted. "So why does he have it?"

"Because he's stupid rich," I said. "We saw all kinds of paperwork about investments and money and number-crunching. I think he has a safe behind a portrait, too."

"Anna did say he works on his other investments," Roxanne said. "He probably owns half of Spain and the café is just for fun."

"He has to be rich as hell," Devon said. "Look at his house."

We paid for our coffee and walked across the street. Roxanne entered her advanced-level classroom on the first floor of the university building. Devon, Brad, and I walked to the third floor for intermediate grammar. We entered our classroom.

Devon led us to our customary seats in the middle of the room. We chose these seats strategically: the two rows in front of us blocked uncomfortable teacher proximity, but our center alignment gave the appearance of attentiveness while allowing us to blend with the crowd.

We arrived ten minutes early. A few Russian girls sat behind us. They spoke rapidly. The room filled gradually with female students; we were amazed that we were still the only males in the class. Devon sat between Brad and me. I reached across Devon and shot Brad with a rubber band.

"Nice shot, Jason!" Brad shouted.

The door opened and Profesora Babe walked into the room. She looked good. Her tight shirt and jeans provoked a usual elbow from Devon.

"Check out the babe today," Devon whispered.

"What a babe," I whispered back.

"She knows what she's doing," Devon said.

Brad picked up the rubber band from the floor. He aimed it at me. Profesora Babe stood in front of the classroom. Every student stopped talking and the room went silent. Profesora Babe took a breath and opened her mouth to say something. Brad shot the rubber band and it hit my left ear.

"Damn it, Brad!" I shouted instinctively.

"*Chicos!*" Profesora Babe shouted.

I felt my face flush with schoolboy fear. I sat perfectly upright. Brad turned his head toward the professor slowly. He hesitated and sat angelically.

"I need two volunteers to stand in front of the class," Profesora Babe said in Spanish.

Still, she knew no English.

I looked at Brad. Devon covered his mouth and suppressed a spurt of laughter.

"Jason and Brad," Profesora Babe said, "come here."

She motioned seductively with her index finger. We

walked slowly toward the classroom stage front.

"Give an impromptu speech about the reading from last night's homework," Profesora Babe said.

Brad gave me a look that said, *Oh no! I didn't read last night*. I started talking. I summarized the reading quickly. Brad meandered his way through a few details. We looked at Profesora Babe and she motioned with her eyes for us to return to our seats. Brad and I bumped knuckles, weaved through desks, and sat in our chairs.

Class ended. I tutored Chema's two boys in an hour, so I walked with Brad and Devon to the café. They went inside. I told them that I would meet them at the bar after I finished tutoring for the day.

I walked through downtown, passed the cathedral, and looked up at its bell tower. It was awe-inspiring. Every time. I cruised on *Calle Gascona*. As I neared the end of the road, I saw Fernando leaning against the doorway of *El Serpiente*. He saw me and waved.

"*Hermano*," Fernando said, "Where are you going?"

"To tutor English," I said.

"Until when?" he asked.

"About seven," I said.

"Come to *El Serpiente* when you finish," Fernando said. "And make sure that you bring the other *americanos* with you."

"Sounds good," I said. "Why?"

"You're in for a surprise," he said.

"Alright," I said, "I'll see you in a few hours then."

I waved and walked across the street. I wondered what Fernando's surprise could be. I thought about it during my walk and, before I knew it, I was in front of Chema's apartment building. The elevator rose and I exited and knocked on Chema's door. He opened it and stood in the doorway; his intimidating presence filled the entire door frame.

"Hello," Chema said with a thick accent.

A cheesy smile emerged under his mustache.

"*Hola*," I replied. "How are you?"

"I am good," Chema said. "And you?"

"*Estoy bien*," I said.

"Please, come inside," Chema said.

I followed him into the living room. Jorge and Paulo were sitting on the couch and they stood to greet me.

"What's up, guys?" I said in English.

"Hello," the boys said in unison.

The boys had grave expressions. Their body language told me that they didn't want to sit through an hour of English tutoring today; maybe they didn't want to be tutored at all. Jorge and Paulo wore khaki pants and red, collared shirts. I noticed wrinkles near the bottom of their shirts and assumed that the shirts had been tucked in all day. *Private school kids*, I thought.

"How was school today?" I asked Jorge.

"It was good," he replied.

"Where do you go to school?" I asked Paulo.

"*Santa Maria*," Paulo replied.

"Do you go there, too?" I asked Jorge.

"Yes," he said.

"*Santa Maria* is a very good school," Chema said. "It's Catholic."

"I attend Catholic school when I was your age," I said to the boys. "You have to tuck in your shirt all day, right?"

"Yes, we do," Jorge said.

Jorge and Paulo smiled.

"I hated tucking my shirt in," I said.

The boys laughed.

"I do, too," Paulo said.

The conversation flowed after the laughter occurred. I asked the boys about last night's Real Madrid game, which forced them to use the past tense. Jorge used the past tense well, but I had to correct Paulo frequently because he continued to speak in the present tense. I looked at the wall clock and realized that we had only fifteen minutes left in our session.

"Ronaldo kick the ball into the goal," Paulo said.

Jorge punched him in the arm.

"Kicked," Jorge said, "Ronaldo *kicked* the ball into the goal."

"Jorge!" Paulo shouted.

I laughed at the familiar older brother versus younger brother dynamic.

"Boys," I said, "do you know what American holiday it is today?"

"No," Jorge said.

Chema leaned his head closer and gave a curious expression.

"It's Thanksgiving," I said.

"What is Thanksgiving?" Paulo asked.

"It's my favorite holiday," I said. "Every family eats turkey, stuffing, mashed potatoes, and other delicious food. There's no school or work. It's a day dedicated to eating with family."

"And why do you do that?" Chema asked.

I explained the legend of the pilgrims' first interaction with

Native American tribes after landing on Plymouth Rock. I told them that the legend was fabricated and white settlers massacred an entire culture through violence and disease for financial gain and cultural pride. I didn't like the symbolism behind the day, but I loved the food and family time the day provided.

"Are you sad that you're not at home with your family?" Chema asked.

I tried to answer and I hesitated. My throat clenched as I fought oncoming tears.

"A little bit," I said.

The tutoring session ended. Chema paid me and I left. I tutored Maria in an hour, so I stopped at a kebab stand. I took my kebab to the plaza in front of the cathedral and sat on a short wall.

I wrapped a scarf around my neck and zipped my jacket to suppress the air's cold bite. I ate my kebab and looked at the cathedral. Its tower was lit and it looked impressive. I thought about my family. Right now, they were eating turkey, stuffing, and mashed potatoes and watching the Detroit Lions annual Thanksgiving football game and telling stories and yelling at each other. I wanted to be there. I sat alone in the cold plaza and finished my kebab.

Families crowded into restaurants near the plaza as I began my stroll to Maria's apartment on *Calle Uria*. Holiday lights illuminated major Oviedo streets. White lights made snowflake patterns across *Calle Uria*. The street, famous for its expensive-yet-fashionable clothing stores, bustled with female shoppers.

Even in layers of thick sweaters, every Spanish woman was attractive. When I reached Maria's building, I pressed her apartment's button and she buzzed me in. I emerged from the elevator and knocked on her door. I heard a light pattering of footsteps and Maria opened the door. I felt my nerves tingle.

"*Hola*," Maria said.

She wore black tights and a long sweatshirt. Her colorful, mismatched socks caught my attention. She wore her hair in a ponytail with no makeup. She didn't need it.

"Hey," I said. "How are you?"

"I'm good," Maria said.

I followed her into her living room. Maria's mother was watching television. She told us to go into Maria's room for the tutoring session.

Maria walked down the hallway and I followed. Her black tights exposed her form, but her thick sweatshirt allowed my mind to wander. An attractive paradox.

Maria closed her bedroom door. She sat on her bed and I sat in her desk chair.

"*No quiero hablar en ingles hoy*," Maria said.

"I'm tutoring you in English, so you have to speak it," I said.

Maria smiled. My heart fluttered.

"How was your day?" I asked.

"Good," she said. "How was your day?"

"Good," I said. "What did you do today?"

"I go to school," Maria said.

"You *went* to school," I said.

"Yes. I *went* to school," she said. "I ate dinner. I shopped. Oh, I bought a new shirt. Do you want to see it?"

"Yeah," I said. "Show me."

Maria walked to her dresser and pulled a red shirt from

her drawer. She took off her sweatshirt. My eyes widened as I saw her thin, low-cut tank top. She put on the red shirt and looked at me. She held out her arms and invited a response.

"That's a cool shirt," I said.

"You like it?" she asked.

"Yes, I do," I said.

Maria took off the red shirt and put it in her drawer. She walked to her bed. Her figure's appeal caught my attention and my eyes followed her movements. She picked up her sweatshirt and put it on.

We proceeded with our English conversation. I corrected her major missteps, but I decided to ignore minor grammar mistakes. Her body language flirted, but the conversation remained professional. The hour session ended. We exited her room and her mother paid me for my time. Maria walked me to the front door.

"What will you do tonight?" she asked.

"I'm going to *El Serpiente*," I said. "Fernando has a surprise Thanksgiving meal for us or something."

"What is Thanksgiving?" Maria asked.

"It's an American holiday," I said.

"For what?" she asked.

"For eating," I said. "Do you want to come with me?"

"But I don't know how to celebrate Thanksgiving," she said.

"You can learn," I said.

Maria's eyes looked toward the ceiling as she pondered her next move.

"Sure, I'll go," she said. "Let me find my shoes."

Maria told her mom that she was leaving and we walked down the stairs and left the building.

"Are you ready to hang out with my American friends?" I asked.

"*Hamblamos en espanol ahora*," Maria said.

"No way," I said. "You have to practice your English."

"Tutoring is over. Now it's your turn to practice," Maria said.

We walked into *El Serpiente* and Fernando greeted us. I saw Brad and Marcos at a table in the middle of the room. We sat by them.

"*Hola*, friends," Brad said.

"Devon and Roxy are on the way," Marcos said.

"Maria," Brad said, "are you ready for Thanksgiving dinner?"

Maria looked at me nervously. Brad's rapid speech intimidated her. I nodded encouragingly.

"Yes," Maria said.

"Alright!" Brad shouted.

Devon and Roxanne walked in a few minutes later and sat by us. Aside from a teenage couple at a corner table, we were the only people in *El Serpiente*. Fernando stood by our table.

"Everyone here?" Fernando asked.

"*Si, jefe*," I said.

"*Perfecto*," Fernando said.

He walked into the kitchen. Thirty seconds later, Fernando and Chef Carmen emerged. Fernando carried a platter of mashed potatoes and a platter of stuffing. Carmen carried a giant turkey.

Fernando's brother, Carlos, walked behind them and carried a platter of sweet potatoes and a gravy boat. The South Americans placed the food on our table. I closed my eyes and inhaled.

My mind whirled with thoughts of my grandma's kitchen. The smell produced euphoria. Brad shouted. I stood and clapped. Devon hugged Carmen and I shook Fernando's hand. The teenage couple in the corner looked curious; distain and envy crossed their faces.

"*Jefe*," Marcos said, "thank you so much."

"It was Carmen's idea," Fernando said.

"Thanks, Carmen!" Roxanne shouted.

"I'm just here to eat," Carlos said.

Everyone laughed.

"How much money do we owe you?" I whispered to Fernando.

He waved his hand and dismissed my question.

"Now," Fernando said, "you eat."

"You first," Brad said.

Fernando, Carmen, and Carlos sat with us. Everyone dug spoons into the various platters and piled the traditional Thanksgiving foods on their plates.

Carmen added spice to the stuffing. The gravy was spicy, too. Her South American culinary flare gave the food a distinct place in my culinary memory. No one spoke for five minutes. We simply ate.

After the food was gone, we thanked Fernando and Carmen again. We bought *cervezas* and tipped extravagantly.

"Maria, did you like Thanksgiving dinner?" Roxanne asked.

"Yes," Maria said. "It was very good."

Brad lifted his glass.

"To Fernando and Carmen!" Brad shouted.

We raised our glasses and shouted wildly. We ordered another round of *cervezas*. Brad finished his beer and stood to leave.

"The turkey made me tired," Brad said. "I'm out of here. I'll see you guys tomorrow."

"Yeah," Marcos said, "I'm going to leave, too. I need to go to sleep."

"*Adios.*"

Devon looked at Roxanne seductively.

"What do you think, Roxy?" Devon said.

"Should we leave?" Roxanne asked.

"Yeah," Devon said. "Jason, what's your plan?"

"I'll walk Maria to her house and cruise home," I said.

"Cool," Devon said, "I'll see you at home, then."

I gave Roxanne a hug and Devon and I bumped knuckles.

"Maria," Roxanne said, "I'll see you soon. You should go to the bars with us this weekend."

"Yes," Maria said, "that sounds fun."

Maria and I walked toward *Calle Uria*. She shivered from the cold. With my hands in my pockets, I held out my elbow. Maria linked her left arm with my right arm. Her warmth eliminated the chill.

The walk seemed infinite, but when we arrived at Maria's front door, the walk seemed too short. I did not want this moment to end. I felt completely enveloped in her.

"Well," I said, "thanks for coming to dinner with me. I hope you had fun."

"I had a lot of fun," Maria said.

"We weren't too crazy for you, were we?" I asked.

Maria laughed.

"No, you have nice friends," she said.

"I'll see you on Tuesday for another tutoring session," I said, "unless you want to come to the bar with my friends and me on Saturday."

"I do want to go to with you on Saturday," Maria said.

"I was hoping you did," I said.

Our arms remained linked. Maria took her keys from her jacket pocket, but didn't move toward the door. I looked at her for a few seconds and she returned my gaze. I removed my left hand from my pocket and tilted her chin upwards and kissed her. She returned the kiss.

Maria walked to the door, unlocked it, and turned to look at me with a smile. I smiled back. The door closed and she walked to the elevator. I turned and walked toward home. The thought of her kiss kept my mind occupied as I walked through the park. I heard competitive shouts form the illuminated soccer game. These games seemed endless.

CHAPTER 20

Devon and I walked into a café near *Parque de San Francisco*. We approached the counter and ordered two coffees. Steam billowed from the *café* until the barista poured milk into each cup. Marcos and Brad were sitting at table near the front window, so we sat with them.

Outside the window, families and teenagers walked from store to store in the bustling intersection at the center of Oviedo. Black clouds masked the low afternoon sun.

"Ouch, do I have a hangover," Marcos said.

"Yeah," Brad added, "last night kicked my ass."

"But you have to love these Saturday afternoon coffee cures," I said.

"Nothing like a little *café* to cure a headache," Devon said.

"I bet you have a bad headache, Dev," Brad said. "You were drunk last night."

"How could you tell?" Devon asked.

"You and Roxy danced for three straight hours," I said.

"And you only stopped to refill your drink," Brad said.

"And you wouldn't stop talking about Lionel Messi," Marcos said. "You said if Messi played American football for the Oregon Ducks, he would be the best college football player in history."

"And I stand by my statement," Devon said.

"Messi's too small," Brad said. "Linebackers would pulverize him."

"He's athletically superior to every college football player to ever play the game," Devon said. "He could evade linebackers."

"You're and idiot," Brad said.

"No way!" Marcos shouted. "Dev's right. Messi would weave between defensive schemes."

"Messi is the same size as I was in seventh grade," I said. "The first time a giant linebacker tackles him in the open field, he's done."

"But defenders slide-tackle Messi all the time in La Liga soccer games and he rises unfazed," Devon said. "He never fakes and injury like every other soccer player does."

"He is tough," I said, "I'll give you that."

Brad waved to our waiter and ordered four more coffees. We drank between our continued argument, paid, and left. We had no destination, so we cruised through the park. Streetlamps lined the paths and created an orange glow. Clouds and trees blocked the low sun and the park seemed dark. We passed an old man who walked alone. The old man clasped his hands behind his back and walked slowly as he absorbed life's aura.

Loud shouts echoed from the cement soccer court to our left. White lights illuminated the urban athletic area. We strolled toward the action. A large crowd surrounded the fence at *La Concha*. South Americans and Africans banged on the woven metal. Fans shouted in Portuguese, Spanish, and African dialects that I couldn't decipher. The African team on the cement looked focused. Sweat poured from their faces. The South American team passed the ball lazily, yet precisely; they were waiting for an opportunity for artistic glory.

I saw the Brazilian on *La Concha*. He wore his country's famous yellow jersey. I recognized Az on the African team. He was playing defense against a South American attacker. The South American dribbled down the left side of the pitch and Az stayed in rhythm with a strong backpedal. The South American juked right, left, right. As he juked left toward the fence, Az exploded forward and slammed the offender into the chain links. The crowd shouted wildly. Devon banged on the fence and Marcos whistled.

A familiar, tough African controlled the ball after Az's defensive check. He sprinted across midfield toward the opposing goal and the Brazilian dashed at an angle to meet him. The African ripped a right-footed shot before the Brazilian arrived. The ball tore through the air and passed the left sidebar and into the goal. The Africans in the crowd roared with support and the South Americans threw their hands into the air, signaling respectful defeat. Az hit the Brazilian on the back supportively. The Brazilian nodded. He strolled toward the sideline and wiped sweat from his face using the bottom of his shirt.

Three South American teammates grabbed their bags and left the field. The sweat on their clothes suggested hours of afternoon play. The crowd thinned, but avid fans stayed in case another game unfolded.

"Who's up next?" Az shouted.

The fans behind the fence remained in observatory positions, making no motion toward the cement of *La Concha*. The Brazilian and two South Americans sauntered to the center of the pitch. Az and an incomplete African squad met them.

"We need three more!" the tough African shouted to the crowd.

"Whatever," Marcos said, "I'm in."

Marcos removed his sweatshirt and jogged to the center of the field. Brad followed. Another South American jogged after them, so Devon and I posted against the fence and watched. I was too hungover to play, anyways.

"I think Marcos and Brad are on different teams," I said to Devon.

"Marcos is walking to the African's side," Devon said.

"Brad and the Brazilian are on the same team, then," I said.

"Looks like it," Devon said.

Both teams exchanged quick goals after kickoff.

"That Brazilian kid is quick," Devon said. "He shakes defenders left and right."

"He can control defenders as well as he can control the ball," I added. "He flicks the ball between his feet too easily."

"But the Africans are really tough," Devon said.

"Yeah, that dude in the red would be a mean lacrosse player," I said. "He rocked me last time we played. Strong elbows."

Marcos stole the ball from Brad and flicked it across the field to Az, who buried it in the back of the net with a well-placed header. Marcos taunted Brad. Brad strutted toward Marcos.

"That steal was B.S.," Brad said.

"I'll keep doing it all day," Marcos taunted.

The game was heated and Marcos and Brad fell into the trap of on-field temper. Marcos walked by Brad and pushed him lightly. Brad retaliated with a harder push. Marcos pushed back with full force, so Brad punched Marcos in the side of the head. Marcos stumbled backwards, regained his balance, and lunged at Brad with a three-punch combo. He landed one punch near Brad's eye. Brad and Marcos became entangled and continued to throw punches, most of which missed the target. Brad's overpowering strength brought Marcos to the ground.

Az scrambled to the ground and pick Brad up and pushed him to the fence. The Brazilian and the rest of the South American squad wrangled Marcos against the other fence. Brad and Marcos struggled to free themselves, but gradually regained their composure through heavy breathing. Az and the Brazilian met at the center of the court.

"*Fútbol* is a pure game," Az said. "We cannot have fighting like this."

"I agree," the Brazilian said. "Sportsmanship is the most important aspect of the game. We are artists and we must treat each other as such."

"We must preserve the purity of the game," Az said.

"Without purity, we cannot have art," the Brazilian said.

They paused.

"What should we do with these Wild West *americanos*?" Az shouted to the crowd around the fence.

The fence shook wildly as the crowd shouted. Az commanded respect from his African peers. The Brazilian commanded the same respect from his South American counterparts. The crowd quieted quickly as Marcos and Brad walked to the center of the court. Brad outstretched his hand to Marcos and Marcos shook it.

"Sorry, *hombre*," Brad said. "I got a little too into the game."

"Me too, man," Marcos said.

The verbal treaty had been signed, but thick tension remained on the field. Brad took the kickoff and passed it to the Brazilian, who passed it to a teammate, back to Brad, back to the Brazilian. His yellow jersey radiated. He juggled three times and back-heeled the ball around his defender. The Brazilian spun to the opposite side and received his own pass. He took two long dribbles, flicked the ball into the air with his left foot and kicked with his right.

"Goal!" Devon shouted.

"We have a tie ball game, folks," I said.

Game point. Brad possessed the ball near midfield. He dribbled right. The tough African in the red shirt charged. Brad lowered his shoulder and the African lowered his. They collided with stopping force. Both men stood their ground, but the ball continued to roll. A South American controlled it and passed across the cement to the Brazilian. In a one-on-one with the goalie, the Brazilian stepped over the ball with alternating feet. The goalie focused on the mesmerizing footwork and the ball snuck through his legs and into the goal. Devon and I cheered along with the few fans that still remained around *La Concha.*

The late fall sun cowered behind the clouds and beneath the horizon. Evening approached. The competitors filtered to the other side of the fence as the afternoon soccer jamboree ended.

"Good hustle," Devon said, as Marcos and Brad walked toward us.

"Thanks," Brad said.

"Hey, Az!" Marcos shouted.

Az and the red-shirted African strolled our direction.

"Good game," Marcos said.

"Thanks," Az said.

The Brazilian wandered our way. He shook hands with Az and the tough guy, and then with Brad and Marcos.

"Are you going to watch *El Clasico* tonight?" the Brazilian asked.

"*Sí*," I said, "we're going to *El Serpiente* in a few hours."

"You should meet us there," Brad said.

"I will," the Brazilian said.

"You too, Az," Devon said.

"I have to work tonight," Az said, "but I'll be around."

We fanned in different directions. Devon and I strolled to a market after we left Brad and Marcos. I bought some orange juice and a baguette. The bread was a few hours old and a bit crunchy, but still delicious.

I showered at our apartment. Devon and I left around 8:00 and walked to *El Serpiente*. The game between FC Barcelona and Real Madrid started at 10:00, but we wanted to claim a prime game-watching table and order a few drinks to prepare for the event.

We strolled through our Pumarin neighborhood. The grocery store near our apartment building was closing and two bars were opening. It was a transitional period in the night. Early evening was ending, but nightlife began to emerge.

Devon and I climbed the staircase to the tunnel and exited

the neighborhood. The orange glow from the streetlights faded as we climbed. Two South American men leaned against the tunnel wall and watched us attentively as we summited the stairs.

"Do you smell that?" Devon asked.

"Yeah," I replied, followed by a slight giggle.

"Smoking a little *mota* in the tunnel," Devon said. "Classic."

We passed the two men. The taller man watched us as smoke bellowed from his pinched fingers, which he hid slightly behind his leg. Devon and I entered the open, well-lit courtyard near *La Universidad* and cruised until we reached *Calle Gascona*. At the top of the cobblestone road, I saw Fernando's brother, Carlos, posted against the wall outside of his restaurant. We waved and turned into *El Serpiente*.

"*De puta madre, tíos!*" Fernando shouted to us from behind the bar.

"*Que tal, jefe,*" Devon said.

I shook Fernando's hand and he led us to a table in front of the television. Soccer fans filled half of the tables in the bar and we felt lucky to acquire a spot in front of the action.

"*Cuantas sillas?*" Fernando asked.

"Four more chairs, *por favor,*" I said.

Devon helped Fernando shift extra chairs to our table.

Marcos and Brad entered the bar a few minutes later and sat with us. Roxanne followed, along with two girls from our study abroad group. Fernando brought beers to our table and added a complimentary plate of *patatas fritas*. With five minutes until game time, the Brazilian from *La Concha* joined our table.

"Place your bets," Fernando said to us.

I placed five Euros on the table and hoped for a Barcelona victory. Devon did the same. Brad, Marcos, and Roxanne bet on a Barcelona victory, while did Fernando and his brother bet big for a Real Madrid win.

Fernando increased the volume on the speaker system so everyone could hear the broadcasters. Kick-off began and the bar crowd cheered.

Barcelona pressed Real Madrid. Ten minutes into the game, Iniesta passed the ball through four Madrid defenders and Barcelona's Xavi received it. Xavi flipped the ball to shoulder height; Real Madrid's goalie flinched. The ball dropped to Xavi's other foot and he chipped the ball above the over-committed goalie. The ball hit the back of the net.

"GOAL!" Devon shouted to the passing Fernando.

Fernando dropped his head and returned to his position behind the bar and began to sulk. I high-fived the Brazilian, who wore his teal Barcelona jersey in support. I took a drink of my Estrella Damm and looked toward the entrance. I saw Anna enter. My heart pounded exponentially. She took three steps into *El Serpeinte* and I raised my hand to wave, and then I saw a familiar Spaniard enter. Alfonso strolled behind Anna and he grabbed her hand. Anna saw my suppressed wave and she led Alfonso to our table. Anna chose a chair across the table from me. Alfonso sat next to her, with Marcos to his left.

"You missed the first goal," I said to Anna.

"*No pasa nada,*" Alfonso said, "Real Madrid will score four more goals. Barcelona will lose."

"No way, *hombre,*" Brad shouted form across the table. "This year's Barcelona team is the best *equipo* in history."

"You're wrong," Alfonso said. "Cristano Ronaldo is the

best player in the world; therefore, *mi equipo, Real Madrid,* is the best team in the world."

"Didn't Messi win the Golden Boot Award this year because he was the best player in the world?" I suggested.

"He did, indeed, Jason," Devon said.

"But Ronaldo should have won," Alfonso said.

"*Tío,*" Fernando said as he brought our table another round of *cervezas*, "The Golden Boot Award goes to the best player in the world. I like Real Madrid, but Messi is the best and most artistic *en todo el mundo.*"

"Messi is an immigrant into my country," Alfonso said. "He belongs back in Argentina."

"I am an immigrant to your country," Fernando said. "Where do I belong?"

"*De dónde eres?*" Alfonso asked.

"I'm from Venezuela," Fernando stated.

"Then that is where you belong," Alfoso said.

The Brazilian lifted his right eyebrow and looked toward Alfonso. In his Messi jersey, the Brazilian lifted his pint glass and drank. He set the glass on the table emphatically; his gaze returned to the broadcast.

David Villa from Barcelona dribbled down the left side of the field. One defender marked him and another approached rapidly. Villa shot the ball without an accurate angle. Real Madrid's goalie stretched his leg forward and the ball ricocheted from it. Barcelona's Pedro leapt and punted the ball into the goal. The crowd cheered wildly as the game clock ticked *21:00.*

The mass continued to grow in *El Serpiente.* Halftime occurred and Fernando brought another round of beer to the table. The group near the door separated and two African men entered the bar. One carried two fistfuls of bootlegged videos. I recognized the other African.

"Az!" I shouted.

Marcos looked toward the door and waved to Az. Both Africans walked in our direction. As they stepped closer to me, I recognized the second African as the tough soccer player from *La Concha*. Az sat on the edge of an opposing booth bench. His sales partner sat in the last empty chair at our table.

"*Quieres una cerveza?*" Brad asked Az.

"No, thank you," Az replied. "I am Muslim. I do not drink alcohol."

"Fair enough," Brad said.

"Respect for your self-discipline, *hombre*," I said.

"How's your night going?" Marcos asked the tough African.

"Good," he said, "Until I saw this Brazilian."

The African patted the Brazilian on the back in good-natured respect. The Brazilian looked toward them and he laughed. He said something in Portuguese. Fernando heard the comment as he passed our table and he smiled.

"Why do you like Barcelona?" the Brazilian asked me in Spanish.

"I didn't know much about *fútbol* until recently," I said. "I followed Barcelona because I had heard of them. I went to a game at Camp Nou. Now, I'm hooked."

"That's a good reason," the Brazilian said.

"What about your reason?" I said.

"My reason?" the Brazilian said. "I lived in an orphanage in Rio when I was a kid. We had a television and Barcelona played games on the television. I studied their movements and I think that I began to play like them."

"But you're artistic with the ball," I said. "That's Brazilian style."

"But my strategy comes from Barcelona's system," the Brazilian said.

A loud shout came from the middle of the bar as halftime ended and the second half began. A few minutes passed on the game clock. I felt a tap on my shoulder. I turned.

"*Hola, Jason,*" Maria said to me.

"Maria, how are you?" I asked.

"I'm good," she said. "I missed the first half of the game because I was watching my cousin's *fútbol* game."

Well," I said, "sit with us."

"*Barcelona dribbles down the left sideline,*" the announcer said in Spanish.

Devon grabbed an empty chair from the group behind us. Messi possessed the ball and sprinted through a defender and neared the top of the 18-yard box. Devon slid the chair next to mine. Messi kicked a slick through-ball to David Villa. Maria sat and placed her hand on my leg lightly. Villa vaulted the ball with his right foot and it hit the back of the net with force.

"That's Messi's second assist of the game," Az said quietly.

"What did you say, African?" Aflonso said.

"That was Messi's second assist of the game!" Az shouted.

"Messi is a lowlife, South American immigrant *puta,*" Alfonso shouted.

The Brazilian raised an eyebrow and stared at Alfonso. Fernando was serving at a table near ours and he glanced at Alfonso also. Fernando shook his head. Az puffed his chest and pointed at Alfonso.

"It doesn't matter if he's an immigrant or not," Az said. "He plays *fútbol*. And he's the best."

Messi possessed the ball at midfield. He launched it through three Real Madrid defenders. David Villa received the ball and kicked the ball hard and into the goal.

"Messi's third assist!" Az shouted.

Fernando brought another round of Estrella Damm to our table. He slammed Alfonso's beer onto the table in front of him.

"That lowlife South American immigrant is playing real well in *El Clasico* right now," Fernando said to Alfonso.

The game clock hit *60:00*.

"At least Messi isn't African," Alfonso shouted.

"*Que*?" Az said.

The tough African stood slowly.

"And what is wrong with being African?" Az asked.

"Oh, quiet down, African," Alfonso shouted. "You don't even drink. Why are you in a bar?"

"Alfonso, stop," Anna said. "You've had too much to drink."

"Don't tell me to stop, Anna," Alfonso said. "Look, African. You're in my country, so get out."

"You don't control me," Az said. "I'm in Spain to work hard independently and I'm in the bar to watch good *fútbol*."

"What does an African know about good *fútbol*," Alfonso said.

"*Hombre*," Brad said to Alfonso. "Chill."

"Alfonzo," I said, "Don't talk like that at our table. We're here to have some fun, but you're crossing the line."

"Shut up, Americans," Alfonso said. "You're ignorant. And what do you know about crossing the line? You used to enslave Africans."

"Clearly that's in the past," Devon said. "So shut the hell up."

"You can't talk to me like that, *americano*," Alfonso said. "You should leave Spain, in my opinion."

Anna looked at Alfonso with a menacing stare. She stood and punched him swiftly in the arm and she left *El Serpeinte*. With one minute remaining in *El Clasico*, Barcelona crossed the ball into the 18-yard box.

"You messed up, *hombre*," Devon said to Alfonso.

David Villa dribbled through two defenders and flicked the ball into the air and into the goal.

Embarrassed, Alfonso stood and followed Anna's path out the door. Az moved and sat in Alfonso's chair.

"Thanks for the assist," Az said to Devon.

"*No pasa nada*," Devon said.

"You know that Alfonso is rich. He'll come after you," the Brazilian said to me.

"*Es verdad*," the tough African said. "Alfonso is high-ranking."

"Alfonso's a punk," Marcos said. "Let him come after us."

The game ended. Barcelona scored five goals and Real Madrid did not score, which ensured us free drinks and a small payout from our earlier bets. We thanked Fernando and everyone gathered outside on the cobblestone. Brad and Marcos walked toward the Cathedral on their way home. Devon strolled down *Calle Gascona* with Roxanne. The Brazilian walked with Az and the tough African toward Pumarin.

"Dev!" I shouted. "Hold up."

Maria and I jogged to Devon and Roxanne.

"I'm going to walk Maria home, so we're cruising with you two," I said.

"Sounds like fun," Roxanne said.

We strolled through the park. Orange glow from the streetlamps lined the maze of pathways. I saw the lights from *La Concha* above the trees.

"Dude," Devon said, "Do you think Alfonso will come after us?"

"No," I said. "At least, I hope not."

CHAPTER 21

I walked into the market below our apartment and bought a small loaf of bread and a bottle of orange juice. I thanked the cashier lazily and lumbered onto the sidewalk. Birds chirped as the Wednesday morning sky lightened progressively.

I saw an old woman walking her terrier across the street; aside from her, I felt like I was the only person awake in the entire city of Oviedo.

After twenty minutes of slow strolling, I arrived at Maria's apartment building. I pressed the button and Maria's voice spoke through the call box.

"*Quien es?*" she asked.

"*Soy Jason.*" I said.

I heard a click and the building's front door opened. I looked at the numerical lights above the elevator door, which told me that the elevator was on the top floor, so I took the stairs.

When I reached her floor, I noticed that her front door

was open, so I pressed against it lightly and poked my head into her apartment.

"*Hola?*" I said.

"Jason, come in," Maria said.

I walked into her living room and looked around, but I couldn't see her. I continued into the kitchen expecting to see a family member drinking coffee, but I saw no one. I walked down the hallway and saw Maria's bedroom light shining through the crack in her door. I knocked lightly.

"Come in," Maria said.

Excited, yet uncomfortable, I pushed the door and walked into her room. She was sitting on the edge of her bed in tights and a sweatshirt.

Though she looked freshly risen from bed, she looked beautiful. I sat in her desk chair and faced her.

"Alright, let's start," I said.

"*Pero tenemos tres minutos antes de nuestra lección,*" Maria whined playfully.

"Well, we can end our lesson three minutes early," I said. "I'm going to be late to class as it is."

I made a conscious effort to remain as professional as possible during our hour-long tutoring session. I pretended like I was there to improve her English-speaking abilities, but I was flirting as hard as I could.

The language barrier between us created an undeniable tension; I could feel it.

We bantered back and forth. I laughed at her when she said something improperly, which made her smile and fire at me with quick remarks in Spanish. I wanted to sit next to her on the bed, but the fact that I was getting paid to tutor her kept me locked in the desk chair.

Soon enough, the hour session finished and Maria began to speak Spanish with a tone of relief, which forced me to switch my thinking pattern back to Spanish. Maria paid me the hourly rate and I stood to leave.

"What's your plan for the rest of the day?" I asked in Spanish.

"I'm going to a biology class in two hours," Maria said. "And after that, I'm going to the *espicha*."

"The what?" I asked.

"The *espicha*." Maria said.

I looked at her blankly.

"You know, the *espicha*." Maria said again.

"What's an *espicha*?" I asked.

"Everybody is going!" she shouted. "It's the fundraiser for the university's biology department. It starts this afternoon and it will go all night. It's at Oviedo's professional *futbol* stadium."

"What do people do at an *espicha*?" I asked.

"Drink, of course!" she shouted again. "The biology department sells *sangria* and *sidra*, but everybody brings their own drinks also. People play games and *futbol* and have fun. Bring all of your friends, please!"

"Sounds like a good time," I said. "We'll be there."

"Come find me when you arrive," Maria said. "I'm selling *sidra* for two hours, but after that, I want to be with you."

Maria smiled softly and I felt my face blush. I waved as I walked out the door.

I pressed the elevator button and paced impatiently. The doors slid open and I melted inside the elevator. I hopped twice with childlike excitement, then leaned against the back wall.

I daydreamed about kissing Maria at the *espicha*. The elevator stopped and shocked me, so I fluttered quickly through the doors and into the lobby and onto the street. I passed a pharmacy and the clock read *8:20*. My grammar class started in ten minutes, so I started to sprint toward the university. Maria's invitation to this *espicha* filled me with endless energy and I ran the whole route to class.

I was three minutes late when I entered the classroom. I was sweating slightly and breathing hard. Profesora Babe looked at me with one eyebrow raised and arms crossed. I lowered my head and hurried to my seat.

"Jason, you're late," Profesora Babe said in Spanish. "What is the answer to question three on the board?"

"Sorry, Profesora," I said.

I replied to the question on the board correctly, somehow. Profesora Babe flashed a sly smile in my direction, then resumed her stern teacher's expression.

I looked at the clock and one minute had passed. Time was dragging and I needed time to move faster. All I could think about was the *espicha*.

I envisioned twenty university students and their parents sipping *sangria* in business casual attire while engaged in discussions about the future of the university while enjoying casual soccer ball passes. This seemed like an elegant engagement.

My daydream ended and I looked at the clock, which told me that another ten minutes passed. Time was taking too long, so I faked a coughing attack and stood with my water bottle in hand and walked into the hallway.

I filled my water bottle and stepped outside onto the staircase to get some fresh air. I let three minutes pass before

I returned to class to give Profesora Babe the idea that my break was necessary.

Finally, class ended after an excruciating lesson of the present-perfect tense. I walked outside with Devon and Brad. We saw Marcos and Roxanne kicking a soccer ball around in front of the stairway, so we walked toward them.

"What's up, boys?" Roxanne said.

"Just excited to be out of class on this beautiful morning," I said.

"You're so optimistic," Roxanne said.

"Isn't he, though?" Devon added.

Marcos kicked the ball to Devon. He messed around with the ball at his feet and passed it to Brad, who picked it up and dribbled it like a basketball.

"Do you guys have plans this afternoon?" I asked.

"Jason, we never have plans," Marcos said.

"Cool," I said. "I was tutoring Maria this morning and…"

"How'd it go, you love machine?" Roxanne asked.

"I just tutored her like I was supposed to do," I said.

"Yeah, I bet you tutored her," Marcos said with an exaggerated wink.

Everyone laughed and prodded with intrusive questions. I felt embarrassed and defensive, but I feigned comfortbility.

"Guys," I interrupted, "nothing happened. Anyways, Maria invited us to this event called an *espicha*."

"What the hell is that?" Marcos asked.

"It's some function that the university's biology department is having this afternoon at the soccer stadium. They're selling *sangria* and *sidra* and people play games to raise money for the department. She said a lot of people go."

"That sounds like an unbeatable cultural experience,"

Devon said. "What do we wear to a Spanish college fundraiser?"

o   o   o

We strolled of the bus at the Oviedo stadium bus stop. The high afternoon sun caused me to sweat in my tank top and khaki shorts. Thankfully, my backwards hat kept the sun off my neck.

I carried a liter of San Miguel in one hand. Devon carried a backpack with sandwiches, while Brad and Marcos each carried six-packs of Estrella Damm. Maria did tell us to bring extra drinks, after all.

The stadium was situated in a natural bowl. As we neared the top of the bowl, we stopped in awe. Thousands of students filled the parking lot of the soccer stadium. The crowd looked like a rock concert mixed with an Autzen Stadium football game tailgate party.

We charged forward through the crowd. I smelled pot smoke and I saw a beer bong before we took ten steps into the mass of students.

"Well, it looks like college is the same everywhere," Brad said.

We pushed our way through the crowd until I saw a sign that read: *Sangria y Sidra*. I lead our group toward the booth. I expected to see a long line, but we strolled to the booth immediately. I saw two unfamiliar girls at the booth, so I walked toward them. Slight panic filled my emotional cartridge. I hoped I didn't miss Maria.

"*Donde esta Maria?*" I asked the taller of the two girls.

"*Esta alli,*" she said, pointing to her left. "Are you Jason?"

"I am," I said, a little thrown off.

"We heard you were coming," she said with a giggle.

I smiled awkwardly and walked to Maria and froze with nerves.

"Hi Jason!" Maria shouted.

She wrapped her arms around me and squeezed. I reciprocated. I felt my heart flutter. I turned and saw my friends staring directly at us.

"That was precious," Marcos said.

"Shut up, dude!" I whispered.

"Maria, how are you?" Roxanne asked.

"I am good," Maria said. "What do you think of the *espicha*?"

"It's unreal," Roxanne said. "There are so many people here."

"There are more people here than there were for the chemistry department's *espicha* last month," Maria said. "We're happy about that."

Maria smiled mischievously.

"The chemistry department must be your rivals," I said.

"Exactly," she said.

The girls at the booth told Maria to go with us, so she took us to the middle of the *espicha* crowd. I crack the top of my San Miguel and took a drink. I gave the bottle to Maria and she did the same. Maria sat on the ground and motioned for us to join, so we all sat cross-legged on the cement parking lot.

Devon dispersed beer bottles to our group and produced a deck of cards from his pocket. We played a Spanish drinking game that Maria suggested. Naturally, she won because my American friends and I didn't know the rules. We talked and laughed and learned about the *espicha* crowd from Maria.

Some Spanish girls were playing with a soccer ball near us. Brad and Marcos stood and approached the girls and, soon enough, they were playing soccer as well. Devon and Roxanne stood to roam the *espicha* grounds, but told us that they would return. I was excited to have alone time with Maria at such a public event. My San Miguel bottle was almost gone and my Spanish was getting more fluid, though Maria laughed as I spoke to her.

"Maybe you need a Spanish tutor more than I need and English tutor," she said.

"My Spanish is perfect and I don't make mistakes," I joked.

We laughed and continued to talk for what seemed like an hour. The sun was beginning to set behind the stadium. I noticed the crowd thinning. Brad and Marcos returned and sat next to us.

"These two girls want Brad and I to leave and go to a bar with them," Marcos said.

"Do it," I said.

"I hate to leave you here though, bro," Brad said.

"Trust me," I said. "I'm fine."

"I figured you were," Marcos said. "*Adios.*"

Brad and Marcos jogged through the crowd to their new *amigas* and they disappeared. Roxanne and Devon emerged through the crowd immediately afterwards. They stood next to us, implying their intentions before they spoke.

"Yo, Jason," Devon said. "I think Roxy and I are going to take off. I'm not feeling too well. I drank a lot of *sangria* from the booth and I haven't had any water all day and it's so hot. We're going to jump in a taxi and go back to our apartment.

You want to roll with us?"

"I'm going to hang out at the *espicha* a little longer," I said. "But I'll see you when I get home, man."

"Alright dude," Devon said. "Maria, thank you for inviting us to this. I had fun."

"You're welcome, *amigos*," Maria said. "Have a safe trip home."

Devon and I bumped knuckles. He and Roxanne turned and walked into the crowd. I felt a sudden wave of nervousness rise in my spine. I was sitting alone with Maria on the other side of town and I was unsure of she wanted me there. *Should I have left with Devon?*

"I'm glad you decided to stay," Maria said.

I smiled.

"Me too," I said.

I leaned over, put my arm around her, and kissed her. The kiss filled me with happiness and emotion and another feel that terrified me: attachment. The sun was fully set behind the stadium.

"It looks like everyone is leaving," I said.

"Let's walk home," Maria said.

"Isn't that far?" I asked.

"Yes," Maria said, "but we can walk together."

She grabbed my hand and intertwined my fingers through hers. We walked toward the *El Cristo* statue, which was barely visible as the sky transitioned form light to dark. Hundreds of people flocked around us, but I only noticed Maria next to me.

As we neared her neighborhood, I realized that I didn't want to let go of her hand. I pulled her close and kissed her again.

"Maria," I said. "I'm leaving for Portugal next week with Jason and Roxy. I'll be there for a few days. Can you please come with us?"

"I want to, Jason," Maria said, "but I have to work at the café."

"Just run away with us for a few days," I said.

"I wish I could, but my parents would kill me," Maria said.

I walked her to her apartment building's front door and opened it for her.

"I'm leaving for the States in a few weeks, Maria," I said.

"Can you please stay in Oviedo?" she asked.

"I want to," I said, "but my parents would kill me if I didn't come home."

I looked into her eyes longingly, wishing for and impossible future. I kissed her one more time and turned and walked home feeling helpless. Aside from stars, the sky was completely dark. I saw *El Cristo* shining on top of a shadowy Mount Naranco as I walked home.

CHAPTER 22

Our train tore through the Spanish countryside. I stared through the window and watched the mid-Iberian landscape as it rushed and blurred. It looked arid. Roxanne and Devon sat across from me in our four-seat train cabin. The seat next to me was empty.

"Too bad Maria couldn't join us," Roxanne said.

"Yeah," said Devon. "Now you're the third wheel."

"Shut up, dude," I said.

"I'm just playing with you, man."

I know, I thought, *but I actually am the third wheel.*

I returned to my vigilant staring contest with the window. My eyes felt heavy, so I let them droop. When I awoke, darkness had extinguished my countryside view. I looked at the clock in the train cabin. *2:00.*

I heard a resonant *pop* from the floor. I flinched from my post-nap daze.

"*Vino?*" Roxanne said. She gave me a clear plastic cup with red wine. Devon raised his cup and I raised mine in response.

"Good morning, sunshine," Devon said to me.

"Where are we?" I grumbled.

"I think we're near the Portuguese border," Roxanne said, "but I'm not sure."

"What time do we get to Lisbon?" Devon asked.

"About six in the morning," Roxanne said.

"Wait," Devon said. "This is a ten-hour train ride?"

"I guess it is," Roxanne said.

"What am I supposed to do for *diez horas*?" Devon bellowed.

Roxanne raised the wine bottle above her head.

"Good call."

We finished the bottle of wine.

o   o   o

"*Estaremos en Lisboa en diez minutos*," the conductor said over the loudspeaker.

I flinched upwards. I punched Devon in the leg and he awoke. Our train pulled into the station and I grabbed my backpack and exited onto the platform. Roxanne saw a bus route map and concluded that the bus we needed would arrive in 32 minutes. She saw a café across the street, so we cruised that direction.

"I need a coffee if I'm going to make it through the day," Devon said.

"Yeah," I said, "We didn't sleep much last night."

After coffee, we rode the bus to our hostel in the center of town. Bright orange and yellow buildings contrasted with the overcast sky. People bustled into alleyway storefronts. Restaurant tables lined the center of wide streets, but they were empty. Corner *cafés* developed lively atmospheres. We entered our hostel lobby and checked in and walked to room 215. Devon opened the door and he tip-toed into the unlit room. Two people slept in two beds. One snored.

Roxanne, Devon, and I claimed the remaining three beds. I changed my shirt and brushed my teeth and threw my backpack into my locker. We left the hostel with aspirations to conquer Lisbon.

We walked down a major road with alleyways intersecting each building. Lisbon had a raw, urban feel. It felt distinctly Iberian with less European influence than Spain. The streets were dirty and the building fronts looked windswept. Graffiti decorated every alleyway wall. The air smelled urban and tasted gritty. I loved it.

We strolled by an elevator designed by the Eiffel Tower architect, and then we saw a bar, so we ventured toward it. Devon ordered three beers and we sat outside at a plaza table. We were silent for minutes.

"I don't want to go back to the States," I said.

"Me neither, *hombre*," Devon said.

"Wouldn't it be nice if we could just...stay," Roxanne said.

"I'm going to do it," I said.

"Good plan," Devon said.

"No, I'm serious," I said. "I'm going to stay in Europe."

"And not go back to Oregon?" Roxanne said.

"Roxy, I think he's serious," Devon stated.

"I am serious."

We paid for our beers and continued the stroll. The road's incline increased.

"The road forks up ahead. Should we turn left or right?"

Devon asked.

"I don't know," I said.

"Flip a coin," Roxanne suggested.

I pulled a Euro coin from my pocket and flipped it.

"Heads is left; tails is right," I said.

I flipped the coin and it landed face-up.

"Heads," Devon said. "We go left. No deliberation."

We turned left at a major thoroughfare and faced a daunting hill with a castle at its peak.

"We're going to a castle!" Roxanne shouted.

As we neared the incline's peak, we entered a stone archway. The cobblestone path to the castle entrance was weathered and dark. We followed the path. I stubbed my toe on an errant stone and Roxanne laughed at me. The path led us to an open courtyard. I saw a stone wall with a medieval cannon near the edge of a cliff that pointed toward the city. I strolled to it and perceived the view of Lisbon.

"You look like a pirate, Jason," Roxanne said.

"I am a pirate," I replied.

"For real man," Devon added. "One leg perched on the cannon. Your beard is getting thick, too."

"I bet Portugal had fleets of pirates when this castle was alive," I said.

"Magellan sailed from Portugal," Roxanne said.

"Or was it De Gamma?" Devon asked.

"I don't know," Roxanne said.

"Magellan and De Gamma were both pirates," I said.

We dashed around the castle grounds and my imagination exploded. I felt like a seven-year-old kid.

We ran to the tallest tower. Devon and I acted like medieval archers and mimicked a castle defense strategy and shot invisible arrows at imaginary attackers below the fort. Roxanne found two stick and threw one to me. A swordfight ensued.

"I win!" Roxanne shouted as she jabbed my stomach with her branch.

"You won the battle," I said, "but the war isn't over."

"Watch your back, Roxy," Devon added.

We strolled through the castle until we saw every corner of the grounds. We needed to eat, so we exited the castle and followed the cobblestone road. We turned left because Roxanne saw a row of brightly colored houses that overlooked the water. She sat on a 50-foot ledge and Devon took a picture.

The cobblestone road led us to a small plaza, which contained five offshoot roads and alleyways in every direction. An old Indian man stood against the doorway of his fruit shop. He was the only person in sight. He wore a turban and white and tan robes. His face was narrow and pointed. I focused on the red dot on his forehead. He had thick eyebrows that gave his face a devious, yet wise demeanor. I looked left and saw an alleyway with stairs that bent around the corner and underneath a building.

"I bet these stairs will take us down to the beach," Roxanne suggested.

"*Vamos*, then," Devon said.

I moved toward the stairs and placed my right foot on the first step. Graffiti covered every inch of the walls that elevated five stories above our heads. I heard a short whistle and turned. The old Indian man was staring at us intently.

"*Ten cuidad*," he said. *Be careful.*

"*Porque?*" I asked.

The man touched his left eye to signify caution, and then retreated into his shop. Devon and I looked at each other with wide eyes. A wave of alertness overcame my body. I walked across the plaza slowly and entered the man's fruit shop. I looked around and saw a few fruit displays with listed prices, but I didn't see the man.

"Hello?" I said. "*Señor?*" My voice quivered as I spoke again.

I heard a noise in the hallway behind the counter, so I waited. Devon popped his head into the doorway.

"Come on, man," Devon whispered. "Let's get out of here."

I exited the store and we proceeded down the alley staircase with hesitant steps. I counted twenty steps in front of me before the path turned sharply to the right into a shadowed tunnel. I looked at the walls and the graffiti looked ominous.

"Jason," Roxanne said, "we don't have to go to the beach."

"Let's see where this path takes us," Devon said.

We entered the tunnel. I scanned the area expecting to see an entire gang of thieves and murderers, but I only saw a light at the end of the tunnel, which led to more stairs. We strolled through the tunnel with ease and I breathed deeply when we emerged. I descended a few steps and saw another short tunnel and, through that, I saw the beach. Tall apartment buildings surrounded us and the two tunnel openings we the only pathways.

"*Americanos?*" said a Portuguese voice from the corner.

I spun to face the voice. A short man in a hooded sweatshirt walked slowly toward us. I noticed a jagged tattoo on his neck.

"We're from Spain," Devon said in Spanish.

"In Lisbon on vacation, then?" the man said. He took to slow steps closer to us.

"Yeah" I said. I puffed my chest instinctively.

"Give me your money," the man said.

Devon and I glanced at Roxanne. She moved behind us. I looked at Devon and he shrugged his shoulders.

"We don't have any," Devon said.

"Yes you do," the man said. "I see your wallets in your pockets."

The Portuguese man pulled a small knife from his pocket and held it casually.

"Buzz off," Devon said.

"Go home, *hombre*," Roxanne added.

The man focused his eyes on Devon and stepped closer to him.

"Give me your money, *hombre*," the man said.

"Take it from me," Devon said.

The man quickened his pace toward Devon and gripped his knife purposefully. I took two hard steps toward the man and punched him in the left eye as hard as I could. He dropped the knife and fell and clutched his face.

Devon, Roxanne, and I sprinted through the declining tunnel entrance and onto the boardwalk by the beach. My heart pounded. I felt adrenaline course through my body and propel my escape.

We dashed to the main road and burst through our hostel door. Devon unlocked our room and Roxanne slammed the door. I sat on the floor and breathed heavily. We sat in silence for what seemed like an eternity.

"What the hell!" Roxanne shouted.

"Is everything alright?" said an Irish man from the top bunk.

Devon and I flinched when the unexpected roommate spoke.

"We're fine," Roxanne said.

"Good," the Irish man said.

He hopped from his bed to floor. He was as tall as Roxanne and he had a blonde mohawk. His beard stubble and stout stature gave him the appearance of a young rugby player.

"My name's Tom O'Leary," he said.

Devon stood and shook his hand.

"I'm Devon," he said. "This is Jason and Roxy. We're from the States."

"Ah, the States," Tom said. "What brings you to Lisbon?"

"We're studying abroad in Spain," Roxanne said. "We decided to check out Portugal for the weekend."

"What brings you here?" I asked.

"My television show finished filming for the season, so I took my money and decided to travel solo around Europe for a while," Tom said.

"Your television show?" Devon said.

"My mates and I have a comedy television show in Dublin," Tom said. "It's a good time."

"I bet it is!" I exclaimed.

"You three look a bit worn out," Tom said.

"You could say that," Devon said.

"Thankfully, I know a traditional Irish cure for exhaustion," Tom said.

"What is it?" Roxanne asked.

"A pint, of course," Tom said. "Let's see what the bar downstairs has to offer."

"Why not," I said.

We walked to the hostel entrance, which doubled as a bar. Roxanne and Devon sat on a couch by a table and I joined Tom. We sat on swiveling barstools near the center of the bar. The open bar space allowed us to see the front door of the hostel through a red glow that came from lights beneath the visible liquor collection.

"What are we drinking?" Tom asked.

"Estrella Damm?" I suggested.

"Never had it," he said. "Bartender, can we have four pints of Estrella Damm please?"

In seconds, four pints appeared in front of us.

"I'll get the first round," I offered.

"Put your money away," Tom said. "I'm buying drinks all night. I can't spend all this television money by myself, can I?"

I thanked him profusely and we carried the *cervezas* to the table. We drank our pints and replayed our day's adventure for Tom. He told us about his comedy show and life in Dublin. We ordered another round. A decent-looking blonde girl walked into the hostel lobby. Tom shouted to her and waved her to our table.

"This is Pauline," Tom said. "She's our other roommate."

"Nice to meet you," Pauline said with a thick German accent.

"How long have you been in Lisbon?" Roxanne asked, looking a bit relieved to have another female presence in the group.

"I arrived late last night," Pauline said. "I checked into the hostel and slept until this afternoon."

"She woke up as I was leaving for a city tour," Tom said. "Where are you from, anyways?"

"Munich," Pauline said.

"I've been there!" I shouted.

"Have you?" Pauline said. "When?"

"For Oktoberfest in September," I said.

"And what did you think?" she asked.

"It was the most amazing festival in world," I said.

"Tell her about your hangover," Devon added.

Pauline laughed. Tom high-fived me and stood to order a pint for Pauline.

We discussed the World Cup from the past summer and Pauline expressed anguish over German's defeat. Tom admitted Ireland's average status in the international *fútbol* world, while I remained hopeful that the U.S. would win a championship in the next two decades.

The sun set early, which drew young tourists into the hostel bar. At the table next to us sat a group of Italians: four attractive women and three round men. They appeared to be close enough to our age. One man walked to the bar and returned with seven shots of brown liquor, which the group drank after an Italian toast.

Devon, Tom, and I clapped audibly to encourage the direction their night was taking. A bearded Italian man stood and motioned for our tables to join.

We didn't have enough movable chairs, so everyone abandoned social graces and we all sat on the floor. Our conversation began in Spanish, which left Tom and Pauline out of the mix, so Pauline switched to Italian, which didn't work for us, so we swayed toward English to accommodate everyone.

"I have an idea!" one Italian man exclaimed.

He jumped to his feet and sprinted upstairs and returned with a miniature roulette wheel, which he placed in the middle of the group. He jogged to the bar and ordered four shots of vodka and for shots of whiskey for each person our circle. Multiple group members assisted him in carrying trays of cheap liquor back to our floor circle. I caught Devon's eye.

"Damn, dude," Devon whispered.

"*Cuando en Lisboa?*" I said.

"When in Lisbon is right," Devon replied.

"Everybody pick a color: red or black," one Italian man commanded. "Red is vodka. Black is whiskey. If you're wrong, you drink."

"Eleanora goes first!" an Italian woman shouted.

I placed a shot of whiskey in front of me as my bet. Tom did the same. Everyone else placed a vodka glass in the center. Eleanora spun the roulette wheel. Tom drummed on his legs with anticipation. The wheel spun for almost one minute and, when it stopped, the ball landed on red. Eleanora pointed to me with wild excitement.

"Drink!" she shouted.

Tom and I raised our glasses and drank our whiskey with ease.

"You made that look easy," Pauline said to Tom.

"It won't be once I start drinking vodka," Tom said.

"You mean rubbing alcohol?" I said.

"Exactly."

After a half hour, my whiskey shots were gone. Four shots glass filled to the brim with nose-singeing, bottom-shelf vodka stared me in the face. Eleanora moved from her location in the circle and sat by me. I faced the center of the circle with my stomach to the floor. She crossed her legs and leaned sideways, using me for support. She invaded my personal space. I liked it. Or at least I thought I did. I placed my bet. *Red.*

"Yes!" I shouted.

The thought of drinking vodka disgusted me. I placed my bet again. *Red.* After a few more spins, I still had three glasses. An Italian man named Mario, or something similar, possessed one whiskey shot. We placed our bets. *Red.*

"Cologne!" Devon shouted "You won!"

Tom high-fived me and Roxanne hugged me and Eleanora pressed harder on my body.

"You win!" an Italian man said to me. "Do you know what that means?"

"I get a trophy?" I said.

"You have to drink all of your remaining shots at the same time," he said.

"Well now," I said. "Some prize."

Devon hit me on the back for motivation. I didn't want to do it. I sat upright and grabbed one shot glass, which I brought it to my lips slowly.

I smelled the vodka and my body shivered involuntarily. I drank the vodka and shivered excessively. I grabbed the next glass. I wanted to get this over with quickly. I brought it to my lips and smelled it and moved the glass away from my face.

"Ja-son," one Italian man shouted. "Ja-son. Ja-son!"

Two more Italians joined the chorus of support. I drank the second vodka shot and shivered.

"One more!" Tom shouted.

"Ja-son!" the Italians echoed loudly.

"Ja-son!" Roxanne shouted.

Devon rolled on the floor as he laughed at the entire scenario.

"Ja-son!" our group cheered.

Other groups of other nationalities at other tables glanced toward me. Some stood and joined the cheering squad.

"Ja-son!"

I held the third, final glass in front of my face. I thought about throwing up, but the transparent, liquid foe taunted me and I accepted the challenge.

"Ja-son!"

I drank the shot and slammed the shot glass on the floor. Wild shouting ensued. I sulked in the corner for a few minutes and let the vodka shadow pass. I was drunk.

We talked with the Italians for an undecipherable amount of time. One Italian man insisted that I kiss Eleanora. I didn't want to kiss her. I could only think about Maria and how much better *sidra* tasted than this nasty vodka. I looked at her face and it moved from side-to-side. Or maybe I was moving side-to-side. I stepped outside to breathe some fresh air. I stumbled to the left and found a small alleyway with a sewer drain. My right hand supported me as a posted against the wall. My face glared at the sewer. My body rumbled. I threw up pure vodka into the drain. I stood and looked around to make sure no one saw me, wiped my face with my sleeve, and returned to the hostel bar.

CHAPTER 23

I opened my eyes and lifted my head. *Where am I?* My head pounded, so I closed my eyes as I progressed to an upright, seated position on my bed. I reach for my water bottle and unscrewed the cap. *Empty.*

I stood. Dizziness captivated me instantly, so I sat and breathed deeply. I waited for a few minutes and tried to stand again.

I fought through the body aches and walked to the sink and filled my metal water bottle and took three sips. *Satisfaction.*

Wearing only blue lacrosse shorts, I stood in the middle of the room and breathed with control in an attempt to suppress my dehydration shakes.

"Good morning, sunshine," Roxanne said in an overly-chipper tone.

"Hey," I grumbled.

"How are you feeling?" she asked.

"Like hell," I replied.

"I bet," she said. "Let's go get some coffee."

"Should we wake up Dev?" I asked.

"No," Roxanne said, "he needs the sleep. I'll leave a note for him."

Roxanne and I left our room and walked downstairs to the lobby. I glanced at the bar and a momentary wave of devastation overcame me. We strolled outside and turned onto a side street.

The sun hung above us. A few white clouds puffed through the sky. A red digital clock in a *farmacia* window flashed: *9:12*.

"It's so early," I said.

"Early bird gets the worm," Roxanne said.

"But we're not looking for worms," I said sarcastically.

"Shut up," Roxanne said.

We entered the *café* and ordered two coffees with steamed milk. We carried our drinks to an outdoor table in the middle of a five-road intersection plaza. The city stirred itself awake and welcomed Saturday.

"What do you think of Lisbon?" I asked.

"I like it," Roxanne replied. "Aside from that knife-wielding crazy person, the people seem pretty friendly. The architecture is cool, too."

"It reminds me of a smaller Madrid," I said. "More raw. More urban."

"You're right," Roxanne said. "It's a little dirty, but it adds to the city's flavor. I dig it."

"And the graffiti is rad," I said.

We sipped our coffees in comfortable silence for a few minutes. An old man with a well-groomed white moustache, a barrette, and a scarf strolled across the intersection and passed our table. He walked a petite, white dog that was groomed like its owner. The gentleman walked slowly and methodically. His head remained elevated and alert, yet comfortable. *Absorbing life.*

My headache subsided gradually. The coffee calmed my hand quivers.

"I can't believe that we have to go back to the States in a few weeks," Roxanne said.

"I know," I said. "It's rough."

I paused and thought about the proper way to phrase my next question.

"Roxy," I said, "what do you think will happen between you and Dev?"

"What do you mean?" she asked.

"Well," I said, "when you go back to the States, you will be in Seattle and Dev will be a few hundred miles away in Oregon."

Roxanne started to speak and then stopped to think.

"I don't know," she said. "I haven't thought about it. We'll probably wait to see what happens. Take it as it comes, I guess."

She exhaled lightly. Her eyes drifted upward, glancing passively at Lisbon's rooftops.

"Sometimes, it's better to avoid expectations," Roxanne said. "What is Dev expecting?"

"I don't know," I said.

"Oh, come on Jason!" Roxanne shouted playfully. "You're his best friend. You live with him. You have to know."

"I have some thoughts, but nothing concrete," I said.

Another wave of silence passed.

"Have you thought about what's going to happen between you and Maria when you leave Spain?" Roxanne asked.

"Yeah," I said. "I'm not leaving Spain."

"Stop joking about that," Roxanne shouted, inserting a light giggle.

"I'm serious," I said.

"So, if you stay in Spain," Roxanne said, "how would you make money?"

"Tutor as much as possible," I replied.

"What would your parents think?" she asked.

"They wouldn't be happy about it," I said.

"What if Maria doesn't fall in love with you?" Roxanne asked.

"Then at least I tried," I said.

"What about the American Dream?" Roxanne asked. "You know. Buy a big house in the suburbs and raise two kids and start with no money and climb the social ladder."

"The American Dream is dead," I said. "I'm just going to make choices and enjoy the outcome."

"No expectations," Roxanne said.

○   ○   ○

Devon was awake when we returned to the hostel. Tom and Pauline were sleeping, so Devon, Roxanne, and I left to explore. The autumn heat evaporated impending cloud cover. I sweated lightly; I couldn't decide if it was from humidity or hangover.

We strolled along the center median of a major road and zigzagged between restaurant tables. A middle-aged man walked in front of us. A gust of wind blew his hat off his head and it rolled toward our feet. Devon picked it up and jogged toward the man.

"Here you go, sir," Devon said.

"*Obrigado*," the man said.

The man reached into his pocket and pulled out a brown, earthy brick that was about the size of a candy bar.

"*Hashees?*" the man said to Devon.

"No, thanks," Devon replied.

Devon turned toward us and attempted to suppress violent laughter.

We cruised through Lisbon until the sun sank. Dinner time approached, so we aimed for a cheap restaurant. We found ourselves in *Barrio Alto*, a neighborhood filled with narrow cobblestone roads, cafes, bars, and elevated apartments.

Roxanne asked a Portuguese woman for a recommendation. The woman motioned for us to walk two blocks until we saw a stone door, so we followed her advice.

Devon opened the door and we sat down in a small cafeteria in what appeared to be a stone cave. We ordered three steaks. Cheap steaks.

The server brought three wooden planks with a steaming, red rock on each, and then he brought out raw steaks. I placed my steak on the hot rock and watched it sizzle.

I sipped on an Estrella Damm and watched people walking through the *barrio* and I pondered. *Where are all these people going? Are they Portuguese, or fellow travelers like us? What have they done on this trip that's different than my trip? This steak is delicious.*

We left the steakhouse and strolled through a nearby plaza. Devon and Roxanne walked arm-in-arm. I walked a step or two behind them.

They fit together. I thought about Maria; I couldn't get her out of my thoughts. I had known her for almost no time at all, but I always thought about her. Maybe this was love at first sight, but I was no romantic sap, so maybe I just thought Maria was really attractive. But why was I so attracted to her?

Her face? Her body? Exotic appeal?

Certainly.

Her wit and intelligence and charisma?

Absolutely.

But was there something more?

"Go Ducks!" a homeless man shouted from a doorway, which broke my trance and inner monologue.

I looked at my chest. I was wearing my green *Oregon Ducks* shirt.

"Go Ducks!" I replied.

"Eugene, Oregon," The man shouted. "I used to live there, at Thirteenth and Alder."

We waved and continued walking.

"Whoa!" Devon shouted in my ear. "What a small world. Here we are, across the world in Portugal, and a random man pinpoints a street corner from our town back home."

"How did he end up here?" I asked.

"Do we want to know?"

o   o   o

We sat on the early-morning return train to Spain. The conductor informed us that we had one hour until we stopped in Madrid.

"That Brazilian music we heard last night was incredible,"

Roxanne said.

"Yeah," I said, "I can't believe we sat in the front row for that live band."

"The place was packed," Devon said. "I'm surprised we got a beer."

"I love *Barrio Alto*," Roxanne said. "You should live there, Jason."

"When would Jason live there?" Devon asked.

"When our program is over and Jason stays in Europe," Roxanne said.

"Wait, Jason," Devon said. "You're staying in Spain?"

"I think so, man," I said.

"I know you always joked about it, but are you serious?" Devon said.

"Yeah," I replied. "Why not?"

"Because you have another year and half of college left," Devon said. "Because you would miss Duck football games. Because you have opportunities in the States after college."

"I have opportunities here, too," I said. "I can be free and explore and adventure and learn."

"You can't live in that fantasy life, dude," Devon said. "You can do all the same things back home."

"I'm going to write to my parents when I get back to Oviedo and tell them I'm going to stay for a while longer."

"How long do you plan on staying in Spain?" Devon asked.

"We'll see what happens with me and Maria," I said. "Maybe I'll move to *Barrio Alto*. Maybe I'll wander through Ireland or Switzerland. Maybe I'll marry Maria and stay in Oviedo."

"You're crazy, man," Devon said. "But whatever works

for you. I think you need to be realistic and think seriously about this before you make a decision."

Our train arrived in Madrid. We had four hours until our train departed for Oviedo, so we walked to the center of the city: *Plaza del Sol.* I found a kebab shop and we entered. I ordered two kebabs and *patatas fritas.* Devon ordered the same. We devoured them. With more than three hours until our departure, we strolled through town. We passed a bar with a red-painted wooden entrance.

"I heard that Ernest Hemingway wrote a book here," Roxanne said.

"Which book?" I asked.

"I don't remember," Roxanne said. "One of his books about Spain. *For whom the Bell Tolls*, maybe."

"Should we get a drink here?" Devon asked.

"What would Hemingway do?" I asked.

CHAPTER 24

Snow fell as Devon and I walked to class. The sky grew lighter as we walked.

"Just another warm Oviedo morning in December," Devon said.

"I'm glad I adopted the scarf fashion from these Spaniards," I said.

"These are so warm," Devon said. "Why haven't I worn a scarf before?"

We entered the campus plaza and I stopped and compiled snow from a grass patch. I crafted a small snowball and launched it at Devon. I hit him in the foot.

"Nice one, Jason," Devon said.

"I can't believe it's our last day of school at *La Universidad de Oviedo*," I said.

"I know," Devon said. "Four months went by way too quick."

Brad and Marcos stood underneath the steel awning above the main staircase. Marcos raised his arms up. Brad yelled at us, but I couldn't decipher his words through the wind.

"What's up, *hermanos*?" Brad said as we climbed the stairs to our second-floor grammar class.

We entered two minutes late and Profesora Babe glared at me. She gave an undercover smile and she commanded us to sit.

"Damn, Jason," Devon whispered as he elbowed me in the rib, "the Babe looks good today."

"Let's ask her to hit the town with us tonight," I said.

"I like that idea," Brad said.

I thought about different strategies in which I could ask Profesora Babe to hang out with our crew after class. *She had to be five years older than us*, I thought. *How can I ask her in Spanish? She's a babe.*

"*Jason?*" Profesora Babe asked. "*Que es la respuesta correcta para numero tres?*"

"What was the question?" I whispered to Devon.

"What will you do once school is over for the term?" Devon whispered to me.

"Well," I replied in Spanish to Profesroa Babe, "my friends and I will go to *El Serpiente* and drink *sidra* with Alex, the boss. We'll reminisce about our time in Oviedo and we'll practice our Spanish. You are more than welcome to join us. We can practice the skill that we've learned in this class."

I smiled cheesily. Profesora Babe smiled shyly.

"Brad," Profesora Babe continued, "*pregunta numero quattro.*"

Devon elbowed me in the rib.

"Nice work, Jason," Devon said.

I walked to *El Serpiente* with Devon and Brad. We stopped by Maria's apartment on the way. I pressed the buzzer button to her apartment number and her mother answered. I spoke into the microphone and asked for Maria and her voice came through the speaker seconds later. She was eating with her family. We invited her to join us at *El Serpiente* after she finished. Marcos and Roxanne met us at the corner of *Calle Gascona* and we walked up the hill to El Jefe's bar for one last night of Oviedo adventure.

Fernando met us at the door and led us to a standing table in the center of the bar. He returned with *sidra* for all five of us *americanos*. Brad raised his glass.

"To El Jefe!" Brad shouted.

"El Jefe," we echoed.

"And to our last night out as Team Fun!" Brad continued.

"*Equipo Divertido*!" Marcos shouted.

We drank more *sidra* and then Fernando brought Estrella Damm to our table. We thanked him. A woman walked through the door and El Jefe tapped my shoulder and motioned for me to look.

"Who is that beautiful lady?" Fernando asked in Spanish.

"My grammar teacher," I replied.

Fernando looked at me with wide-eyed disbelief. Brad stood and waved to Profesora Babe and she sat at our table. Fernando brought a drink for her and he winked as he set it on the table. His Venezuelan charm was in full effect.

"Jason," Roxanne shouted to me, "Maria's here."

I looked toward the door and Maria roamed curiously as she searched for our table. I waved to her, which moved her toward me. She sat next to me and placed her hand on my thigh.

Alfonso arrived with Anna, who saw me and wandered to our table. Anna and Maria looked at each other fiercely, followed by avoided eye contact. Alfonso looked in my direction. I saw Devon glaring at him.

"You leave tomorrow?" Anna asked in Spanish.

"Yeah," I said. "We all have different flights, but we all leave for the States tomorrow. I'm the last one leaving. My train leaves at *20:15* for Madrid, and then I'll catch a plane to the States."

"I'm flying from Oviedo to London, and then to the States," Roxanne said.

"Me too, actually," Devon said.

"No way!" Roxanne shouted.

"I'm leaving tomorrow morning for Barcelona for my connection flight," Brad added.

"How was your trip to Portugal?" Maria asked.

I looked at Roxanne and thought about our early morning café conversation in Lisbon.

"It was fun," Devon said. "We met a lot of cool people. Ate good food. Listened to good music."

"We got attacked by a mugger in an alleyway," Roxanne added.

The group gasped inquisitively.

"Yeah," Devon said. "We were walking down a staircase and this Portuguese dude threatened us with a knife for our money and we got away."

"It was pretty crazy," I added.

"I can't believe this girl beat up a knife-wielding mugger," Alfonso said and point to Roxanne.

"My girl kicked ass," Devon said proudly.

"It must have been an African who tried to rob you," Alfonso said.

"Why do you say that?" Devon asked.

"Because immigrants are desperate," Alfonso said. "Especially Africans. They are black, after all."

"What's that supposed to mean?" Devon said firmly.

"They're not motivated and they're not intelligent," Alfonso said coldly.

"You'd better watch your mouth," Devon said.

Devon stood in anticipation to confront Alfonso, but Alfonso didn't notice.

"And then there are South American immigrants," Alfonso said. "They don't speak real Spanish. They pretend like they have a connection to Spanish culture, but they're dark-skinned and stupid and dirty. They live in the jungle."

"Get the hell out of my bar," Fernando said. "I don't tolerate disrespect."

Fernando stepped closer to Alfonso. So did Devon. I stood and did the same.

"You foreigners think you're tough, huh?" Alfonso asked. "It's fine. At least you're not a woman."

"Anna, why do you date this asshole?" I asked.

"Good question, Jason," Anna said. "I need a good man like you. Goodbye, Alfonso."

Anna stood and walked out of *El Serpiente*. Alfonso stood and walked after her. He stood in the doorway and watched Anna run away. He returned quickly and angrily His face was red and he clenched his fists. Alfonso stomped back to our table and pushed me.

I staggered backwards and bumped another table. He pushed me again. I nearly fell into the aisle. Alfonso's arms contracted toward his chest as he prepared for a powerful push. I stepped forward quickly and punched him in the nose. He staggered and wound up and threw a slow haymaker. I ducked, coiled, and exploded with an uppercut and a right cross that hit Alfonso in the ear. Devon pushed him to the ground and stood over him.

Brad grabbed me and Ferndando picked Alfonso up off the ground and shoved him outside. Fernando returned to the bar and brought us another round of Estrella Damm.

After more rounds of *sidra* and Estrella Damm, we realized that *El Serpiente* was closing for the night. We helped Fernando clean and lock the bar.

"Profesora," Brad said, "thanks for hanging out with us tonight."

"You're welcome. It has been a true pleasure having you boys in class," she said in perfect English.

Profesora Babe kissed Brad on the cheek. He turned red and fought to keep himself from smiling too widely. She looked at Fernando.

"Can you give me a ride home?" Profesora Babe asked Fernando.

"I can," he said suavely.

Fernando walked toward his motorcycle and we walked with him.

"*Chicos,*" Fernando said, "you are true friends. No matter where you go in the world, you will always have true friends here, in Oviedo."

We all shook his hand.

"Thanks for everything, *Jefe,*" I said.

"See you soon," Fernando said.

I stood on the cobblestones of *Calle Gascona* and looked at *El Serpiente* with *Equipo Divertido*. I pictured *El Serpiente* as Team Fun's headquarters.

"We made this our spot, team," I said.

"This was our homework," Roxanne said.

We laughed.

"Well, Roxy," Devon said, "should we go home?"

"Let's do it," Roxanne said.

I gave Roxanne a hug.

"Dude," Roxanne said to me, "it's been real. I'll see you back in the States when you come to Washington to visit."

"*Te vere pronto*," I said. *I'll see you soon.*

"Boys," Devon said, "I'll see you back home in a few days."

"Peace, man."

I walked with Maria down *Calle Gascona* until we reached *Calle Uria.* Christmas lights lined the streetlamps.

"Are you really leaving tomorrow night?" Maria asked.

"I don't know yet," I said. "What's the worst that could happen if I miss my flight? What if I stay in Oviedo?"

"I think you would be in trouble if you stay," Maria said.

"How?" I asked.

"Your parents would be mad," she said. "Your friends would be mad. I wouldn't be."

I kissed her.

"You might see me tomorrow," I said, "or you might not."

EPILOGUE

I stomped through the jungle; the heavy, humid air filled my lungs with each deep inhale. Ruins stood to my right, so I swiped a branch and continued through the dense vegetation to explore. I emerged from the ruins and returned to the main path of Mount Narnco's El Cristo journey. The path straightened and I saw the main goal of today's solo mission in front of me: the towering statue.

The incline seemed steeper than my last hike up the mountain. The higher I climbed, the thicker the snowfall became. I was cold and my head beaded with sweat underneath my hat. My legs became more tiresome with each step.

When the trail reached its peak, it flattened into a snowy view of Oviedo, which nestled itself comfortably inside a mountain bowl. I clutched the railing on the edge of the mountain cliff and looked at the city.

The small, packed apartment buildings seemed tiny from this height. Los Picos de Europa etched themselves into the skyline; their snowcapped peaks towered above the city, yet they stood innumerable kilometers away from me.

I thought about everything and nothing and observed the snow as it dusted the red rooftops. Cars whipped around traffic circles on the two major roads out of Oviedo. El Parque San Francisco would be empty today, except for the fútbol courts. I saw the mountains on the other side of the city. They were taller than Mount Naranco.

ACKNOWLEDGMENTS

This novel is the result of key effort and influence by so many people and I want to thank all of you for your part in its creation.

Thanks to Grant Allen, my editor. He read the first draft of this novel while sailing from the Columbia River into the Pacific Ocean and back again. He provided me with incredible feedback through two revisions and I could not have completed this without his help and wisdom.

Thanks to David Corby for his adventurous spirit. As a Peace Corps volunteer in the Dominican Republic, he's utilizing his Spanish-speaking abilities to change the world; he did the same for me.

Thanks to Ryan Huff for his optimism, adventurous attitude, and willingness to explore. He allowed me to thrive in an environment that exceeded my comfort zone.

Thanks to Alex Gross for the inspiration to create a story, put it down on paper, and actually do something with it. His entrepreneurial spirit is infectious.

Thanks to Sean O'Leary and Nick Osborne for your kindness, adventurous attitude, and drive to have fun at all times.

And, of course, thanks to my wife for providing me with feedback and support throughout all of my writing endeavors. Her ambition, altruism, and passion for life push me to strive to be better every single day.

ABOUT THE AUTHOR

Tom Malone was born and raised in Portland, Oregon. He studied journalism and history at the University of Oregon, Spanish at *la Universidad de Oviedo*, and earned his master's degree in teaching from the University of Portland.

He has taken dozens of road trips throughout the United States and continues to travel throughout the world. Currently, Malone teaches secondary Social Studies near Denver, Colorado, where he camps, fishes, hikes, and snowboards often.

OTHER WORKS BY AUTHOR

Across Americana: A Novel

Ben's plan is unfolding perfectly. He is graduating from college. His dream job is set. Plus, his girlfriend is staying in his hometown and marriage is on the horizon. Then, on his college graduation day, he loses his job offer and his long-term girlfriend. Ben's best friend is leaving for the East Coast at sunrise. With nothing to hold Ben back, he embarks on a spontaneous cross-country road trip to New York City to begin an unforeseeable future. Along the journey, Ben encounters adventures that change his future forever.

o   o   o

Sloan Fitzpatrick: Middle School Journalist

Sloan Fitzpatrick is nervous about his first day of seventh grade. His best friend moved to another state. The school bully grew taller over the summer, while Sloan remained short. Plus, he registered for a Newspaper class just because his crush was the Editor-In-Chief, even though he knew nothing about journalism. After interviewing a city politician for his first assignment, Sloan finds himself wrapped up in the school newspaper. But he also finds himself caught in a political corruption investigation and he's in way over his head. Now, how's he supposed to handle seventh grade?